THE GHOST IN THE ATTIC

A CHARLIE MACCREADY MYSTERY

THE GHOST IN THE ATTIC

A CHARLIE MACCREADY MYSTERY

James M. McCracken

Copyright © 2020 James M. McCracken

JK Press

2nd Edition

ISBN: 978-1-7329347-7-1

All rights reserved. No part of this book may be reproduced or transmitted in any form or by any means, electronic or mechanical, including photocopying, recording, or by any information storage and retrieval system, without permission in writing from the copyright owner.

This is a work of fiction. Names, characters, places and incidents are either the product of the author's imagination or are used fictitiously, and any resemblance to any actual persons, living or dead, events, or locales is entirely coincidental.

CONTENTS

1. CHARLIE MACCREADY — 1
2. SAINT MICHAEL'S — 10
3. THE ATTIC — 32
4. HOWARD'S GIFT — 41
5. THE GHOST IN THE ATTIC — 53
6. THE TUNNEL — 62
7. THE HEADSTONE — 80
8. THE ALTAR BOYS — 98
9. PRIOR ANSELM — 122
10. CHRISTMAS — 143
11. GUS — 171
12. THE NEW PRIOR — 187
13. THE STAKE OUT — 211
14. JEFFREY — 238
15. THANK YOU — 254

DEDICATION

In memory of my grandfather
Casper Earl Mace,
who, despite the cruelties of life,
always loved.

ACKNOWLEDGMENTS

With heartfelt appreciation to Dennis Blakesley, Barbara Fauria, Suzie Fauria, Toni Howell, Robert Howell, Michael Anne Maslow, Mary Miller, Denise Miller and Dianna Scheffler for being my continual sources of encouragement.

CHARLIE MACCREADY

Charlie MacCready could not remember when he came to live with his grandparents, Walter and Ophelia Zenner, at 95 Tam O'Shanter Drive. For as long as he could remember they had always been together and he had always had his bedroom in the attic of their small one-bedroom house. It wasn't all that bad living in the attic. His grandfather cleared out a space just under the small round window that overlooked the front yard and street. His soft bed, a cot with an old worn out feather mattress, sat under the gabled ceiling to the right. Across from it was his dresser, whose legs were sawn off to make it fit under the sloping roof. Beside the head of his bed and beneath the window was a bedside table and a lamp, picked up at a garage sale for fifty cents marked down from a dollar. His most prized possession, however, was a gold locket that contained a small photograph of his father and mother, which he hung on a nail over his bed. It was the last thing he saw before he fell asleep at night and the first thing that greeted him each morning.

Charlie could not remember his parents. He was only two years old when they dropped him off at his grandparents' house in the middle of the night, with promises to return for him in a few days. His mother seemed very upset about something but she wouldn't tell her parents what was troubling her. She cried when she kissed his forehead, his grandmother told him, and then they just disappeared into the night. That was ten years ago, ten years and not a single word.

After a week went by, his grandparents explained, they became worried and notified the police. Their search, however, failed to uncover any clues to his parents' whereabouts. As the years passed without any news, his grandparents gave up speaking about them and settled into the task of raising Charlie.

Still, Charlie couldn't help but hope, while he sat for hours staring out of his tiny window, that someday his parents would come back. Someday he would see a car pull up and his mother and father step out. He would run to them and they would take him home to live with them again.

That hope was put to the test when suddenly, one winter night, his grandfather passed away. That night was permanently etched in Charlie's memory. He had just fallen asleep when a noise below woke him. His attic flashed with red and blue light. He quickly climbed out of his bed and looked outside. An ambulance and a rescue truck were parked outside. Two men in white uniforms were wheeling a gurney down the walk toward the ambulance. In the eerie shadows of the night he couldn't make out who was under the blanket. It wasn't until his grandmother called to him from below that he knew the answer.

The weeks that followed were a blur as his mother's sister Bernice and brother Chester came in and out of the house. Charlie could tell something was up. Every time his aunt and uncle came over, they sent him to the attic and then they would speak in hushed voices to his grandmother. Charlie would ask her what they wanted but she would never say. He could tell whatever it was, it was upsetting her and for that he disliked them more.

One summer night, six months later, Charlie found out the feeling was mutual. He had gone to bed as he normally did, but he couldn't sleep. Instead he tossed and turned in his bed. Then he heard a knock at the front door and the familiar gruff sound of his Uncle Chester's voice. He asked if Charlie was in bed to which his grandmother said, "Yes." The three of them went into the kitchen and sat down at the table and began to talk in normal voices. Slowly Charlie climbed out of his bed and crept to the opening to the attic just above the kitchen.

"Mother," his Uncle Chester began. "You can't stay here alone any longer."

"But I'm not alone," Ophelia protested. "Charlie is here with me."

"Charlie is just a boy," Aunt Bernice chimed in with an indignant tone in her voice. "He can't even take care of himself, let alone be of any help to you."

"But he does help me. We help each other," Ophelia explained.

"That's not the point, Mother," Again, Charlie's uncle spoke up. "The boy belongs in an orphanage, and you belong in a place where people who are trained professionals can care for your needs."

"But he's my grandson, my own flesh and blood; I can't just send him away." Charlie could tell that his grandmother was crying. Her voice trembled as she spoke. "What if Faith and Patrick come back for him? What will I tell them?"

"Mom," Aunt Bernice said in her usual patronizing way. "Faith and Patrick are dead or they would've come back by now."

"How dare you say such a thing," Charlie's grand-mother

snapped. "You do not know that. None of us know that."

"Mother, look at the facts. Faith and Patrick disappear in the middle of the night. The police go to their house and find it in a shamble. No one has seen either hide or hair of them since. We all warned Faith not to marry Patrick, remember?" Aunt Bernice said matter-of-factly.

"I can't believe it. I just won't," his grandmother said and covered her ears.

"This discussion is over." Uncle Chester snapped coldly. "I have been granted power of attorney over you by the courts. And it is our opinion, Bernice's and mine, that it is in your best interests to move into Happy Meadow's Retirement Home, and that the boy be sent to Saint Michael's Abbey and Home for Boys."

"No," his grandmother shrieked and sobbed. "You can't do that to him."

"I can and I have. In two days one of the Brothers will be here to pick him up. Have his things ready. It's time to go, Bernice."

They left without another word. Charlie lay awake and listened to the faint sobs of his grandmother until she fell asleep from her tears. He wondered what was to become of him, and would his parents be able to find him at Saint Michael's? He then began to wonder what sort of place was Saint Michael's. He had never heard of it before, but he knew deep inside, he would not like it there.

Two days passed almost as though overnight. He didn't think it was possible for a person to cry so much, but his grandmother cried silently, seemingly non-stop, since she told him the news. He couldn't believe he wouldn't be with his grandmother anymore, but he couldn't cry. He didn't know why. He wanted to. He just couldn't, and he found he couldn't speak either.

The midmorning sun shone through the tiny window in the attic, and made it easy for Charlie to see his reflection in an old, cracked mirror left behind when the other boxes were removed. Quietly, he stared at his reflection and wondered what was so horrible about him that made his own relatives not want him. He wasn't a strikingly handsome boy, but he was far from ugly. His reddish-brown hair was thick and wavy, and his eyes were a dark brown. Freckles dotted his average-sized nose and cheeks. His ears did stick out from the sides of his head a bit much. He always thought it made him look cute; but now, he hated them. I *am* ugly, he thought to himself. He turned away from his reflection, placed his comb on top of his clothes and closed the old, tattered suitcase, a cast off of his cousin's. As he turned to leave the only home he knew, a sparkle of light caught his eye. He stopped and looked at the locket that hung above his empty bed. Without a thought, he took it, put it around his neck and headed for the ladder.

The kitchen looked bigger without the small table and chairs that once sat in the middle of the room. He spent many hours at that table being home-schooled by his grandmother. However, his fondest memories were the nice, quiet evenings he spent with her snapping beans and shelling peas while listening to her tales of the old days. He sighed quietly to himself and walked into the living room.

The living room was empty except for a few pieces of old newspaper that were left over from packing. The shadows from where the many pictures once hung still lingered on the walls. Charlie set his suitcase down and walked over to the fireplace. The mantle, once adorned with his grandmother's treasured knick-knack collection, was empty. Only a light coat of dust marred the surface.

Charlie was lost in his thoughts and did not hear his grandmother enter the room behind him.

"Charlie, dear," Ophelia called to him gently.

Charlie turned around and looked intently at the small, round-shouldered, white-haired woman in front of him. Her hair was pulled back in its usual tight bun on the back of her head. Her apron, trimmed in blue, matched her eyes behind her half-moon spectacles. She stepped closer to him. He took a deep breath and smelled the clean scent of Ivory soap and rose petals that were distinctly her. She took his hands into hers as she stood before him. Her hands were soft and warm.

"Charlie," she said with a slight smile as her eyes began to tear. "You do know how much I love you, don't you?"

Charlie just looked at her, committing every detail of her gentle face to his memory. He did know that she was perhaps the last and only one that truly did love him and he loved her. Yet it seemed that everyone he loved was taken away from him; his parents, his grandfather, and now her. He vowed to himself that he would never love anyone again.

"If there were just some way we could stay together, you would never have to leave me; but there just isn't, dear child. You do understand that, don't you?" She paused and waited for his reply. "You're going to be just fine at Saint Michael's, you'll see. Saint Michael's Abbey is really a wonderful place. It won't be so bad." She stroked the side of his face gently. "Here, I have something I want to give you," she said in an almost whisper. "You cannot tell anyone I gave this to you, no matter how much they ask, and you must never give it to anyone or let it out of your sight. It's very important," she continued as she dug in the pocket of her apron. "Ah, here it is," she said and pulled out a small brass key. "Keep this with you at all times. And remember what I said." She pressed it into his hand and closed his fingers tightly around it.

"The car's here." Uncle Chester's voice echoed in the empty room. Charlie and his grandmother looked up at the man in the doorway. He was tall and stocky. His hair was dark brown and his almost coal black eyes stared at them accusingly. "What are you two up to?" he asked, and looked directly at Charlie.

"It's none of your concern, Chester!" Ophelia spoke sharply to her son. She turned back to Charlie and her face softened again. "Remember what I said. I'll be in touch, and maybe even come see you, if the warden lets me out." She raised her voice on purpose as she said the last few words, hoping Chester would feel the daggers in her tone. She kissed Charlie's forehead and gave him a hug.

Charlie hugged her back. He didn't want to let go. There was a pain in his chest and he felt as though he were about to cry but his eyes were dry.

Uncle Chester grew impatient as he stood in the doorway watching the two of them. With a disgusted sigh he stepped into the room and picked up the old suitcase with one hand and grabbed Charlie's arm with the other, giving it a sharp jerk.

"Come on, boy," he bellowed coldly. "You can't keep Brother Simon waiting all day."

Uncle Chester led Charlie down the narrow walk to the curb where a black Ford van was parked and waiting. With every step he gave Charlie's arm a purposeful tug.

"You're just as irresponsible as your mother," Uncle Chester snarled. "She was always making everyone wait for her while she lollygagged around. Well, you'll snap out of that soon enough," he said with an almost evil laugh in his voice. "They aren't going to cater to you at Saint Michael's. No sir. You're going to have to shape up, and fast, if you want to stay out of trouble." He gave another wicked laugh. "That'll be the day."

Charlie didn't hear a single word his uncle spouted. His attention was focused on the tall, gaunt-looking man dressed in the long, black, hooded robes of a monk. His hair, what little there was of it, was pure white, which made his dark brown eyes behind his wire rimmed spectacles look more sinister than holy. He stood very straight, his shoulders back and his chin raised. He looked down his long, crooked nose at Charlie as Chester presented him.

"He's all yours, Brother Simon. You can do whatever you want with him. Mind you, he's a bit thick headed and stubborn so you may want to work him extra hard for a few days. Break him of that."

"We'll take that under advisement," Brother Simon spoke in a deep raspy voice. "I assure you."

"Maybe a few months of hard labor will teach him to respect his elders and be more appreciative of the kindnesses we've shown him," Uncle Chester jeered.

Charlie looked at his uncle. What had he ever done to him? In the years he spent with his grandparents he couldn't recall ever saying anything to his uncle and vice versa. Why was he being so mean and hateful?

"Could be." Brother Simon nodded. "I'll pass along your advice to the Abbot. Pick up your bag, young man."

Brother Simon slid open the side door of the van. Charlie looked inside at the three empty bench seats. He stepped forward, and glanced over his shoulder at his grandmother who stood on the front porch. She was crying. A tear came to his eyes for the first time. He clenched his teeth and fought to keep from showing any emotion in front of his uncle. He tightened his hold on the key in his hand. *Keep this with you at all times. It's very important,* his grandmother's voice echoed in his ears.

A sharp slap to the back of his head by his uncle caused

him to look away. He climbed into the van in silence.

"I don't envy you your job," Uncle Chester said as the van's door slid closed. "He's a stubborn one. Hasn't spoken a word in weeks."

"At the Abbey, we have ways of dealing with problem children," Brother Simon said dryly, and bid them good-bye before climbing behind the steering wheel.

Charlie watched his grandmother weeping and waving as the van pulled away from the curb and headed down Tam O'Shanter Drive. They turned the corner and she was gone from sight.

SAINT MICHAEL'S

Saint Michael's Abbey and Home for Boys was situated on the top of a hill a hundred and fifty miles from Happy Meadows, where his grandmother went to live. It was too far to walk and too far to visit every weekend, even if he could find a way. Charlie settled back in his seat and watched the scenery flash by.

At the bottom of a hill was a small village of German immigrants. The buildings were adorned in the traditional German bric-a-brac style with colorful accents of oranges and gold. In the center of the town stood a tall obelisk surrounded by brightly colored flowerbeds, dedicated to the founders of their small village. Festive posters and banners hung from the lampposts announcing the coming of Oktoberfest. Charlie had never heard of it before and wondered what it was all about.

Brother Simon drove the black van quickly through the town. Several of the town's people had to jump out of his way. One old man shook his cane at Brother Simon and shouted at him in German. Charlie tightened his seatbelt and took the chain from around his neck. He unfastened its clasp and slipped his secret key onto it with his locket. He looked up again to see Brother Simon watching him in the rearview mirror.

"Where did you get that key?" he asked in a tone that was all too demanding, and then turned his attention back to the road.

Charlie didn't answer. He swallowed hard and quickly tucked the locket and key under his shirt. He tightened his hold on the suitcase resting on his lap. He wondered why Brother Simon's question about the key made him fearful. He wished his grandmother told him what it was for.

Brother Simon occasionally glanced in the rearview mirror at Charlie. He appeared to not have a liking for children and Charlie wondered why someone like Brother Simon would run a Home for Boys. With a jerk of the wheel the van turned up the narrow road toward the Abbey.

Charlie ducked his head as the van roared through the dark forest. The tall fir trees were so thick it was hard to tell if it were still daylight. Suddenly there was a movement in the trees. Charlie looked quickly, but whatever it was had disappeared. He looked at Brother Simon who appeared to be driving faster, with his eyes intent on the road ahead.

As the van came to the top of the hill, the trees cleared to reveal a parking lot in front of a long, single-story garage building. Brother Simon slowed the van to a surprisingly gentle stop just outside one of the five garage doors. Immediately a short monk scurried over from one of the neighboring garages. His nose was small and pointed and seemed to twitch nervously. His ears stuck out from the sides of his head, which was covered with his short, very straight, very black hair. He smiled warmly at Charlie and gave a small wave in greeting. Charlie couldn't help but smile at the monk.

Brother Simon opened the door and stepped out of the

van. He coldly dropped the keys into the short monk's hand.

"Park it for me, Tobias," he ordered more than asked. Then he turned back to Charlie. "Don't just sit there. Get your things and let's get a move on."

Charlie quickly climbed out of the van and slid the door shut. He hurried over to Brother Simon's side.

Brother Simon tucked his hands under his robes and straightened his back even more.

"Follow me and keep up," he snapped and turned toward the large green lawn that stretched out across the hilltop.

Charlie watched as Brother Simon moved across the lawn. The slight breeze rustled his robes and made him appear to be gliding across the surface of the grass. Charlie tightened his grip on his suitcase and hurried after him.

As they walked across the grass Charlie noticed clusters of neatly pruned trees, like an oasis in a desert, scattered here and there. To his surprise as they passed close by one cluster of trees, Charlie could see in the center a clear pond filled with what looked like giant goldfish. The pond was surrounded by well-tended flowerbeds. He would've liked to have taken a closer look and maybe even rest a bit on the inviting bench that sat under one of the trees, but Brother Simon was still hurrying ahead of him. He shifted his suitcase to his other hand, his arms beginning to ache from the weight, and quickened his pace.

As they rounded still another oasis, a huge four-story, brick building rose up out of the ground a hundred yards away. Its terra-cotta tiled roof was pitched very steep and added another floor's height to the structure. Charlie froze and stared at the building that resembled a castle. Only one entrance was visible from the front. Two large wooden doors were placed directly in the center of the first floor of the façade with a large portico stretching out above its steps like a half-raised drawbridge. Windows that opened from the bottom symmetrically dotted the front of the building. A tall tower rose above the east, front corner of the building, clearly another story higher than the peak of the roof. Charlie became dizzy just thinking about it. He never did like heights. He shook his head and hurried to catch up with Brother Simon.

As they crossed the narrow two-lane driveway that bordered the west edge of the lawn and connected the Abbey to the parking lot, Brother Simon slowed his pace. When he reached the front steps under the portico, Brother Simon turned sharply, facing Charlie. In an icy stare he looked down at him.

"Once you go through those doors you will find that no one is going to coddle you. Your silence will not win you any special sympathies here. You're just another useless urchin. You'd do well to remember that," he sneered and turned around.

Charlie swallowed hard as he took in the words. He couldn't understand why Brother Simon disliked him so much. They had never met before, as far as he knew. He took a deep breath and hurried up the steps to the front doors.

The main entry hall looked bright and cheerful. The large room, two stories high, had a grand marble staircase to the right that led to a balcony on the second floor. A large polished brass and crystal chandelier glowed above them and caused the white marble floor to sparkle beneath their feet. The walls were also white with large ornately framed paintings of old men in robes just like Brother Simon's. Charlie got an uneasy feeling as he walked farther into the room. It was as though the eyes of the paintings were following him. He shuddered and tried not to think too much about it. Directly in front of them and also to the right and left were sets of double doors.

Brother Simon stepped up to the doors on the left and pressed the tiny button on the wall beside them. From inside, the sound of a buzzer echoed. Brother Simon turned again to face Charlie.

"Stay put," he said in his usual cold voice. "Abbot Ambrose will be here in a moment. I've got things to do." Without so much as a good-bye, he walked across the room and disappeared through the doors on the opposite wall.

Charlie was glad he was gone, yet at the same time, he wished he would have stayed until this Abbot Ambrose person came. Charlie's mind raced as he tried to anticipate what the Abbot would be like. Would he be as cold and unfriendly as Brother Simon? Would Abbot Ambrose dislike him too? He shivered as the sound of footsteps on the other side of the doors reached his ears. Charlie drew a quick breath and unconsciously held it. There was the sound of keys rattling and then a click as the doorknob turned. Charlie took a step back. The door opened slowly.

Much to Charlie's surprise a tall, thin man with a white beard and full head of white hair stepped out into the entry hall. He was dressed in the robes of a monk. A deep blue sapphire-jeweled, golden cross hung from a gold chain around his neck. He smiled warmly at Charlie and there was a sparkle in his blue eyes. He appeared to be kinder and gentler than Brother Simon, Charlie thought.

"You must be Charlie." His voice was deep, yet gentle. He held out his hand to Charlie.

Charlie nodded silently and shifted his suitcase back into his left hand and shook Abbot Ambrose's hand.

"Oh, that's right." Abbot Ambrose raised his chin and folded his hands together in front of his stomach. "Your grandmother told me you haven't spoken a word since you heard you were being sent away. I hope you'll give us a chance. We really aren't as bad as your uncle says. However, your grandmother is very worried about you, son. She hopes that you will find your voice soon so you can telephone her. Whenever you're ready, just let me know. So, shall we give you a quick tour and get you settled?"

Charlie's eyes lit up at the thought of his grandmother. Even though it had only been a few hours since he saw her, he missed her terribly. He nodded his answer to the Abbot.

"Okay, then, let's start here." Abbot Ambrose turned around and motioned toward the doors at the end of the entry hall. "Through those doors is our Abbey Church, you'll be seeing a lot of it in the days to come. The stairs, which are off limits, are for our visitors to use. They lead to the visitor's loft in the church. Through those doors is our monastery wing." he said and pointed to the doors that Brother Simon had gone through. "It, too, is off limits to the boys." He turned back to the door through which he had come. "Shall we?" He motioned for Charlie to enter.

Charlie stepped into another hallway. Abbot Ambrose followed but paused to lock the doors behind him. He must have seen the puzzled look on Charlie's face because he gave him a reassuring smile. "The boys here are not permitted to use this entrance. There is an entrance in the back that they use. This way," he said as he started down the hallway toward another set of stairs at the bend.

"On the first floor here we have our offices, including my own, and visitation rooms for prospective parents when they come to adopt one of our resident boys. Also located on this floor just around the corner are the refectories, that's what we call our dining rooms," he explained noticing the puzzled look on Charlie's face. "The kitchen and the laundry also share that hall." He continued as they came to the staircase.

"The basement houses the classrooms you'll be

attending, and the second floor houses our classrooms for our seminary students. We have classes all year around. In the summer months, however, we focus on more recreational lessons such as baseball, swimming and the arts. I don't suppose you're a talented baseball player; we could always use a good short stop." Abbot Ambrose smiled again at Charlie.

Charlie didn't reply. He was busy looking around at the many doors that lined the walls. They were taller than the doors in his grandparents' house. They were made of oak and had polished brass doorknobs. On the wall beside each door was a number and between each door along the wall hung bright colorful, framed photographs of different landscapes and outdoor scenes.

"The mail slots for you and the other boys are located on the landing between the first floor and the basement. You'll want to check there for letters from your grandmother, and also when you write her, you'll want to put it in the outgoing mailbox there. Brother John delivers the mail after breakfast every day, except Sundays," Abbot Ambrose continued as they started up the stairs.

Charlie noticed that once they had reached the second floor, the white marble stairs changed to cold gray concrete. The walls even changed from the bright clean white to a more muted shade.

"The third floor is reserved for our seminary students. They will be returning from summer break in a couple weeks. This floor is strictly off limits to everyone except the seminarians." Abbot Ambrose continued up the last flight of stairs. "And at last we come to the fourth floor. This will be your new home," he said as he opened the heavy fire door to reveal yet another long hallway. "Here on the fourth floor we have the four dormitories and a large living room area for our young residents. We have two types of boys here at Saint Michael's, our residents and our students. We refer to our orphaned boys as our resident boys because they are with us all year round. The boys who are here because they want to take a look at the priesthood, or because this is their last chance before juvenile home, are referred to as our students."

Abbot Ambrose paused just inside the fire doors.

"Each of our four dorms has an overseer we call a Prefect. They each have an office and living quarters that adjoin their respective dorm. Here we have Saint Peter, whose Prefect is Father Vicar. It is our largest dorm." He motioned to his left at the solid wood double doors.

Charlie looked at the life-sized portrait that hung on the wall between the double doors and the door with Father Vicar's nameplate. It was framed in an ornate golden frame. The elderly man with a kind face was dressed in a white tunic with a set of golden keys on a ring that hung from his rope belt. He had a large book opened in one hand and a feather quill in his other. Charlie recognized the image as being of the Apostle Peter and not of Father Vicar.

"Across the hall is Brother Conrad's Saint Thomas the Doubter dormitory." He gestured with his right hand as he proceeded down the hall.

Charlie only caught a glimpse of the portrait of Thomas the Doubter, as he hurried to catch up with Abbot Ambrose. Like the portraits downstairs, their eyes seemed to follow him as he moved down the hall. He shrugged away the uneasy feeling it gave him.

They passed through an arched doorway and the hallway opened up. To the left, a row of sinks was below a long mirror that lined the wall. Two doors, one marked Showers, and the other, Restrooms, were in the center of the row of sinks. To the right was the large living room Abbot Ambrose called The Common Area. Three small groupings of a sofa and two overstuffed chairs were placed in different areas of the room. Accented by a matching braided rug, end tables and lamp, they looked quiet and inviting. Dark burgundy velvet drapes framed each window and softened the daylight along the north wall. Against the west wall were game tables and chairs. Charlie hurried to catch up with Abbot Ambrose as he shifted his suitcase to his other hand.

As they passed through another arch the hallway narrowed again.

"Brother Owen oversees Saint Sebastian dorm," Abbot Ambrose continued his tour and gestured to his left. "Saint Thomas and Saint Sebastian are the smallest of the four dormitories. Each has about ten members. Saint Peter has the most with twenty-two members."

Charlie didn't hear what the Abbot said. He was distracted by the portrait of Saint Sebastian. It was the image of a young man with short, reddish brown hair and brown eyes, with a cloth wrapped around his waist. He stood tied to a post. Arrows pierced his bare chest, arm and stomach. A glowing halo surrounded his head as he stood looking heavenward.

"And here we are," Abbot Ambrose announced as he came to a stop in front of the double doors to his right. "Father Emmanuel oversees your dorm, Saint Nicholas."

Charlie turned away from the portrait of Saint Sebastian to look at the last portrait. Again, it was not at all what he expected to see. When he heard the name, he expected to see a jolly, round man dressed in red velvet suit, trimmed in white fur with a holly sprig on his hat. Instead the sight that greeted Charlie was of a tall, thin man dressed in black robes like those of the monks. His face was kind and gentle as he welcomed the children around him. Charlie stood and lost himself in the picture unaware that Abbot Ambrose was talking to someone else.

"Master MacCready?" he repeated a little louder to get his attention.

Charlie jumped and looked at the Abbot and the monk that stood beside him.

"Son, I'd like you to meet Father Emmanuel," Abbot Ambrose said. "Since your grandmother home-schooled you, we scheduled you to take a placement test in a couple days to determine which grade you should be in. Don't worry about it, it's not too tough," he explained with a smile and a wink to reassure Charlie. "Father Emmanuel will show you to your cubicle and help you get settled. I have things that I need to tend to. I'll see you later at dinner. Take good care of him, Emmy. He's a special young man."

"Not to worry, Abbot. He's in good hands." Father Emmanuel smiled and put his arm around Charlie's shoulders.

Charlie looked at Father Emmanuel. He was more of what he had in mind for the portrait of Saint Nicholas. He was tall and very round. His eyes twinkled when he smiled and his cheeks and bulbous nose were pink. There was something about him that made Charlie feel at ease for the first time that day.

"It's a pleasure to finally meet you, Charlie." Father Emmanuel said smiling down at him.

Charlie nodded and gave a slight smile back.

"Your uncle has told us so much about you," he continued.

Charlie cringed, his mind flooding with all the mean-spirited things his uncle could have said about him.

Father Emmanuel felt Charlie's shoulders tense up. He gave him a gentle, reassuring squeeze and let out a jolly laugh that jiggled his round belly.

"Good thing we never listen to such nonsense," he added. "We here at Saint Michael's like to form our own opinions about our younger members. And since I don't see another head sprouting out of your shoulders or any fangs in your mouth, I'd say he was a bit off in his assessment."

Charlie gave Father Emmanuel a funny look to which Father Emmanuel laughed heartily again.

"Come on dear boy, let's get you settled. I'll show you where you'll sleep." He opened one of the doors to the dormitory and held it for Charlie.

Slowly Charlie stepped inside. The room was larger than any bedroom Charlie ever saw before. In the center of the dorm lay a warm brown braided rug on the floor. A dark green sofa with two matching green and gold, plaid, overstuffed chairs were placed in a circle around the rug. A small, old trunk with a sheet of thick glass on its top served as a coffee table. Two tall floor lamps stood like sentries at either end of the sofa.

Along the north wall, under the row of windows, and down the two outer walls, were single beds of various styles. Beside each bed was a nightstand. Partitions were placed between every other bed, separating two beds into a cubicle. Built into the remaining south wall, on either side of the double doors, were several doors behind which were closets, one for each member of the dormitory.

"So, what do you think of our little home?" Father Emmanuel asked as he rocked back on his heels and patted his stomach.

Charlie didn't answer. He just looked around the room in awe. Everything seemed so big compared to his room in the attic.

"Oh, of course," Father Emmanuel stammered as he

remembered. "Here in Saint Nicholas we have twelve boys from age eleven to seventeen. We feel it's important to have a mixture in each dorm. After all, in a family you have to learn to get along with kids of all ages," he continued as they walked over to the corner in the far left of the dorm.

"Over here is your cubicle," Father Emmanuel explained. "You'll be sharing it with a really nice young man, Howard Miller. He's a resident, too, and I think he's about your age," he said as though it were an afterthought. "You both are a lot alike. I think you'll get along wonderfully." He turned away from the cubicle and walked back to the doors. "Your locker is number thirteen," he said, pointing at the narrow doors that lined the wall on either side of the main doors. "I hung up the cassocks and surplices your grandmother bought. She wanted you to have new uniforms instead of the hand-me-downs. I'll let you unpack and get acquainted with your new surroundings. We'll be having dinner in the refectory just as soon as the other boys get back. They're off at our annual baseball tournament. They're playing our rivals at Saint Luke's Academy for the trophy. See you at dinner, Charlie." With that he lumbered off and disappeared through the double doors.

Alone, Charlie sighed and walked back to his cubicle. He sat down on the bed Father Emmanuel pointed to as being his. It was a single bed, a bit larger and the mattress a bit harder than his cot in the attic. It had a wooden frame with four tall bedposts. He fluffed the soft, feather pillow and put it behind him as he leaned against the tall, flat headboard. From his bed, he could see the double doors and most of the dorm. Above the side of his bed was a window that looked out over the front grounds. From his perch on the fourth floor, a height that at first made him uneasy, he could see the garages that he and Brother Simon just left moments ago. Another thought came to him as he surveyed his view. From there he could easily see the only road up the hill and would be able to see his parents when they came for him; and they will come for me, he thought to himself.

The sound of laughter and the hum of chatter filled the dorm as the doors burst open and a flood of boys poured in. Some were dressed in the unmistakable uniform of baseball players; their shirts were a festive blue and gold, and on their backs were large, gold, embroidered letters SM, for Saint Michael's. The crowd moved as one to the center of the room where some immediately plopped down on the sofa and chairs. Others just stood around or headed to their cubicles.

Charlie rested his chin on his knees and wrapped his arms around his legs as he quietly watched the boys. His pulse quickened as he searched the many faces for one he thought looked like a Howard. Anxiety started to flutter like a butterfly in his stomach. Which one could it be, he wondered? Will he really like me, as Father Emmanuel said, or will he hate me like the rest?

Amid the group Charlie noticed a skinny boy with short, curly, black hair and black rimmed glasses. He was talking excitedly with two boys dressed in their baseball uniforms. When his eyes met Charlie's he suddenly smiled and started toward him. Charlie looked away and tried not to show how nervous he was inside.

"Hi," the boy greeted and held out his hand to Charlie. "My name is Howard. We're going to be bunk mates."

Charlie didn't move. He just stared at Howard and the two boys who walked up behind him. Howard put his hand in his pocket and shrugged.

"Abbot Ambrose told me you haven't said a word since you were told about coming here. It's really not that bad here. Oh, and he also told me that your grandpa died recently. I'm sorry about that. I never knew my grandparents. They died before I was born but my mom used to tell me stories about them, I think. She died too, you know."

Howard paused again and gave Charlie a puzzled look. Abbot Ambrose warned him it wouldn't be easy talking with someone who couldn't or wouldn't speak. No one was quite sure why Charlie hadn't said anything; but Howard had assured him everything would be fine. He was used to sharing his cubicle with new kids. In his fifth year at Saint Michael's, he was now one of the oldies.

"It's okay if you can't talk. I tend to talk enough for two people anyway."

Charlie smiled at that comment. Howard did seem to talk a lot and very fast at that.

"Hey, you smiled." Howard beamed. "That's a good sign." He noticed the tattered suitcase on Charlie's bed. "What do you say we go and get you unpacked before the dinner bell sounds?"

Charlie gave a slight nod and began to move off the bed. Howard picked up the suitcase and turned around only to see a small crowd gathered behind him. Immediately he became protective of Charlie and glared at them.

"What're you losers staring at?" he said gruffly. "Get out of here. Come on Charlie. Just ignore them."

They walked over to the wall of closets and stopped in front of the one with the thirteen on the door.

"This is really neat." Howard said as he opened the door. "I'm right next to you in number twelve." Howard's eyes widened behind his glasses and his mouth dropped open. "Wow. Will you look at that! You have all new cassocks and surplices. It's not very often we see those here. Usually we get the mended ones from the smaller seminarians when they've grown out of them. One of the Brothers in the laundry department collects them, mends them and then tailors them to fit us. They aren't the greatest, but they look good enough. But man, look how nice these are." Howard took out one of the red surplices and held it up. "Wow!" he breathed.

Charlie was confused by the fuss Howard was making. He was not quite sure what he was supposed to do with the clothes. The closest thing he ever saw to it was when he went to Mass with his grandparents. The boys with the priest wore things similar to them. Howard noticed Charlie's bewilderment.

"Yeah," he nodded and hung the surplice back in the closet. "We have to wear them to meals and classes and Mass. Pretty much all day. The only times we don't have to wear them is when we have recreation, and on the weekends, but we still have to wear them to the meals. Each dorm is assigned a color. We're red. Saint Peter dorm is purple. Saint Thomas is yellow. Saint Sebastian is blue. It's so the Brothers can tell where we belong easier." Howard leaned a bit closer to Charlie's ear. "I hate them, and if you ask me, I think we wear them because the Brothers are too old to remember our names."

Charlie smiled again. He was beginning to like Howard. He was funny and quite a character.

"See, there you go again." Howard beamed. "You're smiling. I think you're going to be okay, Charlie."

Howard opened the suitcase on the floor and froze. Slowly, he picked up the framed photograph and stood up. He stared at it and tears came to his eyes.

Charlie felt bad as he looked at Howard and the picture of his parents. He put his hand reassuringly on Howard's shoulder. Howard looked up and forced a smile.

"Your parents look like they're nice people," he said, staring at the picture. "My mom died when I was six. I was in first grade. She had an operation on her back and was in a body cast. Dad said she wasn't supposed to go up the stairs but she did. She lost her balance and fell down. She broke her neck. I found her when I came home from school." He looked away from the photograph. "My dad remarried shortly after that. His new wife didn't want any kids around, and so dad put me in here. I haven't heard from him since. He signed the papers for me to be adopted out if anyone wants me." He shrugged and handed Charlie the photograph.

The framed photograph slipped from Charlie's hands and landed on top of his clothes in the opened suitcase. As Charlie quickly bent down to pick it up his locket and key fell out from under his shirt. The tinkle sound caught Howard's attention and he stared at the oval locket and key curiously.

"What's the key for?" he asked.

Charlie quickly grabbed the key and stuck it under his shirt. He looked at Howard with wide eyes. Howard could see that Charlie was uneasy and so he smiled.

"It's okay," he assured him. "You might want to put your picture on your nightstand to keep it close," he said as he returned to unpacking Charlie's suitcase. "You sure don't have many clothes." Howard commented in a chipper voice. "That's okay because you really don't need a lot. When you're wearing your cassock, you'll only need a tee shirt and your jeans under it. Otherwise it gets too bulky and uncomfortable."

Just then the sound of a bell rang throughout the fourth floor. Charlie jumped nearly dropping the framed picture he just picked up.

"That's the bell for dinner. We have ten minutes to get ready and get downstairs," Howard talked fast again and opened his locker. "You best put that down and take off your shirt and get out one of your cassocks," Howard urged him.

Charlie set the picture down on one of the shelves in his closet and took off his short-sleeved plaid shirt. He stared at the black cassocks and red surplices in his closet and wondered which to put on first. He glanced over at Howard and noticed that he pulled his well-worn black cassock over his head. Howard noticed Charlie looking at him.

"You put the black one on first," Howard told him. "You'll find it quicker when you go to take it off if you leave all put the top three buttons buttoned. That way you just have to put it on over your head. After you button up your cassock you put on the red surplice." Howard pulled on his red surplice as he gave Charlie instructions. He then straightened his glasses and ran his fingers through his hair. "Ready," he said confidently and closed his closet door.

Charlie was still buttoning his cassock when the second bell rang. Howard grabbed one of Charlie's surplices and closed his closet door. He pushed Charlie toward the hall doors.

"Keep buttoning as you walk," he instructed as they pushed through the double doors and into the hallway. "We don't want to be late tonight. Here, put this on." He threw the red surplice over Charlie's head and pulled it down. Charlie slipped his hands through the full billowing sleeves and then glanced in the mirrors as they rushed past them.

"Perfect," Howard said as he looked at Charlie. "Come on. Hurry."

Howard and Charlie joined the sea of red, yellow, blue and purple clad boys as they wound their way down the stairs to the first floor. At the end of the stairs the boys separated into four straight rows, each with their own color, outside the refectory doors. A deafening silence replaced the noisy chatter and sound of footfalls.

"Here, stand in front of me," Howard told Charlie

quietly.

Charlie slipped into line just as the sound of swishing robes was heard from behind them. Charlie turned to see who it was but Howard nudged him.

"Don't look around," he whispered.

Charlie quickly turned back to face the front of the line. His curiosity was satisfied in just a few short moments when the four prefects took their places at the front of the line.

When the doors opened the purple robes of Saint Peter dorm entered first. The blue robes of Saint Sebastian were next; then the red robes of Saint Nicholas and finally the yellow robes of Saint Thomas.

The refectory was a long room with a high ceiling. Tall windows lined the east wall and looked out on the forest. Along the west wall, beginning to the left of the double doors, hung six large portraits, in gold ornate frames. The portraits were of elderly men all dressed in the robes of a monk. Each had a large crucifix on a golden chain hung about their necks. A brass nameplate was centered under each of the paintings, but Charlie couldn't make out the fine print. Four long wooden tables set in rows that ran the length of the hall. At the head of the hall by the entrance, a raised platform elevated the head table. Behind it hung a navy-blue velvet curtain. At either end of the curtain was a doorway leading to the kitchens.

Each dormitory prefect stood at the head of their long table as their charges walked single file down one side and back up the other until each one stood behind their chair. Once everyone was in their place, the prefects took their places beside Abbot Ambrose at the head table.

Abbot Ambrose stood silently at the center of the head table. His eyes surveyed the roomful of boys. His stern expression melted into a warm smile and his eyes twinkled.

"Tonight," he began in a cheerful voice. "We have cause to celebrate on two counts. First, we want to welcome a new member to our family, Charlie MacCready. He will be a member of Saint Nicholas dormitory. I hope you'll all make him feel at home."

The room broke into applause as all eyes turned toward him. Charlie ducked his head to hide his embarrassment at being singled out in front of strangers. His embarrassment and the applause didn't last long though as Abbot Ambrose continued.

"Our next cause for celebrating is our spectacular defeat of Saint Luke's Academy and being awarded the championship trophy."

The Saint Peter table broke into loud cheers, whistles and applause. Abbot Ambrose glared at them for their outburst and then smiled letting them have their moment. Father Vicar, a thin man with thinning dark black hair and eyes just as dark, looked panic-stricken and raised a quieting bony hand. As the table returned to silence, Abbot Ambrose continued.

"Our big hitter of the day is none other than our team's captain Master Dougary Duggan. His five home runs resulted in a total of seventeen points for our team. Congratulations, Master Duggan. Please come up and receive the award for Most Valuable Player."

Charlie turned around and watched the commotion at the Saint Peter table. A thin, yet toned young man with straight, rather long brown hair stepped forward. He appeared to be comfortable with the attention, something Charlie wished he could be.

Again, the room broke into applause, with the exception of Howard and two other boys at the Saint Nicholas table. Charlie noticed it immediately, and was confused. Howard looked at him and leaned toward him.

"I'll explain later," he whispered and then straightened up.

The applause died down as Dougary returned to his table and stood by his chair. His buddies from Saint Peter patted his back and offered their congratulations.

Charlie jumped when Abbot Ambrose clapped a small block of wood against the head table. He looked around as the room fell silent and as one, everyone bowed their head. Charlie looked up at the head table. Abbot Ambrose smiled at him kindly and bowed his head. Charlie did the same.

After Grace was said, everyone sat down in silence. The sound of the block of wood hitting the table again signaled the start of the meal. The boys were free to talk among themselves. Charlie watched as five monks wheeled carts of food out of the doorway to the right of the head table. The monks silently served their tables. Charlie turned his attention to the boys all around him. He wondered if they were all orphans as his uncle had said.

Howard was busy talking to the two boys seated across from them. The boy directly across from Howard was thin and blonde haired. His eyes were blue behind his wire-rimmed glasses, which gave him the air of being studious. The boy across from Charlie was pudgy. His sandy blonde hair looked as though someone had placed a bowl on his head and cut around it. His eyes were so dark they reminded Charlie of pieces of coal.

"Charlie," Howard nudged him and nodded toward the two boys. "This is Rick Walters. He's a student." He motioned toward the blonde-haired boy. "And this is Gustav Kugele. Gus has the cubicle next to ours. He's one of us, a resident." Charlie cringed at being referred to as a resident as he looked at the pudgy boy.

"Hi, Charlie," they both greeted as one.

Charlie didn't respond. Instead he looked at the plate that was just set in front of him. The smell of beef stew filled his nostrils and he realized he was hungry. He hadn't eaten all day; hadn't thought of food. There was just too much happening. He picked up his fork and began to eat.

"So, where are you from?" Rick asked and looked directly at Charlie.

Charlie looked up, his mouth full.

"He's from Hillsborough." Howard jumped in.

"I was asking Charlie." Rick glared at Howard.

Gus looked at Rick and then at Howard and wiped his mouth with his napkin. He was used to their sparring but it still made him nervous. He moved his plate and chair over a bit.

"So, I hear you don't talk," Rick continued and looked at Charlie. "Tell me," he leaned forward. "Is it can't or won't?"

"He ca—" Howard started to answer, but was silenced by Rick's halting glare.

"I know you can talk, Howie." He turned back to Charlie. "But I was asking Charlie."

Howard put down his fork and knife. It was obvious to Charlie that he was annoyed at Rick for pressing the issue. Howard leaned toward Rick.

"Look you little idiot," he lowered his voice and tightened his jaws. "If you don't let up, I'll make sure you get work crew for the rest of the summer."

Rick's eyes suddenly widened and he glanced at the head table. He looked at Howard, then settled back in his chair and continued to eat in silence.

Howard grinned proudly at Charlie and noticed his confused expression.

"Work crew is the monks' way of punishing us. We

have to give up our free time to do chores. Right now, if you get work crew, you're sent to help the monks harvest the crops. It is hard and dirty work and something to be avoided at any cost," Howard explained.

Charlie nodded that he understood.

Howard smiled, and returned to eating.

Charlie was glad when dinner was through. He could retreat to his cubicle and shut out the rest of the world. After Abbot Ambrose clapped the block of wood against the table everyone rose and stood behind their chairs. One by one, the tables emptied as they filed out of the refectory behind their prefects. As soon as they reached the stairs, the neat rows dissolved into a flurry of color as everyone headed back to their dorms to change their clothes.

THE ATTIC

The next two weeks passed quickly for Charlie. The placement test he had taken put him in the eighth-grade class along with Howard, Rick and Gus, much to his relief. The test now over, Charlie settled into his life at Saint Michael's. Even though he felt a friendship with Howard, Rick and Gus, he still wouldn't speak. He knew deep down any day that one of them could be adopted and they would be gone. No, he wouldn't allow himself to be hurt again.

Howard filled him in on who was who around the home. Dougary, the baseball star, was a student, one of the boys for whom Saint Michael's was their last hope before juvenile home. His parents, being wealthy and prominent in town, were able to strike a bargain with the judge when Dougary ended up in trouble with the law for theft, assault and running away from home. So he was sent to Saint Michael's instead of the local juvenile home.

Dougary's buddies, Travis Bleckinger, a short stocky boy with blonde hair that resembled straw, Austin Fulton, a reedy boy with a hook nose and glasses, and Larry Hertz, who resembled a bulldog more than a boy, were all students and trouble makers. They were all members of Saint Peter dorm and, coincidentally, members of the baseball team. They formed a sort of gang which tormented Howard and the other members of Saint Nicholas dorm because they were the youngest members of the home, and most of them were residents with no parents to come to their defense.

Howard also explained that most of the students went home on one weekend a month and on holidays. This gave them at least one weekend a month of peace without Dougary and his goons, and made life a bit more bearable.

He also filled Charlie in on the elite club of the Altar Boys. It was a twelve-member group who were selected by Abbot Ambrose to serve as altar boys for the monastery. They could be identified by their white surplices with lace around the sleeves and the bottom hem. These boys were granted special privileges such as being able to roam the front grounds freely and use the main entrance. They also had access to the monastery wing and the private gardens in addition to the sacristy in the Abbey church. No one knew the exact criteria Abbot Ambrose used other than the boys tended to be at least twelve years old. Once you were selected a member, you were a member until you were adopted, graduated or reached your eighteenth birthday. Charlie could tell by the way Howard talked about it that he really wanted to be a member of the Altar Boys.

Howard also explained about the realities of adoption as he saw them. "Couples want to adopt young boys," he told Charlie. "Every year your chances of being adopted become fewer. Once you become a teenager, you might as forget ever belonging to a family. I've only three more months left." As he said that, Charlie noticed there were tears in his eyes.

The day of the seminarians' return had come. At breakfast, Abbot Ambrose announced that all members of the fourth floor would be confined to the fourth floor for the entire day. "As a safety precaution," he explained. "We don't want anyone to be trampled as the seminarians get moved in. And we have a special favor to ask of the members of Saint Peter dorm and Saint Nicholas dorm. Please do not stand in the windows and act like monkeys. Last year we received several comments from the families of the seminarians."

Howard and Charlie lay on their beds in their cubicle, looking through a stack of old comic books. Howard's former bunkmate gave the books to him when he was adopted a few months earlier. Gus lay on his bed on the other side of the partition from Howard, listening to a small radio that was held together with a piece of masking tape. He busied himself by gluing Popsicle sticks together in no particular order or shape. Two boys played checkers on the sofa, while over their heads a sponge cut in the shape of a football flew back and forth as two older boys played catch.

The makeshift ball landed for the sixth time on Rick, who was seated in one of the overstuffed chairs and trying to get a head start on some of his classes. He slammed his book closed, grabbed the sponge ball, and threw it away from the boys. He muttered under his breath for them to play someplace else as he headed back to his cubicle in the opposite corner of the dorm from Howard and Charlie.

Howard looked up when the thud of Rick's book caused everyone to jump. He watched Rick and shook his head.

"Well I'm just having too much fun." he sighed sarcastically. "I've got to get out of here or I'm going to go nuts."

Charlie looked up from his comic book.

"You with me?" Howard asked with a rather sinister smile.

Charlie smiled and nodded. He couldn't resist the adventure. He closed his comic book and sat up.

"Come on," Howard whispered as he looked around and put his comic book away. As soon as he was sure it was safe, the two headed for the door.

"And just where do you two think you are headed?" A voice from behind them said as their hands touched the doors.

They both spun around. Their hearts pounded in their chests.

"Don't sneak up on people!" Howard snapped at Rick. "What business is it of yours anyway?"

"Because if you two get caught leaving this floor it means work crew for the entire dorm and I don't want to spend my weekend working in some stupid hop field." Rick returned just as curt with his fists resting on his bony hips.

"Oh, don't worry," Howard sneered. "We're just going to the bathroom." He pushed the door open and walked out. Charlie followed without a word and glanced back as the doors closed in Rick's face.

Howard started toward the bathrooms, but paused and looked around. When he was sure no one was watching, he turned back toward the fire doors at the end of the hall.

"Come on," he whispered and quietly tiptoed over to the doors. He glanced over his shoulder one last time to be sure no one would see them, then leaned against the fire door. He held a finger to his lips, as if Charlie really needed to be told to be quiet. Slowly the door just enough for him to slip through and Charlie followed. The door closed behind them, and Charlie found they were in a stairwell.

"This leads down to the main lobby," Howard whispered, and pointed to the stairs. "Those lead to the monastery wing," he said, pointing to the fire doors opposite the doors they had just come through. "Everyone except members of the Altar Boys is forbidden to enter there."

Charlie listened as Howard explained. He was beginning to wonder what they were doing in the stairwell but he didn't have to wait long.

"See there." Howard pointed to the ladder on the wall that led to a doorway in the ceiling. "That's the attic."

Charlie couldn't help but notice the twinkle in Howard's eyes as he grinned from ear to ear.

"No one's allowed up there so we have to be very quiet. Come on."

Before Charlie could object, Howard had mounted the ladder and was opening the attic door. Charlie quickly followed him, not really sure why. Once inside the attic, Howard closed the door and the attic went dark for a moment.

A few seconds later, as his eyes adjusted to the dark, Charlie could see light streaming in through the half-moon windows built into the dormers that were evenly spaced along the roofline. Unlike his attic back home, he could stand straight up and walk about freely. He didn't need to stoop. The attic was huge and ran the full length of the building.

"We can even walk over the monastery wing," Howard said. "There's lots of neat old junk up here." He made a sweeping gesture with his hands at many boxes, trunks and old furniture everywhere.

"Most of the guys wouldn't dare come up here," he continued as they walked over their dormitory ceiling. "There's an old story about it being haunted." Howard stopped and peered out one of the half-moon windows.

Charlie looked out the window, but his fear of heights kept him at a distance from the dormer. The view appeared to be the same as from the window over his bed, just higher. He could clearly see the driveway that ran from the Abbey portico along the west edge of the huge lawn to the parking lot, the garage building, and the road down the hill before it disappeared into the forest.

"We're right above your bed, Charlie." Howard informed him. "If you look straight down you can see the portico over the entrance." Howard leaned against the window a bit more. "This is where they say it happened." His voice changed to an almost haunting tone.

Charlie shot Howard a curious look. It didn't go unnoticed. Howard sat down on the bare wooden floor. Charlie crawled over to him, careful not to look out the window.

"The story says that about forty years ago an orphaned boy was locked up here over night by a group of hoodlums from Saint Peter dorm. It was supposed to be a practical joke because the boy was afraid of the dark, but it didn't end up that way.

"As night fell and the sun went down, the attic grew darker and darker, and the boy grew more and more afraid. They say he clawed at the locked attic door and screamed and begged to be let out. All the while the hoodlums laughed and made creepy noises. They continued all night.

"In the morning, however, one of the older boys from his dorm found out what the bullies had done and came to the boy's rescue. He found the boy huddled by this window, his hair completely white and his skin as pale as a ghost. There were dark circles under his eyes, which were wide with fear. The boy stared blindly into the attic. His friend called to him, but the white-haired boy didn't answer. When the older boy walked over to him, the white-haired boy, panicked thinking his friend was a monster or something. He pushed him away. His friend lost his balance and fell against this very window. It shattered and he fell to his death. He landed on the top of the portico. It took the Brothers months to get the blood cleaned off the bricks.

"As for the white-haired boy, he disappeared. Some say that he's living in the woods around here, waiting until he can get his revenge on the bullies that tormented him." Howard shrugged. "I don't believe it," he said in his normal voice. "You'd think after forty years someone would've seen him lurking around in the trees. He'd have to be at least fifty-three years old, wouldn't you think?

"Ah, it's just a stupid old story told by the older boys to scare the younger ones." Howard stood up and dusted off his jeans.

Charlie shivered as he thought about the story. He was never one to be afraid of the dark or the attic for that matter. He did not even believe in ghosts, but this story did pique his curiosity.

"Come on," Howard quietly called to him. "I'll show you another way out of here."

Charlie stood up, dusted off his pants, and followed Howard deeper into the attic. He guessed they were getting closer to the bathroom area.

"Here," Howard said, stopping and looking down. By his feet was what appeared to be a vent over the bathrooms.

Charlie took a closer look. It was an old vent; the air pipe had been removed a long time before. The vent was over one of the stalls in the bathroom.

Howard looked down through the vent to make sure the coast was clear and then he pried the vent open. "Come on," he instructed. "Just hold onto the sides and lower yourself onto the top of the stall then you can climb down onto the toilet and wait for me."

Charlie did not like the idea. His heart pounded as thoughts of falling filled his mind. He hesitated but then seeing Howard looking at him, urging him to hurry up, he carefully followed the instructions and found himself safely on the floor in the bathroom. Howard climbed onto the stall walls and replaced the vent cover then hopped down to the floor.

"Crawl under the wall to the next stall and flush the toilet. We'll meet by the sinks. Okay?" Howard whispered.

Moments later they were walking back to their dorm. Charlie was relieved that their little excursion was over, yet he was glad that he had gone with Howard.

"Hey, where've you two been?" Rick demanded as they returned to their cubicle.

"What's it to you?" Howard answered smugly. He turned to Charlie. "Just because he's six months older than me and gets better grades, he thinks he's the boss. But you're not my father!" Howard snapped at Rick.

"Well, you better not be sneaking up to the attic again. You know it's off limits. If you get caught up there you both will be in so much trouble you won't know what hit you."

"If you don't shut up, I'll hit you!" Howard said.

"You were in the attic?" Gus poked his head around the partition and looked at the three.

"Will you keep your voice down!" Howard shushed him. "And no, we weren't in the attic," he lied.

The bell rang signaling it was time to get ready for dinner. Howard ignored Rick and Gus and left to get dressed. Charlie noticed Rick's condemning stare and Gus's awed expression at the thought that he had visited the forbidden attic. Without a word, he followed Howard to the closets.

"Later on, I'll show you something else," Howard said as he pulled his surplice over his head. "You aren't going to believe this, just you wait." He smiled and his eyes had that twinkle again.

Charlie nodded and smiled at the thought of going on another one of Howard's little adventures.

"You know," Howard said as he combed his hair with his fingers. "I think we're going to be best friends. Let's go, buddy."

Charlie closed his closet door and followed after Howard. Yes, he thought to himself. We are going to be best friends.

HOWARD'S GIFT

The sun shone brightly on the last day of summer break. After breakfast, Howard and Charlie raced back to their dorm to change their clothes. Charlie was anxious to see where Howard would take him. As they hurried down the hall to the stairs, they bumped into Dougary and his three thugs, Travis, Larry and Austin.

"So, where are you two girls off to in such a hurry?" Dougary looked down his nose at Howard and Charlie.

"None of your business." Howard brushed him off. "And we're not girls."

"Oh, but you're wrong," Dougary came back. "It is my business. Why don't you show him, Travis?"

"My pleasure." Travis sneered. He stepped forward, rubbing his fist into his hand. Austin and Larry stepped behind Howard and Charlie, blocking their escape.

Charlie was actually becoming a bit nervous. The last thing he wanted was to be involved in a fight. He tried not to show his feelings as he looked at Larry and Austin.

"Now, this is gonna hurt you a lot more than it will us,"

Travis laughed wickedly.

"Excuse me," a voice came from behind them. "Am I interrupting something?"

Austin, Travis and Larry jumped at the sound of Father Emmanuel's voice. They quickly took a less threatening stance and moved away from Charlie and Howard.

"No," they all said and shook their heads. "Not at all. We were just having a friendly little chat. That's all."

"Well," Father Emmanuel smiled knowingly. "Why don't we let the four of you continue your chatting next Saturday as you help the Brothers in the hop fields?"

"But—" Dougary protested.

"Want to make it two Saturdays, Master Dougary?" Father Emmanuel said more than asked.

"No, Father," Dougary answered sheepishly.

"Good. Not another word then." Father Emmanuel smiled at Howard and Charlie and motioned with his eyes for them to leave before he continued down the hall.

Howard and Charlie laughed all the way down the stairs.

"Did you see the look on Dougary's face when Father Emmanuel gave them work crew?" Howard laughed.

Charlie nodded and followed Howard quickly out the back door.

Outside the back door and away from the building was a large field. A running track encircled two baseball diamonds complete with bleachers. Howard ignored the calls to join the baseball game and led Charlie toward the right, toward the monastery wing.

"This is another place we are not supposed to go," he said, and shrugged as they continued to walk. "But I'll show you, anyway."

The backside of the building was just as stark as the front.

From this side, Charlie realized the building was made in the shape of a giant E on the ground. As they passed the center wing, Howard explained to Charlie that it was the Abbey church, and pointed to the stained-glass windows that lined the walls nearly two stories above them. To Charlie's surprise they appeared dark and gray instead of the bright colors he had seen from the inside.

When they approached the monastery wing, Charlie noticed that a tall laurel hedge formed a wall in front of them. As they drew closer, Charlie could see a wrought iron gate in the center of the hedge. He began to grow nervous as Howard approached the gate. If this area is off limits, why was he showing it to me, he thought to himself. Is he trying to get me in trouble?

"What are you two doing?" a voice said as Howard reached for the latch.

Charlie and Howard jumped and spun around. Their hearts pounded in their throats.

"Don't sneak up on people like that." Howard snapped as he tried to catch his breath. "You could give someone a heart attack."

"Well, you shouldn't be snooping around places where you don't belong," Rick said smugly and tried not to laugh at them.

"Oh, bug off, you self-righteous pain-in-the-butt," Howard snapped, and turned around to peer inside the cloistered gardens.

"Well, I guess I'll just have to tell Abbot Ambrose you aren't interested." Rick shrugged and turned around, pretending to be leaving.

"Not interested in what?" Howard snapped as he turned around sharply, his curiosity roused.

"Oh, nothing important." Rick started to take a step.

Howard jumped at him, grabbing his arm and spinning him around. Rick could tell that Howard was upset.

"What is it, you scrawny little brat?" Howard demanded; his fist raised ready to punch Rick.

"Okay. Okay." Rick laughed and freed his arm from Howard's tight grasp. "Abbot Ambrose wants you to get cleaned up and come to visitation room three right away. There is a couple there who want to meet you. I can't for the life of me understand why."

Howard's eyes lit up. Charlie knew Howard had been there for nearly five years, and was less than three months from giving up all hope of ever having a family again. He looked at Howard and forced a smile.

"I'll catch up with you later," Howard said, and ran off, leaving the two behind.

Charlie watched Howard leave, and then looked around. His mind was reeling as he tried to sort out his thoughts and feelings about what he had just heard. He turned back to the cloistered garden gate, not thinking or seeing anything at all.

It's happening again, he thought to himself and the familiar lump rose in his throat.

"Oh no you don't," Rick said, turning Charlie around. "You aren't going in there while I'm here to get the blame. Come on." He steered Charlie back toward their wing. "We can go for a walk this way. There are still plenty of things to see over here without getting into trouble."

The two headed toward the baseball fields. Charlie wasn't in the mood to watch a game but he let Rick lead him across the field anyway.

"You don't strike me as the athletic type," Rick said as they drew closer to the backstop. "But since you're going to be here for a long time, you might as well know a little bit about the tradition here. Each summer all the dorms select a team from their members. We then have playoffs between the teams. The best team then gets to represent the school against other schools. Sometimes, like this year, some of the best players from the other dorms are added to the team.

"There are eleven schools in our league. All the teams compete against each other for five weeks. Then the four top-ranking teams play in the finals. The winning team gets the trophy for a year and the highest scorer gets a medal. Unfortunately, this year it went to Dougary. He's such a jerk." Rick clenched his teeth. "Come on, let's go for a walk."

Charlie sighed; he really didn't want to walk around listening to Rick. In fact, he wasn't sure just what he thought of him. Rick was nice enough, but Howard was more like himself, not the best in school, but not the worst. Still, Charlie found himself walking along a narrow brick path not far from the field.

"Have you seen the cemetery?" Rick asked.

Cemetery? Charlie thought to himself. Why would there be a cemetery up here? He shook his head in answer to Rick's question.

"It's just over there." Rick pointed up the path a bit.

Charlie looked in the direction and saw a waist-high hedge, neatly trimmed. A small chapel building stood on the other side, complete with stained glass windows. As they drew closer, the tops of some of the larger monuments became visible just above the hedge.

"They don't use the chapel anymore," Rick stated plainly as they stood looking over the hedge.

"Whenever someone dies here, the Brothers toll the big bell in the tower once for every year of the dead person's life. Sometimes when you count the tolls you can guess who died. You wouldn't believe how long some of these monks live. The

Brothers that ring the bell are exhausted afterward. Just beyond the trees over there in the far corner, I'm told," Rick said as he pointed away from the main cluster of monuments, "is where they bury the boys who die here. During 1918 there were quite a few boys that died in the flu epidemic. Luckily there hasn't been any boys die here in a long time.

"Come on, I'll show you the swimming pool," Rick said and started to walk off.

Just then the bell rang for lunch. Charlie was relieved. His stomach was beginning to let him know that he was hungry, especially since he didn't eat much at breakfast; also, he was tired of Rick's constant talking and their tour. Charlie bolted back to the dorm to change clothes, leaving Rick far behind. Spurred on by the thought that he would meet up with Howard, he ran faster and faster.

When he reached the dorm, Howard was nowhere to be seen. Charlie changed his clothes, and then checked their cubicle one last time before heading downstairs for lunch. As he walked down the stairs he tried to look ahead to see if perhaps Howard had already changed and was waiting downstairs. It was hard to see over the heads of the taller boys, but it soon became obvious to him that Howard was not there. A sinking feeling in the pit of his stomach took away his appetite.

The meal seemed to drag on. Charlie barely ate any of his food. He kept looking at the empty chair beside him. Even though he had only known Howard for a couple weeks, he couldn't imagine living there without him. They had bonded like brothers. It was as though they had known each other all their lives. Now it was happening all over again, he thought to himself.

Charlie was never so glad to finally be through with the meal. As all of the boys began to file out of the refectory, Abbot

Ambrose stepped down from the head table. He nodded as the boys all passed by him. When he saw Charlie, a smile spread across his thin lips and he stepped forward.

"Charlie," his voice was kind. "I was wondering if I might have a word with you."

Charlie's heart sank even more as he anticipated what the Abbot wanted to tell him. He nodded and then followed Abbot Ambrose into the corridor.

"We can talk over here, it won't take long," he said as he ushered Charlie into one of the visitation rooms.

As they entered Charlie was hit by the scent of flowers, roses to be exact. He looked at the side table just inside the door to his left. A large crystal vase sat filled with freshly cut roses. In the center of the room were a sofa and two straight back chairs. A coffee table sat in front of the sofa, the sunlight from the window on the opposite wall reflected off its shiny wooden surface.

"Please, have a seat, Charlie." Abbot Ambrose directed him to the sofa while he took a chair across from him.

"Charlie," he began softly, "You've probably heard that Howard had visitors today. They're a nice older couple and they're wanting to adopt a boy about Howard's age. They weren't able to have children of their own. They could offer the right boy a good life, a good home and the love of fine parents."

Charlie couldn't look at Abbot Ambrose; instead he looked at the floor. He tried not to think about the tightening in his throat and chest. He felt as though he couldn't breathe.

"I think you should know," Abbot Ambrose said sympathetically seeing Charlie's sad expression. "Howard turned them down."

Charlie looked up suddenly. His mouth opened in shock. He knew how much Howard wanted to belong to a family, to be adopted. He couldn't believe his ears. He turned them down?

"Yes," Abbot Ambrose said as though reading Charlie's mind. "He told them that he didn't want to leave you behind. He even tried to convince them to adopt you too, but they only wanted one child. So he said he wasn't the boy for them."

Abbot Ambrose paused and looked at the twelve-year-old boy in front of him. He wondered if he really understood the huge sacrifice Howard had made on his behalf. Did Charlie appreciate it? He stroked his white beard, deep in thought.

The tightness Charlie had felt in his throat and chest was gone. His ears kept echoing the Abbot's words "He turned them down." He blindly looked about the room and wondered where Howard could be? He needed to see him to understand why he did it. He had the chance to leave but he stayed.

"That's all I wanted to say," Abbot Ambrose spoke firmly. Charlie focused his eyes on him. "You would do well to think about the special sacrifice Howard made on your behalf. You may go."

Nervously Charlie stood up. He nodded to Abbot Ambrose and then hurried out of the room. He had figured out where he might find Howard but he would have to be careful. He ran up the stairs as he formed his plan.

Moments later, Charlie stood in the attic waiting for his eyes to adjust to the afternoon sunlight that poured in through the half-moon windows. Once they did, Charlie could see clear to the far end of the attic. There were many more boxes and old trunks than he first thought from their visit a week ago. He ignored them and turned his attention toward the window above their cubicle, the one that Howard had shown him. Slowly, quietly he crept across the wooden floor. The boards creaked softly under his feet. Sure enough, Howard was sitting on the floor by the window. Charlie took a deep breath and walked toward him. His robes rustled as he moved.

Howard looked up and gave him a slight smile. "So, you found me," he said in a rather depressed tone and turned his head away.

"Why did you do it?" Charlie asked. His voice was hoarse. "It's what you've wanted for five years."

Howard looked at Charlie, his eyes wide in shock. "You talked!" he gasped.

Charlie ignored Howard's surprise. "You told me yourself about the odds of being adopted once you hit thirteen. I'm not worth it."

"That's not true," Howard answered flatly. "You're my friend. I can't leave you here."

Charlie looked at Howard in silence.

"It just seemed like the right thing to do." Howard shrugged.

"Howard, I don't know what to say." Charlie shook his head, letting Howard's words sink in. He pulled up his robes and sat down on the floor across from his friend. "I'm glad you didn't go. I mean, it just seems like everyone I ever care about leaves me or is taken away. When I was two years old, in the middle of the night, my parents took me to my grandparents and left me there. They said they'd come back for me, but they never did. Then, one night last winter, my grandfather died. After that it was just grandma and me. Things were fine until my mother's older brother, my Uncle Chester, stuck his fat nose in. I overheard him talking to my grandma one night. He said that she needed to go to a home for old people and that I needed to go to an orphanage since my parents were dead. Grandma doesn't believe that and neither do I. Once my parents find out that I'm here, they'll come for me. I'm sure of it."

As Howard listened to Charlie, to his determined hope, he couldn't help but feel sorry for him. He had seen it so many times in his five years at Saint Michael's. At first the new boys were in denial, hoping to wake up from a bad dream and be back at home with their parents. It usually took about a year for it to sink in that this, being an orphan and being at St. Michael's, was their reality. Their only hope for a home and a family now was adoption. When he looked at Charlie, he hoped he was wrong, that his parents were alive, that they really would come for him.

"When they do come for me," Charlie continued. "I'll ask them to adopt you and then we can be brothers forever." Charlie beamed with a bright smile. "Wouldn't that be great?"

"Yeah." Howard smiled. "Well, we best be getting—"

Suddenly there came a noise at the far end of the attic above the monastery wing, a sound like heavy footsteps. Charlie and Howard jumped and looked at each other. Howard held a finger to his lips to tell Charlie to keep very quiet. Cautiously they peered around the stack of boxes.

In the distance they could see a monk with his hood raised over his head to hide his face from view slowly walk up the center isle toward them. He appeared to be searching for something among the many boxes and trunks. He stopped and carefully removed a stack of boxes from the top of an old trunk. There was a jingling of keys and then a click as the lock on the trunk popped open. The old lock actually sounded as though it broke, Charlie thought. The monk choked from the dust that flew into the air as he opened the trunk.

"What's he doing?" Charlie whispered.

"I don't know." Howard shook his head.

"Do you know him?" Charlie asked keeping his eyes glued

THE GHOST IN THE ATTIC

on the scene in the distance.

"I'm not sure," he answered. Just then a ray of sunlight hit a golden object on the mysterious monk's hand. Howard gulped in air. "It's Brother Simon," he breathed. "If he catches us up here, we're going to be in big trouble." Howard turned away from the sight and sat with his back against the boxes.

"What shall we do?" Charlie asked and kept a lookout.

"Keep quiet for one thing." Howard answered. "Maybe he'll go away and not stay up here too long."

"Right." Charlie agreed and kept watching Brother Simon. The gaunt monk looked up and down the attic and then took a package from under his cloak. Charlie thought it looked like a thick book. Charlie wished he were closer so he could get a better look at what it was, but he didn't dare move a muscle.

Brother Simon quickly placed it into the trunk and closed the lid. He tried the latch but it wouldn't lock. He restacked the boxes on top of the trunk and turned away to leave.

Suddenly, a noise came from the opposite end of the attic over the student wing, a deep, mournful, moaning sound. Brother Simon turned around sharply and looked in Charlie's direction. His eyes narrowed as he peered into the distance. Charlie quickly ducked back behind the boxes and held his breath. His heart pounded in his chest. He heard the noise, which at first scared him, but the possibility of being discovered was even more frightening.

Charlie listened as he held his breath. The sound must have frightened Brother Simon because the sound of heavy footsteps running away echoed throughout the attic.

The sound of the attic door slamming shut brought Howard and Charlie to their knees. They looked around cautiously.

"He's gone," Charlie breathed with a sigh of relief.

"What was that sound?" Howard remained nervous as he

looked in the opposite direction.

"I don't know." Charlie looked too but then looked at Howard and smiled. "Don't tell me you think it's the ghost?"

Howard looked at Charlie and tried to hide his fear.

"No," he lied. "Let's just get out of here."

They both bolted for the door back to the fourth floor. Neither one looked back to see who had made the noise. They were focused on getting back down the ladder.

"Hey, Charlie." Howard called him quietly as he stepped off the ladder.

Charlie turned around to look at him.

"Don't tell anyone why I turned those people down, okay? If Dougary and his creeps find out they'll make it sound like it was something else, you know? It would be disastrous for both of us."

"Don't worry." Charlie smiled. "This will remain our secret."

THE GHOST IN THE ATTIC

"Hey guys, wait up," Gus called as he hurried after Howard and Charlie.

They stopped at the top of the stairs and turned around. Charlie smiled, seeing Gus running to catch up, his cassock unevenly buttoned and his red surplice still half pulled over his head. Gus struggled to pull it the rest of the way on as he juggled his thick World Cultures book and binder in his other hand. As he neared, he tripped over his untied tennis shoe laces, and dropped everything as he fell on the floor.

"Come on, Gus." Howard sighed quickly, coming to Gus' aid and helping him to his feet. Charlie collected the pens, book and binder, while Gus tied his shoes. It was obvious to Charlie that despite Howard's teasing, he really did like Gus.

"You need to redo the buttons on your cassock before you trip again." Howard said impatiently. "But it will have to wait or we're going to be late for class, and you know what Brother Simon does to tardy people."

"I know," Gus panted, out of breath. "I'm sorry. I overslept."

"We know." Charlie smiled.

"So, did you hear it again last night?" Gus asked as they all quickly made their way down the stairs.

"Hear what?" Howard pretended not to know.

"The moaning in the attic," Gus whispered fearfully. "You know, the ghost."

"Oh," Howard scoffed and gave a little laugh. "That was just the wind."

Charlie looked at Howard. He had heard the noise too. In fact, when he looked over at Howard, he saw him staring at the ceiling, his covers pulled up to his chin.

"It didn't sound like the wind to me," There was a note of hostility in Gus' voice. "I know the difference between wind and the sound a ghost makes. I'm not stupid, as everyone seemed to think."

"You don't really believe in that stuff, do you?" Charlie asked.

Gus looked at Charlie with widened eyes. "Oh, it's real, Charlie," he said. "Just ask Brother Tobias, the mechanic. He'll tell you. Say, when you guys were in the attic, did you see anything?" Gus looked at Howard and then back at Charlie. "I mean, did you see the ghost?"

Charlie shook his head but Howard let out a forced laugh.

"Of course not, silly! That's the whole point of being a ghost. You're invisible."

Gus thought for a moment. "Oh, yeah," he agreed. "I was just testing you guys. I knew that."

Charlie smiled. He saw through Gus's attempt to save himself from being embarrassed by his slip of the tongue. Still, he liked Gus.

They reached the basement just as the bell rang for class. The three gave a collective groan and picked up their pace but without actually running, since running in the halls was strictly forbidden and anyone caught would get work crew for a month of Saturdays. As they entered the classroom, they let out a sigh of relief. Brother Simon wasn't in the room. They quickly took their seats.

"Hey Howie," a voice called to him from the back row. "You little girls lucked out this time."

Howard, Charlie and Gus ignored the heckler and settled into their desks.

"What's the matter, Howie? Cat got your tongue," chided Travis.

"That's it, just try to ignore us." Dougary nodded and glared at the back of Howard's head. "You're mine. I owe you big time for last Saturday. You better watch yourself."

Larry shot a spit wad at Howard. It hit him in the back of the head. He elbowed Austin and the two snickered.

Howard turned around sharply just as Brother Simon entered the room.

"Master Miller!" Brother Simon's voice was cold as ice. "Turn around or you'll be spending Saturday in the fields."

Howard jumped and quickly obeyed as Dougary and his buddies snickered under their breaths.

World Cultures was the most boring of all the classes Charlie had. Brother Simon's monotone reading and lecturing was enough to put even Rick to sleep. The one positive thing, however, was that Brother Simon hated basketball and sports in general as much as he appeared to hate children. In fact, on game nights, when all of the other teachers let them go without homework, Brother Simon usually handed out double his usual amount. The homework load proved to be too much for Dougary and his buddies, who had failed the course the year before and had to retake it. It was the one thing that brought a smile to Brother Simon's otherwise stern face.

Brother Simon began class as usual with a long lecture. As he paced up and down the aisles, he appeared to be looking at Howard and Charlie most of the time. It made Charlie feel uncomfortable. When the bell rang out, they were in luck again. Brother Simon failed to give them any homework.

Out in the hall again, Howard, Charlie and Gus headed for their next class. They were thankful that Dougary and his goons had class in the opposite direction, and wouldn't be tormenting them again.

"So, why should we talk to Brother Tobias?" Charlie asked, reopening their earlier conversation.

"Because he was around in those days." Gus whispered. "You know, when *it* happened."

"He doesn't look old enough." Charlie said as he quickly did the math. "He'd have to be in his fifties by now, and he surely doesn't look that old."

"He was ten when it happened; don't let his looks fool you." Gus sounded sure.

"Come on, Charlie, don't tell me you're starting to believe it too?" Howard rolled his eyes.

"No," Charlie answered. "I don't believe in ghosts, but I did hear something last night, and I know it wasn't the wind. Someone flesh and bone had to have made that noise. I'd just like to know who it was and why, that's all." Charlie turned back to Gus. "Has anyone ever tried to find out the real story behind this ghost story?"

Gus thought for a moment then shook his head. Howard let out a heavy sigh and stepped in front of them.

"No one has because it's just a story," Howard said in a very annoyed tone. "The older kids are always trying to scare the younger ones and new kids. I only told you the story so you wouldn't believe it in case one of them tried to scare you. So, can we just drop it?"

Charlie looked at Howard. Something about the look on his face told Charlie that Howard believed it more than he was letting on, and he was just as frightened as Gus was. Charlie smiled.

"Sure," he nodded but made a mental note to see Brother Tobias as soon as possible. But first he would have to find a way, since the front grounds were off limits.

As they settled down to lunch later that day, Rick seemed to be excited more than usual. Almost as soon as Abbot Ambrose signaled that it was okay to talk, Rick launched in to his big news.

"Have you heard? Last year two members of the Altar Boys turned eighteen and moved out, and just last week Clifford was adopted by a couple named Murphy, so that makes three openings for the club. I've got to get into that club," Rick said.

Charlie could almost see the wheels in Rick's head turning, as though he was trying to formulate some plan on how to get in.

"Say, wasn't that the name of the couple that wanted to adopt you, Howard?" Gus asked, as he thought hard to remember.

Howard shrugged and tried to play it off. "It could've been. I don't really remember," he lied. He glanced at Charlie. Charlie looked down at his plate, trying not to feel guilty.

"So, what do you have to do to be selected as a member of the Altar Boys?" Charlie asked, and tried to steer the conversation away from the Murphys.

"That's just it, nobody knows," Rick admitted and settled back in his chair. "Abbot Ambrose chooses the replacements on his own. Usually he does it at the end of the first quarter of school, around Halloween. So, maybe he looks at our grades." Rick's eyes lit up.

"If that were true," Howard forced a laugh. "Then why was Randy chosen? He failed three classes including Physical Ed.?"

"Oh," Rick said as the hopeful look in his eyes faded away. "That's right," he sighed and slumped a bit in his chair.

"Well, whatever it is," Gus frowned. "I'll never make it."

"Don't be too hard on yourself, Gus." Charlie smiled. "So what do we know about the members?" he asked looking at Howard and Rick.

"As for ages, three of the members are seventeen, two are sixteen and three are fifteen and one is fourteen." Rick submitted.

"Yes, and there are four from Saint Peter, two from Saint Sebastian, two from Saint Thomas and only one from our dorm," Howard added. "So, what does that tell us? Nothing. That's what."

"Well, don't make it sound so hopeless." Rick snapped at Howard. "There has to be some method to the selection process."

A blank look came over Howard's eyes. Suddenly he looked up, then he started to move his head around as though he were following an invisible fly. Without warning he grabbed at the air and brought his clenched fist in front of his face. Slowly he opened it.

"Andrew," he announced with a grin and returned to eating his lunch.

"Very funny," Rick scoffed.

Gus and Charlie looked at each other and bit their tongues to keep from laughing out loud.

The rest of the meal passed in silence. Rick was obviously put off by Howard's sarcasm and Charlie's quiet snickering.

Gus could care less about the club, feeling as though he didn't stand a chance. At least that was what he said.

The afternoon seemed to fly by for Charlie, Howard and the rest of the boys. With classes over, they had returned to their dorm to change clothes and relax before the dinner bell. Charlie was too tired from running all day to classes. He didn't bother to change his clothes; instead he just dropped down onto his bed and stared up at the ceiling. His thoughts soon drifted back to their conversation about the ghost in the attic. Then something Gus said started to cause him to wonder. He sat up.

"Howard, do you know a way to get to the garages without being seen?"

Howard, who was lying on his bed with his eyes closed, gave Charlie a disgusted look. "You aren't going to let this thing go, are you?"

"Howard, you know as well as I do that the noise we heard last night was *not* the wind. And what about that day in the attic? Even Brother Simon heard something," Charlie explained.

Howard turned over on his side and faced Charlie. "Don't tell me you're starting to believe in ghosts."

"No," Charlie answered with a note of disgust in his voice. "Besides, the sound we heard last night wasn't the moans of a boy. They were much deeper. More like what a man would sound like. Dead people don't age."

Howard thought for a moment. Charlie was right. The noise did sound more like a man, but who? Now his curiosity was piqued. He sat up on the edge of his bed and thought about a way to reach the garages without being seen. He shook his head.

"I don't know." He hated to admit.

"Well, how did Gus talk to Brother Tobias then?" Charlie asked.

"Good question." Howard turned toward the partition. "Hey Gus, you over there?"

"What?" came his groggy reply.

"Come over here," Howard ordered. Charlie gave him a stern look. "Please," he added. Charlie smiled.

The partition shook and the springs of Gus' bed squeaked signaling that he was on his way. Seconds later he appeared at the foot of Howard's bed. He leaned against the wagon wheel footboard as he yawned.

"What?" he asked as he looked at Howard with glassy, half-opened eyes?

"How did you manage to talk to Brother Tobias at the garage without getting caught?"

"Oh, I took the tunnel." He yawned again.

"The tunnel?" Charlie repeated in a whispered surprise. "Wow!"

"What tunnel?" Howard asked disbelievingly.

"The one behind Our Lady of the Subway," Gus said sleepily.

"Our Lady of the Subway?" Charlie looked at Howard. "Who's that?"

"That's the name Steve and Mike in Saint Sebastian dorm gave the statue of Mary in the grotto next to the cemetery." Gus yawned again. "Can I go back to bed? I want to get some sleep before dinner."

"Sure, go ahead," Howard said. He appeared upset that he hadn't known about the tunnel before. After all, he had been at Saint Michael's three years longer than Gus.

"Thank you," Charlie called as Gus retreated to his bed. The bedsprings squeaked and the partition shook as Gus settled back down for his nap.

"A tunnel," Charlie repeated. "This is so cool."

"Well, we'll have to wait until this weekend to check it out. In the meantime, we better keep this to ourselves," Howard whispered. "The last thing we need is for the rest of the guys to find out and then the tunnel will be guarded."

"Okay," Charlie agreed. "I wonder why they have a tunnel?" he thought out loud.

"Oh, there you go again." Howard shook his head. "Let's worry about one thing at a time."

Charlie looked at his bunkmate and smiled.

THE TUNNEL

Saturday morning finally arrived. Charlie was not sure which he was more excited about, talking to Brother Tobias about the noises in the attic, or the fact that there was a tunnel on the grounds. He could not believe their luck. At breakfast that morning, Abbot Ambrose announced that he, Father Emmanuel, and Father Vicar, would be taking the upperclassmen to town. They would be assisting the Brothers with the Abbey's booth at the Oktoberfest. They would not be back until dinner.

Charlie rushed through his breakfast and hurried outside to meet up with Howard. Howard had left breakfast early, saying he needed to do something before they met at the backstop on the athletic field.

The sun shone brightly in the autumn sky. There was a bit of a nip in the air and Charlie could see his breath. He shivered as he waited by the backstop and wished Howard had let them change their clothes. Some other boys dressed in the jeans and sweatshirts walked by and gave Charlie a funny look. Charlie ignored them and under his breath told an absent Howard to hurry up.

Howard opened the back door and ran down the steps to the walkway. He spotted Charlie and headed off to meet him. He folded up the large piece of parchment paper he carried and tucked it into the pocket in his cassock.

"It's about time," Charlie said and shivered in the cool of the morning. "People were giving me funny looks. I was afraid that at any minute one of the Brothers would come out and ask me what I was up to."

"Relax, Charlie. You worry too much." Howard smiled and put his arm around Charlie's shoulders. "Let's go."

The two headed down the path toward the cemetery, the same path that also led to the swimming pool. Since it was still quite early, they didn't run into many boys along the path. When they did, they changed the subject of their conversation and tried to act natural. Charlie shook his head at Howard's clowning attempts.

"So, where were you this morning?" Charlie asked as they walked.

"I was doing some of my own investigating." Howard smiled to himself proudly. "It seems that the tunnel was constructed during World War II as a way for the Brothers to travel from the main road to the monastery without being in the open. It took the Brothers working around the clock three months to complete the tunnel; all of it being dug out by hand. The Brothers, fearing the tunnel might be discovered by the enemy, dug dead end tunnels and loops to confuse any uninvited guests."

Charlie was fascinated by what he heard, but what he heard also raised more questions.

"How did you find this out?" he interrupted Howard's explanation.

Howard stopped and looked at Charlie. "I have my sources." He smiled. "Besides, what does it matter as long as we have the information and the map?" He pulled out the piece of parchment paper from his pocket.

"Where did you get that?" Charlie asked as he looked excitedly at the map. "This is old," he said, noticing the yellowed and tattered edges.

"I got it. What does it matter from where? What's with all the questions?" Howard said, and folded up the map. "I also thought enough to borrow a flashlight from the maintenance closet. Don't let me forget to put it back." Howard took the flashlight from his other pocket and turned it on to be sure it worked.

"Good thinking," Charlie said and kicked himself for not thinking about the tunnel being dark. Now the possibility of getting lost on one of the loops or dead ends set his stomach into flutters of nervousness. This safe little adventure was quickly turning into something more serious. However, he began to reason that if Gus could do it, then he should be able to make it. After all, Gus was not the bravest of the boys, and besides, Howard had a map.

As they approached the cemetery, Charlie noticed a tall mound of stone and earth off to the side of the path. Ivy had grown over the top of the mound and hung down across the alcove that was formed in the side of it. The makeshift grotto housed a life-sized statue of the Virgin Mary. Her paint was cracked and peeling, showing what appeared to be years of neglect. In the past couple months, he had walked down that very path countless times. Why had he not noticed this before? Charlie quickly shook the thought from his head and chose to think about the matter at hand.

"Now, according to my source," Howard was careful not

to slip and say who. "The opening to the tunnel should be right behind the statue in the shadows."

Cautiously they approached the grotto, making sure that no one was watching them.

"Look!" Howard pointed the beam of the flashlight at the back of the grotto wall. "There it is."

Charlie felt his stomach flutter. A wave of anxiety swept over him and he was not as sure about doing this as he had been earlier in the week.

"You better go first," he said as they climbed up beside the statue. "I mean, since you have the flashlight and map."

"Okay." Howard nodded. He was not nervous about going into the tunnel in the least. In fact, knowing that Gus did it was enough to convince him he had to. After all, he was not going to let Gus show him to be a failure and a coward.

Carefully, he inched his way around the statue and into the opening of the tunnel.

"Come on," he whispered, not wanting his voice to carry clear through to the other end of the tunnel.

Charlie slipped behind the statue and into the tunnel with ease. The opening was large enough that a full-grown man could easily make it through. The inside of the tunnel looked like an old mineshaft with timbers and boards securing the walls and ceiling. At first, they walked downhill at a steep incline. Charlie tripped a couple times on the hem of his cassock and bumped into Howard, before they finally reached the level ground.

"How far down do you think we are?" Charlie whispered as they slowly inched their way along the dark tunnel. The air was stale and thick with the smell of dirt.

"I don't know exactly," Howard answered. "I never thought to ask a—, my source." He almost slipped.

Suddenly, they both stopped as the beam of the flashlight

showed they had reached an intersection. Howard shone the light to the left and then to the right.

"Which way now?" Charlie asked.

"I don't know." Howard took out the map and handed it to Charlie.

They studied the map for a few moments and then Howard shone the light to the left.

"This way," he said. "The right is a dead end."

They started off down the tunnel again. The air seemed a bit cleaner and cooler. Howard flashed the light at the ceiling.

"Air vents," he said as he spotted a pipe opening.

"This is some tunnel." Charlie shook his head and took a deep breath of the fresh air.

"I'll say," Howard agreed. "It sure has held up well for being so old."

Again, Howard stopped. "What in the world?"

He shone the beam of the flashlight on an apparent fork in the tunnel. He pulled out the map again. They looked it over and then looked back at the fork. Howard shone his light down the fork to the right.

"This appears to be fairly recent," he said shining the light on the bare dirt walls. "Look, it's not finished like the rest of the tunnel."

"I wonder where it goes?" Charlie thought out loud.

"One adventure at a time, remember?" Howard said as he flashed the beam down as far as it would go into the new fork. "Our tunnel is to the left," he said and tucked the map back into his pocket.

"We'll have to come back and check it out later." Charlie nodded, making a mental note.

The two proceeded down the path to the left. They were sure they had made the right choice when they came to the next intersection. It was on the map and clearly marked. They picked up their pace, and before long they emerged from the tunnel to find themselves in what appeared to be a broom closet in the basement of the garage. Cautiously, they opened the door and stepped into the one-room basement. It was a small musty room with one window too small for a person to climb through. Beside the closet stood an old locker. A group of three old oil barrels half-covered by a canvas tarp stood in the center of the room. On the opposite wall, a wooden staircase connected to the first floor above.

As they looked around the dimly lit room, they became aware of voices above them. They recognized one voice immediately, it was Brother Simon. He sounded upset about something and the other voice tried to calm him. The conversation came to an abrupt end, and the sound of footsteps coming toward the basement door sent Howard and Charlie scrambling to find a hiding spot. Howard ducked behind the oil barrels and covered himself with the tarp while Charlie hid beneath the stairs. The door swung open and Brother Simon lumbered down the wooden steps, sending dust and dirt onto Charlie below. Charlie covered his mouth and nose to keep from sneezing.

Brother Simon wasted no time. He walked straight to the closet and without looking back, which Charlie and Howard were grateful for, he disappeared. Charlie waited until he was sure they were safe before he emerged from beneath the stairs. He then motioned to Howard that it was safe to come out.

"Look at you." Howard laughed as they met at the foot of the stairs. Charlie's surplice was soiled and dusty. His face was smudged with dirt and his hair had cobwebs in it.

"What about you!" Charlie said as he tried to dust himself off.

Howard too was covered with a layer of dirt. Now he was beginning to regret that he had been so insistent they not change clothes.

"Come on." Howard shook his clothes to get as much of the dust off them as he could. "Let's hurry up and talk to Brother Tobias and get back to the dorm."

The stairs led right into the first parking bay. Charlie looked around. The garage was actually one long room with several large doors. The black van that brought Charlie to Saint Michael's was parked in the furthest parking bay. An old rusty blue pick-up was parked in the next bay nearer. In the third, the center bay, a Cadillac was parked with its hood opened. Brother Tobias was bent over the engine with his back to them.

"Hello Brother," Howard called as he casually walked toward him. Charlie grabbed Howard's sleeve and gave him a wide-eyed look of disapproval. "What? Would you rather we sneak up on him and scare him half to death?" he asked and started off to greet the monk.

"Well, no. I suppose not," Charlie had to agree and followed Howard.

Brother Tobias stood up and turned around. He smiled while wiping his greasy hands on an old rag. His dark, almost black, beady eyes sparkled in the light that came through the opened garage doors.

"Hi boys!" he greeted them in a rather high-pitched voice for a man. "I don't get many visitors out here. Ah," he smiled as he looked at their soiled clothes. "Looks as though you discovered the tunnel."

"Well, actually, we were told about it as a way to come to see you," Charlie admitted and shook his hand.

"Me?" Brother Tobias cocked his head. "I'm flattered. Why on earth would you want to talk to me?"

"We were told you could tell us about the boy who fell from the attic window about forty years ago," Howard spoke up.

"Oh, you mean the famous ghost story." Brother Tobias' smile faded. His eyes began to dart around the garage and his hands began to tremble.

"We're trying to get to the bottom of it," Charlie added.

Brother Tobias shook his head. "No. No," his voice squeaked. "I'm sorry but I can't help you." He turned away.

"But we've been hearing noises at night," Charlie continued.

"I'm afraid I can't help you." Brother Tobias shook his head. Howard noticed Brother Tobias' hands trembling more.

"But Gus said you told him—" Charlie blurted out.

Brother Tobias stopped and turned back around. "You mean the little chubby boy?"

"That's him," Howard answered. He couldn't help being curious by Brother Tobias' reaction.

"Well," Brother Tobias thought quickly, "he came to me because one of the boys told him the story. So, I just said I was there to scare him. I must have been too convincing. I better be getting back to work and you boys had best be heading back to the dorms before you are caught out here. I'd hate to see you spend your free time on work crew."

"Thanks, Brother." Howard smiled and started to leave.

"But, what about—" Charlie protested.

"Come on, Charlie." Howard grabbed his arm and pulled him away. "We have bothered Brother Tobias long enough."

"But he's not—" Charlie continued to pull against him.

As they reached the door to the basement, Charlie looked back at Brother Tobias once more. He still appeared to be quite nervous as he kept wiping his hands and looking about the garage as though he was searching for something. Howard gave

Charlie's arm a tug to get him started down the stairs.

"I don't understand why he wouldn't talk." Charlie shook his head. "And you, why did you pull me away?"

"Didn't you hear what he said?" Howard turned around to face him as he pulled out the flashlight. "If we didn't leave, he would have given us work crew. I for one don't want to spend my Saturdays cleaning toilets or some other God-forsaken job. Come on." He turned around and turned on the flashlight.

Charlie thought for a moment and then quickly followed Howard so as not to be left behind. He didn't believe for a moment that Brother Tobias was only trying to scare Gus, and he couldn't understand why Brother Tobias was so nervous. He remembered when he first met Brother Tobias, the day he came to live at Saint Michael's. He appeared to be nervous then too. Perhaps it had something to do with Brother Simon, Charlie thought to himself, but what and why?

Before he knew it, they had reached the grotto and were back on the path back to the dorms. Their trip back through the tunnel seemed shorter.

"We'll have just enough time to shower and change our clothes before lunch," Howard said as they hurried along.

"Boy, I guess I'm too late." Rick said catching up to the two. "Are you both okay?" There was an honest sound of concern in his voice.

"Too late for what?" Charlie asked not slowing down.

"What are you talking about?" Howard snapped impatiently at Rick.

"Dougary, Larry, Travis and Austin were looking all over for you," he answered ignoring Howard's biting tone. "They haven't forgotten about having work crew because of you two."

"Oh, who cares?" Howard brushed him off.

Rick looked at them curiously. "Well if they didn't get a

hold of you, what happened to you guys?"

"You could say we went on a wild goose chase," Charlie answered disappointedly.

The two had just finished their showers and changing into their clean clothes when the bell for lunch rang. Charlie stuffed his dirty clothes into his laundry bag and closed his closet door.

"Come on, Howard. I'm starved." Charlie put his arm around Howard's shoulders and the two headed off for the dining hall.

The refectory appeared to be noisier than usual. They boys from Saint Sebastian dorm were having a birthday party for one of their members. Charlie looked at Howard, who just shrugged his shoulders and bit into his hamburger.

Gus leaned forward, his mouth full of French fries. His surplice dipped into a spot of ketchup on the table. "Did you guys find the tunnel and get to talk to Brother Tobias?"

Rick looked at Gus sharply, then at Howard and Charlie. "So, that's what you two were up to," he said in his usual scornful manner. "You know if you guys get caught on the front grounds, you'll be in so much trouble that even work crew would seem like a holiday."

"Oh, relax Rick," Howard brushed him off and continued eating.

"Don't worry, Rick," Charlie's tone was much kinder. "We have no intention of going back there. Besides, Gus, Brother Tobias was only pulling your leg. He doesn't know anything about the story."

Rick's expression changed to confusion. Why was Gus in the know and he was left out? "What story? What are you guys talking about?"

"The ghost in the attic," Gus replied with a mouthful hamburger.

Rick gave a laugh. "You guys are chasing a ghost?"

"No!" snapped Howard, glaring intensely at Rick. "We don't believe in ghosts."

"We're just trying to figure out how much of the story is true and what really happened," Charlie explained.

"Well, if you ask me—"

"We didn't," Howard quickly interrupted Rick.

Rick glared at him. "I think you guys are wasting your time. You should be spending your few days before mid-terms studying instead of wasting it on some wild ghost chase."

"Blah. Blah. Blah." Howard ignored Rick. In recent weeks he had become annoyed at the way Rick talked to him. His tone of voice, his condescending looks and the way he treated him like a child all of the time had become too much. After all, he was nearly thirteen, hardly a child anymore.

The rest of the meal was spent in silence. None of the four dared say another word. Charlie could tell that Howard was still steamed at Rick, and Rick was upset with the both of them. Gus retreated into his shell as he always did during times of tension. The last thing he wanted to do was say something that would direct all the hostility toward him.

After lunch, Howard suggested that he and Charlie go to the library and check out the old yearbooks for any clues. He did not say it to Charlie, but he felt as though Brother Tobias was definitely hiding something and he wanted to find out what it was.

The library was quiet, as usual. The librarian, the short, elf-like monk Brother Joel, looked up from his desk behind the checkout counter as they entered. A quick finger to his lips reminded them both that talking was strictly forbidden. According to the rumors around the fourth floor, Brother Joel on more than one occasion smacked a boy's knuckles with a ruler for breaking the silence. Even the thought was painful to Charlie.

From the checkout counter, the librarian could see the entire library. All the rows of bookcases were set at an angle in an almost sunburst design. He could even see the study desks that were set up at the ends of each row. There was definitely no hiding from him.

Charlie followed Howard to the section of the library where they kept the old yearbooks and old history books on the Abbey. Charlie had only been in the library once before, found it overwhelming, and left before finding the book he was looking for. He was impressed with Howard's ability to find what they were after. He watched as Howard ran his finger along a row of thin books of various colors.

"I don't believe it," he sighed in a whisper. "They're all gone."

"What are gone?" Charlie asked.

"The yearbooks," Howard answered. "All the yearbooks from the forty years ago are gone. Who would have taken them?"

"Why don't we ask Brother Joel?" Charlie whispered.

"He won't tell who has them," Howard sighed. "They are very strict about not telling who checks out what books. To tell would be worse than a priest telling what he heard in the confessional. Come on."

The two left the library, and spent the rest of the afternoon in their cubicle. Charlie wrote another letter to his grandmother, telling her about his adventure in the tunnel and the mysterious disappearance of the books in the library, while Howard read in his comic books.

The upperclassmen were back from town an hour before dinner. They chattered excitedly about how much fun they had, and about how the townspeople had treated them to root beer, pretzels and strudels. They all brought back souvenirs of their trip. One boy sported a new German hat with a red feather, another showed off the stockings he bought, and each had a bag of candies and pastries. Howard ignored the excitement and stayed on his bed pretending to read, when actually he was very jealous. In his five years at the Abbey, never once was he permitted to go to the Oktoberfest. It was always the same story, when you were older.

At dinner, Abbot Ambrose took his place at the head table, along with Father Emmanuel and Father Vicar. It was good to have them back, Charlie thought to himself.

Rick was still brooding about lunch and so ate in silence. Gus, fearing Rick's wrath, kept silent, and let Howard and Charlie do all the talking. They talked about the comic books and Charlie's letters to his grandmother.

Finally, Abbot Ambrose signaled the end of the meal with a loud clap of the wooden block. The room immediately fell silent, and everyone turned toward the head table. Abbot Ambrose rose to his feet and walked around to the front of the table.

"As you all are quite well aware, Halloween is fast approaching," he began his announcement. Instantly hoots and cheers roared from the Saint Peter table. Father Vicar motioned for them to be silent but smiled defiantly at Abbot Ambrose's back. Abbot Ambrose glared directly at the rowdy boys and continued. "This year we strongly recommend that you do not repeat any of the antics of last year's party. Father Pacome did not appreciate the fish in the ponds being traumatized as some boys either jumped into or were thrown into the ponds. And frightening Sister Claire, our cook, and chasing her across the front grounds as she is trying to go home is not funny in the least." There was a faint snickering coming from the Saint Peter table as Travis elbowed Larry. "May I remind you, Master Bleckinger and Master Hertz, that the front grounds are off limits to all residents of the fourth floor except for the Altar Boys." He then looked at the rest of the students. "This year anyone caught on the front grounds will not only earn work crew for themselves but for their entire dorm as well." A groan rose from all of the tables. "For a month," Abbot Ambrose added. All the students gasped. "That would sting a bit wouldn't it?" he nodded. "Just be sure you obey the rules and you'll have nothing to worry about.

"This year the committee for planning the party will meet with Brother Conrad. Any questions?"

Rick's hand immediately went up. Howard groaned under his breath and shook his head. Rick looked at him out of the corners of his eyes and stuck his nose in the air and held his hand higher.

Abbot Ambrose looked at Rick and then took a quick look around the room, apparently hoping someone else would have a question first. To Charlie it seemed as though the Abbot was on to Rick's brown-nosing. Seeing no other hands, Abbot Ambrose turned back to Rick.

"Yes?" he asked with a sigh.

Rick stood up next to his chair. "Abbot Ambrose, we know that the selection for replacements to the Altar Boys is coming up. Could you tell us when you'll be announcing the new members?"

A smile spread across his thin lips and he stroked his beard thoughtfully. The Altar Boys Club was very special to him. It held some of his fondest memories from when he was a student years ago. "The announcement will be made as it always is every year at breakfast on All Saints' Day," he answered plainly.

Rick raised his hand again as he continued to stand by his chair.

"Yes, Master Walters?" Abbot Ambrose leaned back against the table and folded his arms over his chest. He tried not to sound too exasperated with Rick, so he smiled under his white beard.

"Is there a list of requirements that you could share with us all for someone who wants to become a member of the Altar Boys?" Rick tried to sound intelligent as he posed his question.

Abbot Ambrose visibly frowned. "I hate to disappoint all of you," he said as he looked directly at Rick knowing he was not speaking for the whole assembly. "That information is confidential."

Rick opened his mouth to start to object but Abbot Ambrose raised his eyebrows and silenced him. Rick slid back into his chair and glanced at Howard, who was grinning while he stared at him. Rick looked away.

"Well, since there are no more questions, we will conclude our meal." Abbot Ambrose ended the question and answer session.

Outside the refectory, Howard could not resist. "Ah, Abbot Ambrose, we were wondering if you could tell what criteria you use to select members for your elite group of boys?" he mocked in a shrill voice and then started laughing so hard his eyes watered. "Way to go, Rick," he laughed.

"Oh, shut up, you heathen," Rick snapped, and hurried up the stairs.

Charlie looked back at the refectory doors just as Abbot Ambrose emerged. He excused himself from Howard and Gus with a lame excuse that he had forgotten something in the refectory and would meet up with them soon. He actually wanted to catch the Abbot before he slipped away.

"Ah, Abbot Ambrose?" he called as he hurried to catch the abbot before he went outside for his usual after-lunch walk.

Abbot Ambrose turned around and smiled when he saw Charlie. "Yes, son?"

"Do you have a moment?" Charlie asked nervously. "There's something I'd like to talk to you about."

"Sure," he nodded. "Let's go to my office."

Charlie was impressed by the Abbot's office. He'd never seen the inside of it before. A large oak desk was set to one side facing the door. Behind it, built into the entire wall, was a matching oak bookcase with many shelves. Each shelf was packed with books of various sizes and colors. Charlie was awestruck as he tried to imagine Abbot Ambrose reading all of them. It was especially impressive since he was having trouble reading a book half the size of the smallest one in the bookcase.

Off to the side of the desk were three chairs placed around a small coffee table. A floor lamp sat between two of the chairs. Abbot Ambrose turned it on and then sat down in the chair beside it. He invited Charlie to sit across from him.

"Now, Charlie," Abbot Ambrose smiled. "With what may I help you?"

"Well," Charlie began nervously. "I wanted to talk to you about the Altar Boys replacements. Oh, I know the requirements for choosing the members is private, but I just wanted to ask you—" Charlie paused and looked around the room as though searching for the right words.

"Yes?" urged Abbot Ambrose with a gentle smile. He could see how nervous Charlie was, and he almost felt sorry for him.

"I was wondering if you would consider Howard. There, I said it." Charlie relaxed a bit as he waited for the Abbot's reaction.

"Master Miller?" came Abbot Ambrose's surprised response. He had expected Charlie to ask for himself to be considered. He stroked his white beard and thought for a moment. "Why him?"

Charlie took a deep breath. He had been thinking a lot about this and had an answer. "I know he would never admit to it, but I do know that Howard wants more than anything to be a member. He doesn't say anything, but I notice the look in his eyes whenever the subject comes up. The one time we talked about it, he said he doesn't stand a chance of ever being selected."

"Why does he think that?" Abbot Ambrose's expression grew very concerned.

"Because he says that the Altar Boys are, well, Holy Joes. They obey the rules, I mean. They help with Mass. They also help with the older Brothers, reading to them, visiting them and helping them out with little chores and stuff like that.

"I don't know if you've noticed but Howard's not like that. He bends the rules and sometimes even breaks them. He's got a temper, and he gets annoyed easily by Rick and Gus. But he's not really a bad person. He was nice to me when I first came here and he didn't even know me."

As Abbot Ambrose listened, he stroked his beard and even smiled a time or two. He then cocked his head and looked at Charlie.

"What if I told you, Charlie, that I had asked him to be nice to you? Would that change how you feel?"

Charlie looked directly into Abbot Ambrose's blue eyes. His mind was suddenly filled with questions. Was Howard only being nice to him because he had to be? Was his friendship only a duty? Did Abbot Ambrose really ask him to be nice to him?

"No," he said boldly. "No, it wouldn't change my feelings. Even though you asked him to be nice to me, he did more than that. He gave up being part of a family because he didn't want to leave me behind, and I know you would never ask him to do that. He did that on his own, because deep down inside he really does care about others. Probably more than he would ever admit to."

Abbot Ambrose smiled. "You're very perceptive for a boy your age, Charlie. Master Miller is lucky to have a friend like you." Abbot Ambrose stood up and Charlie took his cue that it was time to go. "I can't promise you anything, son, but I will consider what you've said."

Charlie nodded. "I understand. I thank-you for that." He turned toward the door.

"One other thing," Abbot Ambrose halted him.

Charlie turned around as he opened the door.

"I did not ask Master Miller to be nice to you. He did that on his own, too." Abbot Ambrose smiled.

Charlie smiled back. "Thank-you."

THE HEADSTONE

Charlie walked out of Brother Simon's classroom ahead of Howard and the rest. He was glad he was finally finished with his midterms. It had been a busy two weeks studying and cramming at the last minute for the tests. He had no time to even think about the ghost in the attic. He even became so used to the moaning above him at night that it no longer scared him. In fact, he felt sorry for whoever it was.

Howard and Gus emerged from the room looking as though they had been in a real struggle. Gus' hair stuck out from all sides owing to his nervous habit of running his hands through his hair whenever he was stressed. Howard's pencils were chewed down to the lead and his shirt collar was soaked with sweat.

"So, how bad do you think we failed?" he asked Charlie as the three waited for Rick.

"Oh, I imagine I will be taking this course over and over and over. I'll be a senior and still taking this eighth-grade class." Charlie laughed.

"What about you, Gus?" Howard turned to him.

"If this were a regular school, my parents would be called

in for sure. I guess that's one good thing about being an orphan." Gus said, and immediately his eyes filled with tears.

Howard laughed heartily. "You said it, Gus boy." He put his arm around Gus' shoulders and gave him a reassuring one-armed hug. It seemed to do the trick. Gus's tears dried up.

"If you two girls are through kissing on each other, we'd like to get through here," Dougary said in a disgusted tone.

Howard glared at him and moved aside. He had not forgotten about Dougary's threats of revenge. Luckily, they were too busy with midterms also to pursue them.

"We're watching you, maggot," Travis snarled as he and the other two passed by.

"Oh, I'm so scared," Howard mocked them.

"And you should be," Larry added as they disappeared up the stairs.

"What's keeping Rick?" Charlie cocked his head and looked into the classroom. "What?" he said as he saw Rick and Brother Simon talking. "I don't believe this."

"What?" Gus and Howard said together and then took a look for themselves.

Rick smiled and said his good-byes as he walked out of the classroom and into the corridor. His smile faded as he looked at all the shocked faces in front of him.

"What's with you guys?" he asked innocently.

"No, what's with you and Brother Simon? Since when have the two of you been so chummy?" Howard asked.

"For your information, Brother Simon likes intelligent people." Rick again had a haughty tone in his voice.

"That's what I said, 'what's with you and Brother Simon?'" Howard ribbed.

"Oh, don't be funny," Rick snapped. "Just because you haven't a brain in your head doesn't mean everyone else doesn't either."

Charlie could tell that this discussion was about to get heated, so he stepped between the two of them. "So, have you got your costumes ready for tonight?"

Howard glared at Rick, and then looked at Charlie and nodded. "Yeah, I think I've got a winner." He nodded as the thought about the mask he found in the drama closet.

"What about you, Gus?" Charlie turned looked over his shoulder at him as they started up the stairs.

"I've still got a lot of work to do on it but I'll be ready. You guys will be really surprised." He smiled.

"Good thing we have the rest of the afternoon free. Do you need any help?" Charlie offered.

"Oh no." Gus shook his head. He wanted to surprise them with his idea. He had worked for months planning out his costume for this year's party. He even convinced Father Pacome to let him use a corner in the Abbey's garden for his project. Every chance he had, he would go out to the garden and check on its progress. No, this was going to be the winner, he thought to himself proudly.

"You aren't putting that pumpkin over your head," Rick said in a rather bossy tone. "You'll suffocate yourself!"

Gus' mouth dropped open as he looked in shock at Rick but then quickly tried to cover up. "What makes you think I'm going to do that?"

"You aren't the only one who talks to Father Pacome. He told me what you were up to so don't try to deny it," Rick continued.

Gus looked from Rick to Howard to Charlie, his mouth open and his eyes filled with tears. His months of hard work were ruined. Without another word he rushed ahead of them and into the dorm.

Howard and Charlie turned and looked at Rick disbelievingly.

"Boy, I never thought you would stoop that low. You just can't let him alone. What did he ever do to you?" Howard shook his head and walked off.

Rick looked at Charlie. His blue eyes filled with hurt. "I—I didn't mean to hurt him. I'm just worried he'll hurt himself." His voice was soft, not its usual harsh tone.

Charlie looked at him, into his eyes. He was torn between believing him and walking away as Howard had done.

"If you really mean it, then you owe Gus an apology. But not just words, try showing it," he said and walked away.

Rick stood for a moment and watched the door to the dorm close. He did mean it. He was concerned about Gus's safety. He really didn't want him to get hurt. Slowly he walked over to the door and opened it.

Gus sat in his cubicle on the floor next to the pumpkin he had nurtured all summer long. His head was bowed and it was obvious that he was crying. Five months of hard work, ruined, wasted. His hopes of surprising everyone and having the best costume this year and win the blue ribbon, gone.

Rick slowly walked over to him. He really did feel awful for spilling the beans.

"Gus," he said quietly. "I'm sorry I blabbed about your costume. I never meant to hurt you."

"Go away," Gus said without looking up.

"It's not ruined. You could still do it. Not everyone knows; just the four of us is all. Between the two of us I'm sure we can figure out a way to make it safe."

"No," Gus cried wiping his runny nose with his sleeve. "It's no use."

"Come on, Gus. You can't quit just because I'm a jerk. I'll

help you," Rick tried to apologize.

Gus looked up at Rick. "You will?"

"Yes." Rick nodded.

Gus smiled faintly and nodded.

"What we need is some old newspaper and a knife." Rick knelt down next to Gus.

"I already have them under my bed," Gus said and reached under his bed and pulled out a paper bag.

"Good." Rick smiled. "Now, when you cut the hole, you have to make it big enough for your head to fit through. Let's measure your head."

Howard and Charlie sat on their beds listening to what was happening in the cubicle next to theirs. Howard looked at Charlie.

"What do you know," he said with a slight smile. "He has a heart after all."

~§~

That evening, lanterns lit the corridor outside the refectory. Bales of hay and dried cornstalks leaned against the walls. Instead of the usual neat quiet lines of boys, a noisy mob of goblins and monsters huddled. Charlie raised his eye-patch so he could take a better look around. He wasn't the only pirate in the group but it didn't matter to him. He searched for Howard, Gus and Rick.

Howard hunched his back and swayed as he walked down the stairs. He groaned under the rubber mask of the Hunchback that he found. His old surplice from the year before made the perfect shirt with a piece of rope tied about his waist as a belt. He stuffed his pillow under his T-shirt to give his back a convincing hump. He spotted Charlie almost immediately and waved to him but stayed in character.

Charlie smiled as he watched Howard. He was amazed by his creativity and amused by a hunchback with glasses. Then his mouth dropped open as he spotted Gus coming down the stairs behind Howard.

Gus's pumpkin head was perfect. The jagged mouth and triangle eyes and nose were very artistically cut. Charlie could not help but wonder where Gus found a pair of overalls and who had sewn the red patches onto the knees. Charlie recognized the red material. It was from an old surplice. Gus wore a flannel shirt with bits of straw poking out above the bib and out of his sleeves. Charlie hurried over to him just as gasps were heard from the other boys.

"You did it!" Charlie whispered proudly.

"Hey, Gus," Howard grinned beneath his mask. "If you don't win, then I'll eat this mask!"

"Where's Rick?" Charlie asked and looked around.

"Right here," he answered and walked around the corner.

"Oh, what a scary costume." Howard recoiled and said sarcastically.

Charlie glared at Howard. "What happened?" he asked Rick.

"I helped Gus and I guess time just got away." Rick shrugged but smiled at Gus. "Doesn't he look great?"

"I'll say." Charlie agreed.

The refectory doors opened and a fog bellowed out. Shrieks, witches' cackles, screams and eerie music poured out into the hallway. Slowly, the mob moved inside.

The usual dinner formalities were put aside as everyone relaxed and had fun. Even Abbot Ambrose participated, dressed in jeans and a flannel shirt and straw hat. Father Emmanuel with his round belly looked very out-of-season dressed as Santa

Claus. Father Vicar was dressed as Death, complete with a sickle. Brother Owen was dressed as an angel and Brother Conrad as a sorcerer.

After dessert was finished, Brother Conrad and the party committee stood up. "The festivities are just getting started," Brother Conrad began. "Tonight's contest is a scavenger hunt. Each dorm will select ten of its members to be their team. Then each team will be given a list of twenty things to collect. The team that collects their list first and meets back here in the refectory win the prize for their dorm."

"What's the prize?" someone yelled out. Charlie recognized Dougary's voice behind the stupid gorilla mask.

"The prize will be waiting for them after the party in their dorm."

The St. Peter's table erupted in hoots and hollers as though they had already won.

Steve, the sacristan, stepped forward dressed in a nun's habit. He held up his hands and shouted over the noise. "However, before the contest begins, everyone needs to place their vote for best costume of the year. The winner would be announced after the hunt."

The members of the committee quickly passed out the ballots as they circled the tables.

The Saint Nicholas dorm members huddled around Father Emmanuel and selected their team. Then they all listened as he read the list out loud to them. He paired them off by twos and gave them each two items to retrieve. Howard and Charlie had to go outside and retrieve the Bible left in the chapel in the cemetery and then grab one of the life preservers from the swimming pool. Rick and Gus would go the opposite direction and gather a beaker from the basement chemistry lab and then handful of lint from one of the dryers in the laundry room. Ted

Wilson and Cody Brown would retrieve a lantern from the garage and a baseball hidden among the flower beds on the front lawn. The other four members, the youngest of the team, were assigned to gather the easiest items on the list. After all assignments were handed out everyone waited for the signal, a loud witches' cackle, to begin.

"I really hope Gus wins tonight," Charlie said as he and Howard headed off to the cemetery. "He worked so hard, probably harder than anyone."

"Yeah, he deserves to win," Howard agreed. "I voted for him."

"Me too," Charlie admitted.

The path to the cemetery was completely deserted. It appeared as though not every team was given the same list of things to gather, or if they were, they weren't filling them in the same order. Goblins, ghouls and pirates rushed all around screaming, howling and laughing. A smile came to Charlie's lips as he was caught up in the excitement. Never had he had so much fun on Halloween. When he was with his grandparents, they kept him home. They said it was safer with all the stories of poisonings and child muggings. Charlie didn't believe them since he had never heard anything on the news. Still, he obeyed them and stayed home helping them hand out candy.

Suddenly his smile faded as he thought about what his grandmother was doing. Although her letters said she was doing fine, he doubted that she was happy. Her handwriting didn't appear to be as neat and flared as in the past. Silently he wished he were with her right then, even if it meant staying in doors away from the excitement.

"Come on, Charlie," Howard called.

Charlie didn't realize he had begun to lag behind. He quickly picked up his pace and caught up with Howard.

The night sky was clear. Stars twinkled against the darkness. The bright moonlight cast long eerie shadows across the cemetery as Howard and Charlie stopped at the gate. Howard hesitated for a moment as he looked around.

"I don't like this," he said and his voice quivered. "It's kind of creepy, isn't it?"

"We'll be okay," Charlie tried to sound reassuring but he had seen way too many horror movies about zombies and cemeteries. Even he was a bit apprehensive, but as long as Howard was there, he felt they would be okay. His grandmother used to say, "There's safety in numbers." He hoped she was right.

Slowly Howard opened the wrought iron gate. It gave off a loud painful creaking sound that caused both Howard and Charlie to jump.

"Let's leave the gate open," Howard whispered as they passed through.

Tall headstones lined both sides of the narrow path to the little chapel. Charlie squinted in the dim light to read the names carved into the marble slabs. The names were of deceased Abbots. Charlie tried to remember some of the names under the paintings in the refectory to see if they matched but he could not. Spread out in neat rows behind the larger monuments were smaller white marble crosses. Charlie suspected they were for the monks. He glanced back at the gate before he turned his attention back to the chapel.

The chapel was built like a miniature church with a steeple and a set of normal sized double doors that came to a point at the top. On both side walls and at the back were simple stained-glass windows. Howard stopped and turned back toward Charlie. He pulled his mask up, wearing it on his head like a hat, and took a deep breath of fresh air.

"Okay, you go inside and grab the Bible and we'll get out of here," he said almost like an order.

Charlie looked at him. "Why me?"

"Because you're faster," he answered quickly. "I've got all this stuff on and it—" he fumbled.

"Okay. Okay." Charlie nodded. "Be right back."

Charlie stepped forward and took hold of the brass doorknob. Slowly he opened one of the doors and looked in.

The chapel was dark inside. Charlie looked over his shoulder at Howard and shivered.

Suddenly the door swung open. Before Charlie or Howard could move, they were knocked to the ground. Someone was on Charlie's back, pinning him to the ground. The attacker grabbed Charlie's hands and tied them behind his back. He kicked and struggled to see who it was but couldn't. He opened his mouth to scream and felt a cloth being shoved in it to silence him. His screams for help ended up muffled grunts. A pillowcase was then pulled over his head. He was in darkness.

As his attacker raised him to his feet, Charlie could hear the faint grunts that he assumed were Howard's. He hoped that Howard was putting up a real fight and that perhaps he had seen who attacked them.

Without anyone saying a word, Charlie was spun around in circles then led away. Charlie couldn't tell where they were taking him. For a while they were on the path because the ground was hard beneath his feet. Then they left the path and were walking on the soft spongy grass. It was hard to keep from tripping on the uneven ground when he couldn't see where he was going. He could tell at one point they were walking downhill but then they were walking uphill. He was so confused. Who would be doing this to him? Was this part of the game, he silently wondered?

Suddenly they stopped and the hands on his shoulders pushed him down until he sat on the ground. He was moved back against a solid object and his hands were untied for a brief second and then quickly retied. A rope was tightened around his waist. He tried to struggle but couldn't get free. Next someone gripped his legs. He kicked but it was no use. He felt a rope tightening around his ankles.

"What are you doing? Why?" he grunted. This isn't funny anymore, he thought to himself as he pulled on the ropes around his wrists.

The hands that were pressing against him were removed. Suddenly a bright light was shone at his face. The pillowcase was removed but the bright light momentarily blinded him. Charlie closed his eyes and heard the sound of footsteps running away.

It took a while for his eyes to readjust to the night. When they did, he saw Howard tied up in front of him. The rope around his feet was the same rope that tied Howard's feet. If he moved then the ropes around Howard's legs tightened.

Charlie blinked hard and tried to see through the darkness. Howard didn't seem to have fared so well. His mask was on the ground next to him. His nose was bleeding all over the piece of material stuffed in his mouth. Howard squinted and tried to see in the darkness but without his glasses he couldn't see a thing.

Charlie pulled at the ropes that imprisoned his hands. He used his tongue to push at the material in his mouth. Muffled grunts escaped his stuffed mouth. He looked to see if Howard was trying to free himself too but he couldn't be sure. Finally, the cloth fell from his mouth. His tongue felt dry. He swallowed hard.

"Howard!" he yelled.

Howard jumped. He pulled at his ropes round his hands.

He tried to move his legs but it only tightened the ropes around Charlie's legs and caused him to scream out in pain.

"Howard. Stop it!" he screamed. "Howard, spit the cloth out of your mouth."

Howard did as he was instructed and once the cloth was gone, he gasped for air.

"What's going on?" he cried. "Where are my glasses? Where are we?

Charlie looked around. To his left and right he saw headstones. He looked over at Howard and then he realized they were still in a cemetery. Only, he had never seen these headstones before. He peered into the distance and couldn't see the chapel. He tried to look over his shoulders but the stone slab blocked his view.

"We're still in the cemetery, I think," Charlie said.

"What!" Howard screamed and started pulling on the ropes. "I can't stay here. I've got to get out of here. Help! Help!" he screamed as panic started to set in.

"Howard stop it! Stop it!" Charlie yelled. "Calm down. It's okay." Charlie's eyes teared because the pain in his legs.

Howard stopped writhing. He looked around him but everything was out of focus. "What are we going to do?"

"I don't know," Charlie answered.

"They'll come looking for us." Howard said with a bit of uncertainty. "When lights-out comes, they'll notice we're gone and come."

"Yes. They'll come," Charlie tried to sound reassuring. He was still trying to free his hands as they talked. Charlie glanced to Howard's left and froze. "Howard, beside you," he gasped.

Howard jumped again and started to squirm. "What? What is it? Who's there?" he yelled.

"No, Howard. The headstone next to you, it belongs to a

boy. He died forty years ago and was only fifteen. His name was Joseph Oswald," he replied. He looked at the headstone to Howard's right and strained to read the date of death. Nineteen hundred thirty-five it read. "Howard, it's him."

"Who?" Howard said as he tried to look.

"The boy who fell from the attic," Charlie said.

"How can you be sure?" Howard asked.

"I'm not but now we have a name. Maybe there'll be something in the library or maybe one of the monks will know," Charlie speculated.

Just then there was a noise behind Howard. A dark shadow rose up in the distance. A chill ran up Charlie's spine. His eyes widened in fear. He could not move. He could not speak. His eyes were fixed on the shape. It drew closer and closer.

Howard suddenly heard a noise behind him. He twisted and tried to turn around.

"Who's there?" he yelled into the darkness. "Who's there?"

There was no answer. The dark shadow drew closer still. Charlie could see the figure appeared to be wearing the robes of a monk. He tried to calm his growing fear but could not. His heart pounded in his chest as the figure stopped only a few feet behind Howard.

Charlie strained harder to see into the shadows. The shape of the figure's head became clearer. He recognized the familiar shape of the ears that stuck out from the sides. Fear's grip relaxed and Charlie found his voice.

"Brother Tobias," he called.

"What're you boys doing here?" he asked looking at them.

"Someone tied us up here," Charlie said excitedly.

"I can see that." Brother Tobias nodded and then bent down and freed Howard's hands. "Are these your glasses?" he asked.

"I found them by the chapel."

"Yes," Howard gasped and grabbed his glasses and put them on. "Thanks."

"You should have Brother James take a look at your nose," Brother Tobias said as he noticed the dried blood on Howard's upper lip.

Howard felt his nose. It was sore but not bleeding anymore. Now that he could see, he set to work untying the rope around his legs while Brother Tobias freed Charlie.

"Thank you, Brother," Charlie said as he rubbed his wrists. "So, what are you guys doing out here?" he asked again.

"We were on a scavenger hunt," Howard answered as he freed his legs and Charlie's. "Someone jumped us at the chapel and then we were tied here and left."

"I see." Brother Tobias nodded.

"Where are we?" Howard asked has he looked around. "I've never seen this part of the cemetery before."

"You are in the children's cemetery," Brother Tobias answered. "Well, you'd better get back to your dorm. It's about time for lights-out I imagine."

"Thanks, we will, but which way?" Charlie stood up and helped Howard to his feet.

"Through that cluster of trees." He pointed in the direction he came from. "On the other side you'll find yourself in the monastery's cemetery. You'll recognize it."

The two started to leave in the direction Brother Tobias had pointed out but then Charlie stopped and turned around.

"Brother Tobias, what're you doing out here?" he asked bluntly.

"Pardon me?" Brother Tobias asked in a tone that said he was offended by the question.

"I'm sorry," Charlie said. "I was just wondering how you

came to find us."

"Well," Brother Tobias looked around as though trying to find an answer. "I was on my way back to the Abbey when I heard your call for help."

"Oh." Charlie nodded. "Thanks again." Charlie turned around and started back for the dorm.

Howard looked at him curiously and hurried after him. "What was that all about?" he asked.

"Doesn't it seem odd that Brother Tobias would be on his way back to the Abbey at this hour? On his way back from where?" Charlie answered. "He's hiding something."

Howard thought about what Charlie said as they walked back to the dorm. He thought about where they were, so far off the path and in a secluded area. How could Brother Tobias have known where to find them? Why had he been out so late? Things just didn't add up. He shook his head.

The first floor was quiet as they stepped inside the back door. All of the decorations in the hall outside the refectory were gone, just as though the party never happened. They turned and headed up the stairs.

As they reached the fourth floor, they noticed Father Emmanuel, Brother Owen, Brother Conrad and Abbot Ambrose huddled in the center of the hallway. They looked up as the two boys walked through the fire doors. The look on the four monks' faces were ones of deep concern.

"Oh, dear boy, what happened to you?" Father Emmanuel said as he bent down in front of Howard and looked him over.

"I wish I knew." Howard answered.

"I'll get some water and towels," Brother Conrad said, and rushed off toward his room.

"I'll call Brother James," Brother Owen said, and followed Brother Conrad.

"Where did you boys disappear to?" Abbot Ambrose asked, as he looked Charlie over.

Charlie looked at Howard and then back at Abbot Ambrose and Father Emmanuel. "We were going into the chapel in the cemetery to get the Bible for the scavenger hunt when someone jumped us. They tied us to headstones in the old cemetery and left us there. We would still be there if Brother Tobias hadn't come by."

"Ah, yes, Tobias." Abbot Ambrose nodded. "That's right."

Charlie looked curiously at the Abbot. What did he mean by that? He wondered.

"Who would do such a thing?" Father Emmanuel said and shook his head. "That is just awful and mean."

Howard suddenly remembered the threats. "I can't prove it, but I bet I know who it was."

Charlie looked at Howard in shock and then realized who Howard meant.

"Who?" Abbot Ambrose insisted to know.

"I think it was Dougary and his thugs Travis, Austin and Larry." Howard answered.

"Why do you think that?" Brother Conrad asked as he knelt down beside Howard and gingerly began to clean his face.

"Because ever since they got work crew a month ago they've been threatening to get even with us," Charlie answered. "The more I think about it the more I think it was them. But there is no proving it."

"I wouldn't be too sure," Father Emmanuel said.

"What's all the ruckus?" Father Vicar asked as he came out of Saint Peter dorm.

"Someone jumped Howard and Charlie and tied them up in the old cemetery," Abbot Ambrose answered.

"Oh, that's too bad." Father Vicar replied with an insincere smile.

"Tell me, where were Masters Duggan, Bleckinger, Fulton and Hertz during the scavenger hunt tonight?" Abbot Ambrose asked flatly.

"Why they were here in the building hunting up things from their own list as far as I know." Father Vicar looked shocked that anyone would accuse his boys of doing such a deed.

"Well, we'll just have a talk with them in the morning," Abbot Ambrose said.

"No." Charlie looked at him pleadingly. "Please, don't."

Father Emmanuel gave Charlie a shocked look. "Why not?"

"Don't you see, if it wasn't them, they'll be even more upset at us for accusing them," Charlie answered. "And if it was them, we can't prove it because we didn't see them."

"Brother James will be here in a second. He's getting his medical bag," Brother Owen said as he returned.

"Thank you, Owen." Abbot Ambrose nodded. "I agree, Charlie. We won't say anything to them. However, Vicar, I would appreciate it if you would keep a closer eye on them these next few days."

"But you heard him—" Father Vicar started to object.

"And you heard me," Abbot Ambrose said flatly.

Father Vicar's thin face went expressionless. "Yes, Abbot," he answered and then returned to his room without another word.

Charlie didn't like the look on Father Vicar's face when Abbot Ambrose reprimanded him. It was obvious to him that Father Vicar disliked the Abbot a lot. For some reason Father Vicar reminded Charlie of his Uncle Chester and that made him shudder visibly. He hadn't thought of his uncle in months and wished he didn't now.

"Well, as soon as Brother James checks you both over, you should get to bed. We have a big day ahead of us tomorrow," Abbot Ambrose said. "Good night."

"Good night," they all said as Abbot Ambrose headed toward the monastery wing.

"Well, I guess I'll turn in," Brother Owen said and then followed Abbot Ambrose down the hall to his room.

"You'll be fine," Brother Conrad assured them as he finished washing Howard's face.

"What's happening tomorrow?" Charlie asked.

"It's All Saints' Day," Howard reminded him.

"We have Mass in the Abbey Church and then afterward we have open house." Father Emmanuel said as he led them down the hall toward their dorm.

THE ALTAR BOYS

Charlie and Howard were tired. By the time Brother James, the Abbey's resident registered nurse, had finished checking over their bruised wrists and ankles thoroughly, it was well past midnight. Howard had the worst injuries, a black eye and fat lip. He kept looking in the mirror and groaning at his reflection.

"At least your glasses weren't broken," Charlie tried to console him. "Your eye and lip will heal in a couple of days. You'll be okay."

"Boy, when I get my hands on Dougary," Howard seethed.

"Come on, let's go to bed," Charlie said, and started toward the dorm. "Things will look better in the morning."

"Okay," Howard sighed. "Hey," Howard gasped as he suddenly remembered. "I wonder if Gus won the contest?" He picked up his pace.

"Oh yeah!" Charlie smiled at the thought. "I sure do hope so."

The dorm was dark when they entered. The sounds of the boys sleeping peacefully filled the air. Quietly Howard and Charlie made their way to their cubicle. They undressed and crawled into their beds and drifted off to sleep.

The morning bell seemed to have rung just as Charlie had fallen asleep. He turned over and looked at the clock on Howard's nightstand. He couldn't believe that six hours had passed. Slowly he sat up and stretched. Howard was still asleep.

"Hey, what happened to you guys?" Gus asked as he walked around the partition. "We all waited in the refectory for you to come back but—"

"It's a long story," Charlie interrupted and yawned. "We were jumped at the chapel and tied up in the old cemetery."

Gus' mouth dropped open and his eyes widened. "Oh my, were you scared?"

"Yeah." Charlie nodded. "Hey, Howard." He nudged him. "It's time to get up."

Howard groaned and rolled over. "What time is it?"

"Six forty-five." Charlie answered. "So, Gus, who won the contest?"

"Saint Peter dorm." Gus frowned. "At the last second, Dougary and Travis ran in with the Bible from the chapel to win."

Howard looked up at him and then over at Charlie. Charlie seemed to read his mind and shook his head sternly.

"When they went back to their dorm, they found a big bowl of candies, cakes and pastries and stuff like that. They kept coming out into the hall and gloating as they ate it all." Gus glared as he thought about it. "I hope they're all sick this morning."

"Well, look what the cat dragged in," Rick said as he walked up. His mouth dropped open when he looked at Howard. "Oh my God, what happened to your eye?" he gasped.

"That Dog-boy jerk sucker punched me last night at the chapel," Howard said through clenched teeth as he gingerly touched his cheek under his sore eye.

"I'm sorry," Rick said and actually sounded as though he meant it. "Hey, did you hear?"

"Hear what?" Charlie asked.

Rick put his hands on Gus's shoulders and smiled from ear-to-ear.

"You didn't?" Howard said and smiled.

"Yes, he did," beamed Rick proudly. "You are looking the winner of the best costume award."

"Way to go, Gus," Howard said, as he playfully slugged him in the shoulder.

"Congratulations," Charlie added. "I'm so happy for you. That was one impressive costume. No one else had one like it."

Gus blushed. "I couldn't have done it without Rick's help."

"Nonsense," Rick scoffed. "You grew that big pumpkin. It was perfect."

"Oh no," Charlie gasped and sat down on his bed. His smile faded into a very serious look.

"What?" The other three asked and looked very concerned.

"How are you going to top this next year?" he smiled and laughed.

"Oh, don't worry." Gus smiled. "Rick and I already have a plan."

"I see." Howard nodded, suspicious of their suddenly closer friendship.

The second warning bell rang, and the four boys jumped. They immediately dashed off to the showers and then dressed for breakfast.

Howard explained to Charlie that every year the Brothers had an open house on All Saints' Day. After Mass the boys were to stay dressed up and mingle with the guests, some of who were there to check out the boys for possible adoption. The previous year, four boys from Saint Nicholas dorm were eventually adopted by couples who had been to the open house. "Needless to say," Howard pointed out. "I'm sure this year all the orphaned boys will take extra care to look their best."

At breakfast Howard and Charlie noticed that Dougary and Travis were staring at them. Charlie told Howard to just ignore them but Howard could not. He kept glaring at them as they snickered and whispered to Austin and Larry.

When breakfast was finished, Abbot Ambrose rose. Rick grinned and looked at Howard and Charlie. Charlie knew what was coming, the announcement of the new members of the Altar Boys. There would be three names announced, three chances for Howard to be chosen. His pulse raced and his hands sweat.

Abbot Ambrose walked around to the front of the head table. He looked at all of the young faces and smiled warmly.

"I know this is the moment that some of you have been waiting for, when I will announce the three names of the new members of the Altar Boys. However, before I do, I want to give a little explanation of what exactly being an Altar Boy means. This may also answer some of your questions as to what I look for in a potential member." He looked at Rick and smiled.

"The Altar Boys not only assist the priests of the Abbey with offering Mass daily but they also aid the Brothers who care for the older members of the monastery. As you know, they are granted access to the front grounds as well as the monastery wing and cloistered garden, as they will take some of the older members on walks. But with this added freedom of movement comes a very important responsibility. As a member of the Altar Boys you are expected to uphold the dignity of Saint Michael's. You must always be courteous, polite, and respectful as well as neat and clean.

"This being said, when your name is called please come

forward and receive your new surplices." Abbot Ambrose instructed and then gave a slight cough to clear his throat.

Charlie looked around the room. He was surprised to see how many boys appeared to be anxious with hopeful anticipation. He looked at the members of the head table. Father Emmanuel looked at him and smiled. His puffy cheeks were pink and his eyes sparkled as though he knew something the rest of them did not. Charlie turned to Howard. He had wanted to tell him about his visit to Abbot Ambrose but he stopped himself. He didn't want to get Howard's hopes up unnecessarily, so he bit his tongue.

Howard sat staring at Rick with a grin on his face. He delighted in seeing Rick squirm.

"The first member is," Abbot Ambrose said in a loud voice.

Rick closed his eyes and held his breath. Howard laughed and elbowed Charlie to have him look. Charlie smiled and wondered how long Rick was going to sit there with his cheeks puffed out like a blowfish.

"Master Howard Miller."

Rick choked and opened his eyes.

"What?" he said in disbelief and looked directly at Howard. "Him?"

Howard sat in wide-eyed, stunned silence staring at Rick. Slowly the room erupted in applause. He looked around blindly, still in shock.

"Come on up here, Master Miller," Abbot Ambrose urged.

"Go on, Howard." Charlie beamed proudly and tugged on his arm. "You did it. You finally made it. You're an Altar Boy."

"But—but—" he shook his head. Then, as the words sank in, he slowly rose to his feet. As he started to smile, he felt a pain in his cheek below his black eye. He put his hand over the side of his face and continued to smile.

Father Emmanuel rose to his feet. He reached behind the curtain and pulled out a white surplice.

Abbot Ambrose continued. "As an Altar Boy you will no longer wear your dorm's color, even though you'll remain a member of the dorm. Instead you'll wear a white surplice."

Howard stood before the assembly as Brother Conrad helped him remove his red surplice. Father Emmanuel then stepped forward, smiling like a proud parent, and presented Howard with one of his new surplices, which he quickly put on. He grinned and held the bottom hem out, inspecting the three-inch, flat lace trim. He examined the lace on the sleeves. When he looked up, he straightened his back and puffed out his chest proudly.

Charlie smiled at Abbot Ambrose. For a moment their eyes met and Charlie nodded his gratitude.

"Now we still have two more names." Abbot Ambrose raised his hands to quiet the noisy chattering.

As the room fell silent, Rick turned to Charlie. "I can't believe it," he said under his breath. "Howard?" He shook his head. "The biggest goof off in the school?"

"Don't worry, you still have a shot at it," Charlie tried to remind him. "You heard Abbot Ambrose; he still has two more names to go."

"Master Charlie MacCready," Abbot Ambrose said loudly.

Charlie sank back in his chair as the refectory let out a collective gasp and all heads turned to look at him. He could feel his face turn as red as his surplice, embarrassed that he had been caught talking and not paying attention. He felt very uncomfortable when he noticed everyone staring at him. He looked at Gus.

"Go on, Charlie," he grinned at him from across the table. "You made it. You're an Altar Boy!"

"Me?" Charlie looked at Abbot Ambrose. "Me?" he mouthed.

"Yes, Charlie, you." Abbot Ambrose smiled and held out a welcoming hand.

The room erupted in polite applause as Charlie stood up still disbelieving. Beside a clapping Father Emmanuel, Howard stood grinning through the pain in his cheek. His hands were pink from clapping.

"Him?" Rick gasped in shock. "Oh, this is too much, really. Talk about the Abbot's pet."

Gus turned to face him. "Come off it, Rick. Be happy for someone else for a change. It won't kill you. Besides if you aren't named this time you could be next be next year."

Rick looked at Gus as though he said a bad word; his mouth dropped open and his eyes widened.

"Now we still have one name to go," Abbot Ambrose continued when the applause died away. "I have thought long and hard about this, and weighed my decision carefully. I have to admit this was a first for me; I actually met with my first choice to discuss my dilemma. He was very helpful and we reached a decision together. I won't name him but he knows how much I appreciate his help.

"Our last new member is—" Abbot Ambrose paused and looked around the room. "Master Rick Walters."

Rick's pout turned into a smile. He held his head high and he stood up. The applause was less than enthusiastic as he walked forward to accept his new surplice. He ignored Gus's attempts to congratulate him. Gus settled back in his chair, and continued to clap for Rick anyway. As he watched Rick change into his new surplice, he glanced at Abbot Ambrose. As their eyes met, Abbot Ambrose smiled. Gus nodded and continued to applaud.

As soon as the three new members of the Altar Boys were dressed in their new robes, Abbot Ambrose concluded the meal with a prayer. The room then emptied in its usual silent manner, each table silently filing out behind their dorm prefect. When they reached the hallway, they dispersed.

Gus watched from a distance as all the other Altar Boys huddled around Rick, and Howard. They were all talking excitedly and congratulating them.

"You're not regretting your decision are you, Master Kugele?"

Gus jumped and turned around to face the Abbot. "A little," he admitted. "But I'm glad you chose Rick. He wants it so bad. Plus, he really is a good guy. I couldn't have won the costume contest without his help."

"It was a very generous thing you did," Abbot Ambrose said. "You should be proud."

Gus smiled and nodded. He watched Abbot Ambrose walk down the hall toward his office. Glancing back at the Altar Boys, he sighed and headed up the stairs.

Charlie slowly walked into the hall. He looked at the empty stairs and then at Rick in the middle of the noisy huddle. Slowly he joined them, receiving congratulatory pats on the back from the older members.

Charlie still couldn't believe he was chosen to be an Altar Boy. It all seemed unreal as he stood listening to Steve Chambers and Randy Fischer, the sacristans and head of the Altar Boys, explain their new duties. Steve was a senior and a member of Saint Sebastian dorm. He was tall, thin and blonde. From what Howard once told him, Steve was orphaned when he was three. The monks took him in and raised him since. The rumor among the dorms was that Steve was going to enter the monastery after graduation.

Randy was also a senior, but a member of Saint Thomas dorm. He was about three inches shorter than Steve, with dark brown hair and brown eyes. He wasn't an orphan. Like a lot of the boys, to Charlie's surprise, Randy came to Saint Michael's as a last resort, having been expelled from his two previous high schools for disorderly conduct. Once at Saint Michael's he settled down, and along with Steve, was appointed as sacristan. Together they were entrusted to care for the vestments, prayer books, and supplies for the priests of the Abbey.

"Brother James," Steve continued to explain. "Has given me the names of the monks you three are assigned to. You'll meet with them before Mass and assist them during. They each have a pew on the second floor above the sanctuary. After Mass you'll help them back to their room. Then we'll meet back down here for lunch. After lunch you'll return to them and spend a couple hours with them doing whatever they want. Some of them like to go for a walk, but today they may just want to visit and get to know you.

"Rick," Steve turned to him first. "You've been assigned to Father Mathias. He's on the second floor, cell twenty-nine."

Rick nodded silently.

"Howard, you see Brother Gregory," Steve continued to read from his list without looking up.

Howard looked at Charlie and shrugged. It was obvious that he had no clue as to which monk Brother Gregory was. Charlie smiled at him. It didn't matter what the name of the monk was that he would be assigned to, Charlie thought to himself. He wouldn't know who they were anyway.

"And Charlie." Steve looked at him and smiled. "You have been assigned to Father Prior Anselm."

Charlie looked at him in surprise. While he didn't know the Prior, he did hear stories about him. He glanced over at Rick who was visibly upset and glaring at him.

"His cell number is thirty-seven," Steve concluded. "So, welcome to the group, any questions?"

Steve looked at the three of them and smiled. "Okay, then we're off."

The Altar Boys formed two lines behind Steve and Randy as they headed down the hallway toward the main entrance. Howard, Charlie and Rick quickly joined the end of the lines.

Charlie thought about the things he once heard from Clifford, the boy adopted by the Murphys, about the Prior. He began to feel nervous in the pit of his stomach. He remembered that when Clifford returned to the dorm one Sunday after spending time with the Prior, he muttered that the Prior was a cranky old man. He said he could not believe how mean the Prior was to him. Another time, he said the Prior even threw a book at him, because he wasn't fast enough with a task he was asked to do.

"I can't believe you get the Prior." Rick clenched his teeth. "I've been here longer."

"I don't think that is what determines who gets whom." Howard shook his head. "If that were the case, I would have been assigned the Prior." He smiled at Charlie. "I'm sorry, but I'm glad I wasn't."

"That's okay." Charlie shrugged. "Hey Rick, you can have him if you want. I'll trade you."

Rick smiled.

Suddenly the lines came to an abrupt stop. Steve turned around and looked at Rick.

"No," he snapped. "You've been given your assignments for a reason. Now once you enter the monastery wing, you are to keep silent until you are in your Brother's room."

"I'm sorry." Charlie said weakly. He was embarrassed

Steve heard their murmurings. He looked at Howard for reassurance. Howard nodded and smiled which put Charlie at ease.

Steve turned back around and they resumed their walking.

"Well, I guess you must be Abbot Ambrose's pet," Rick sneered.

"What does it matter, Rick?" Howard defended Charlie as he tired of Rick's jealousy. "You made it into the Altar Boys. Why don't you just lighten up?"

Rick glared at Howard. "I have a right to talk if I want to."

"That is enough, Rick. Not another word." Steve snapped again. "As sacristans, Randy and I have to give Abbot Ambrose a report on how well each of you is handling your assignment. I would hate to have to give him an unfavorable report about you. We haven't had a boy stripped of his privilege of being an Altar Boy yet, but there's always a first time for everything."

Rick bit his lip and gulped hard at the thought. He had wanted to be an Altar Boy for so long and even the thought of being removed was chilling.

Steve looked at each of them before he opened the fire doors to the main entry hall. "No more talking."

Charlie tried hard not to laugh. Steve's timing couldn't have been better. He nodded to Steve, who held the door for them as he passed into the main hall.

The group followed Randy over to the staircase and up the stairs to the balcony. The view from the balcony was a lot different from downstairs. The banister rail and balcony rails were polished brass. The floor was covered with a thick dark green and gold diamond patterned carpet. On either side of the balcony was a sign for the restrooms, men on the right, women on the left. The large double doors to the Abbey church were in the center of the wall at the back of the balcony. Two Holy

Water basins made of white marble were on either side of the door. Charlie thought they looked like indoor birdbaths. The boys huddled around Randy outside the doors to the monastery wing and waited for Steve to catch up and open the door.

As they entered the hallway, Charlie was struck by its similarity to the hall on their floor. The walls were a muted shade of white, not bright at all. The floor was a gray, slate color but very shiny. Along both walls of the hall, spaced across from each other were the doors to the monks' rooms or cells, as Steve called them. Charlie didn't like the sound of the word cell. He envisioned a prison with barred windows and heavy metal doors. Steve assured him none of the Brothers were there against their will. Beside each door a small wooden cross was hung. Beneath the cross was a plaque with the room number engraved on it.

Steve and Randy instructed them to be back at the refectory in time for lunch. He reminded them that the lunch bell they were used to hearing on their fourth floor didn't ring in the monastery wing. They'd have to be alert and watch the clock. They then departed to their duties.

The three boys walked slowly down the hall. Charlie looked at the numbers on the little plaques. Every once and again he'd glance at Howard with a worried look on his face. Meeting new people wasn't something that came easily to him.

Rick's door was first as the numbers started at twenty and increased as they walked further down the hall. He looked at Howard and Charlie, who both nodded encouragingly at him and waited a few feet away. They hoped to see what Father Mathias looked like when he answered the door. Rick knocked once. The door opened slightly and Rick slipped inside. Neither Howard nor Charlie was able to see a thing.

Howard looked at Charlie and shrugged. They continued

down the hall. Charlie found his door first at the bend in the hall, but waited until Howard had found his, almost to the end of the monastery wing. They knocked and looked at each other.

Charlie jumped as the door in front of him opened almost immediately. Standing before him was an old, hunched over, man. His spectacles were perched on the tip of his bulbous nose. His face was weathered and wrinkled and his cheeks sagged from age. The front hems of his robes were worn from being drug on the floor.

"Don't just stand there boy, come in," His voice was gravelly. "And don't forget to close the door behind you. Don't need any more drafts," he snarled.

Charlie quickly did as he was told. When he turned around from closing the door, he was surprised by the Prior's room. To the left of the small entry hall was a large bathroom. A sitting room opened up at the end of the entry. Unlike the hall outside, it was bright and cheerful. Potted plants sat atop a low bookcase under a large window that overlooked the front grounds. A small white sofa sat against the right wall. Across its back lay a stained glass patterned afghan. Above it, on the same dull white walls like the hallway, hung bright, colorful scenic photographs in nice brass frames. On the opposite wall, above a straight back, winged chair hung old black and white photographs, a stark contrast to those above the sofa. Beside the chair was a doorway into a small, very sterile looking bedroom.

Prior Anselm sat down in his chair and looked Charlie over.

"Do I know you?" he asked, his voice sounding distant. "Sit down, boy," he said in a gruff voice, motioning toward the sofa.

Charlie walked over to the sofa and sat down. He smiled nervously.

"So, what's your name boy?" the Prior asked as he settled into his chair and pulled another afghan around his shoulders.

Charlie raised his eyebrows curiously since it was already quite warm in the room.

"Charlie MacCready, Father," he answered quickly.

"Charlie, eh?" Prior Anselm nodded to himself and seemed to be lost in his thoughts. "Good name. So, you are the new kid. What happened to your parents?"

Charlie looked around as he thought. "I don't know. When I was two years old, I was left with my grandparents. My parents said they would come back for me but they never did."

"I see." He nodded again. "Are you looking for a new family, then?"

Charlie looked at him in surprise. "No, sir. I already have a family."

"Of course, you do, boy. The fourth floor is full of boys with families that are willing to take care of them." The sarcasm was definitely coming through in the Prior's tone.

Charlie looked at the floor. Deep down he knew the Prior was right. There was no one in his family who was willing to care for him, except his grandmother, and she wasn't able to stand up to his Uncle Chester.

Prior Anselm noticed Charlie's sullen expression and a twinge of guilt stung his conscience. "Ah, snap out of it, boy," His tone was still gruff but softer. "I didn't mean for you to go and get all upset with me. I was just running off at the mouth again. I do that from time to time. I'm old."

Charlie looked up and smiled slightly.

"So, I suppose you've already heard that I'm a cantankerous old goat with a bad temper. Eh?"

Charlie was shocked by the Prior's comment. He had no idea the Prior knew what the boys were saying about him behind his back. He felt a bit embarrassed about it and could feel his face redden.

"Don't look so shocked, boy. I know what they're saying about me. I've worked hard to earn that reputation." He gave Charlie a toothy grin. "So, what do you think?"

"I don't know you well enough, Father," Charlie replied quickly.

Prior Anselm laughed out loud. "Good answer, boy. So, what do you want to know about me?"

Charlie thought for a moment as he looked around the room and then back at the Prior. "Are you a cantankerous, mean old man?"

Again, Prior Anselm let out a hearty laugh. His pale cheeks became pink. His gray eyes watered.

"Oh Charlie, I think we're going to get along just fine," he chuckled and wiped his eyes.

Charlie relaxed and sat back on the sofa. He looked again at the photographs on the wall above the Prior. His curiosity grew and he wanted to get a closer look at them. They appeared to be group photographs taken on the front grounds but he couldn't make out who they were or when they were taken.

"Is there anything I can get for you?" Charlie asked.

"No. No." he shook his head. "It's almost time for Mass."

Charlie nodded and tried to come up with some way to find out about the pictures without pushing his luck.

"So," he tried to sound disinterested. "Did you take those pictures?" He pointed to them.

Prior Anselm cocked his head and then turned back toward Charlie. "No, I did not," he answered.

Charlie could sense that he didn't want to talk about them so he quickly asked. "What about these?" He twisted around to look at the pictures that hung over his head.

"Yes," he beamed.

"Wow! You're really good."

"Thanks, but I'm afraid it's were," Prior Anselm sighed as he looked at his shaking hands. "These old hands aren't as steady as they once were."

"You could use a tripod," Charlie tried to sound encouraging and turned around.

Prior Anselm smiled. "It was a long time ago, Charlie. I'm afraid I'm just too tired these days."

"I'm sorry," he said and the room fell silent again.

"Prior Anselm, how long have you been here, if you don't mind my asking?" Charlie changed the subject.

The Prior's eyes stared off into the room as he thought. "I came to Saint Michael's when I was fifteen. That was nearly sixty-five years ago."

"Wow," Charlie gasped. "What was it like then?"

"Oh my," he smiled as he thought back. "It was a different world back then. I came to the Abbey as a seminarian. I remember my first day. My parents drove me to the Abbey in our old Ford pickup truck. It was a long, bumpy, two-day trip from our farm. My parents were not sure they were doing the right thing letting me go. My dad especially wasn't happy. I was a big help to him on the farm. But he did have my nine brothers to help him. It wasn't as though I was leaving him alone to care for the farm. It wasn't a big farm by farming standards today, but it was a lot of hard work.

"When we drove up the long winding dirt and gravel road and the trees cleared, I saw the Abbey for the first time and I knew I was home. I've never regretted my decision."

"Yeah, it's an impressive building." Charlie nodded. "I was scared when I saw it for the first time."

Prior Anselm smiled. "Yes, this building can be quite

overpowering. But this is the new Abbey building. It wasn't here when I came. The old Abbey is the one that was my first home."

"The old Abbey?" Charlie asked curiously.

"Oh yes," the Prior nodded. "This is our third building actually. The first was located at the foot of the south side of the hill. The second was on what is now called Black Butte. We moved into this one three years after I came here."

"What happened to the other buildings?" Charlie asked. His curiosity was piqued and he sat forward eagerly listening to the fascinating story.

"Well, it's time we start heading toward the Abbey Church for Mass," Prior Anselm reminded Charlie.

"Oh, yes," he sighed. He really wanted to hear more about the Abbey. His mind was flooded with questions. He suddenly realized that Prior Anselm was there when Joseph Oswald fell. Perhaps he could tell him what happened.

It was hard to concentrate during Mass. Charlie's mind kept wandering. He kept thinking about lunch and telling Howard everything he'd learned about the Prior. When the final song was over and the Mass had ended, Charlie helped the Prior back to his room. He told him he'd return after lunch, and then hurried off to find Howard.

By the time he reached he first floor, the boys were just about to file into the refectory. Charlie slipped into his place in line. After the prayer was said and the signal was given that it was okay to speak, he began to talk excitedly to Howard in a hushed whisper.

"This afternoon when I go back, I'm gonna ask," Charlie said and then looked up. Something was wrong. He looked around. Gus wasn't in his seat.

"Where's Gus?" he asked.

Rick continued to eat his lunch but took the time to shrug his shoulders as though he didn't care. "Who?" he asked with a twinge of superiority in his voice.

Charlie glared at Rick. "You haven't changed a bit. You make me sick," he said in disgust and looked away.

A chill ran up his spine as he spotted Gus across the room. He was sitting at the Saint Peter table. Charlie turned to Howard.

"We can't just sit at another dorm's table, can we?"

"No." Howard shook his head.

"Then why is Gus over at Saint Peter table? And wearing a purple surplice."

Howard cocked his head and looked across the room. When he spotted Gus, he sat back in his chair. He looked over at Father Emmanuel, who was busy eating his lunch.

"I'll ask Father Emmanuel," he said and left the table.

Charlie watched as the two put their heads together and whispered. Howard nodded as he listened. Father Emmanuel patted him on the back and smiled, but Howard did not. He slowly returned to his seat.

"Well?" Charlie urged.

"He switched dorms," Howard sighed and shook his head in disbelief.

Charlie looked over at Rick and glared. "What did you do to him this time?"

"Me?" Rick gasped. "I didn't do anything, Mr. Abbot's pet."

"You best not have." Howard glared harder at him. "He moved his things this morning."

"But why?" Charlie felt the familiar sinking feeling in his stomach. Suddenly he was no longer hungry.

"We should talk to him after we get back from tending the Brothers," Howard suggested.

"I'll meet you back at the dorm, then we can go together," Charlie suggested.

"Okay." Howard nodded.

After lunch Charlie headed back to Prior Anselm's room. His thoughts were no longer on the conversation he had that morning. Instead he was preoccupied with the news about Gus' sudden move to Saint Peter dorm. He began to wonder if it had something to do with what he overheard that morning.

Prior Anselm noticed that Charlie was quiet. He tried to read a book as Charlie watered his plants and began to dust the bookcase but the silence was deafening. Finally, he set his book down and looked at Charlie over the top of his reading glasses.

"Okay, Charlie, what's bothering you?" he asked. His voice was softer than it had been earlier that morning.

Charlie looked over his shoulder at him and stopped dusting. He fiddled with the cloth in his hands as he thought.

"It's nothing really," he sighed.

"I see." Prior Anselm nodded and picked up his book again.

"I just don't understand why he would do it." Charlie sat down on the sofa. "Especially moving into Saint Peter dorm with the likes of Dougary and Travis." Charlie made a face like he had bit into something sour.

Prior Anselm set the book back down in his lap.

"Why should that be a problem?" he asked and removed his glasses. He rested his hands on the book in his lap.

"It's just they've always teased him and have been so mean to him. I don't understand it. Why would he do it? I thought he liked us." Charlie shook his head in disbelief.

"Who are you talking about, Charlie?" Prior Anselm scratched his head.

"Gus," he sighed again. "Ever since I came to Saint

Michael's it's always been the four of us, Howard, Rick, Gus and myself. We don't always get along but we work it out. We've always done everything together and we look out for one another. I just don't understand it."

"Why do you think it has to do with you?"

Charlie thought for a moment. He didn't know why; it was just a feeling. Deep down he suspected it had something to do with the three out of the four of them being chosen to be Altar Boys. However, he didn't know for certain.

"I don't know," he shrugged.

"Well, maybe we should cut this afternoon short so you can go talk to him."

Charlie looked up and smiled. "You wouldn't mind?"

"No. Not at all," Prior Anselm assured him. "You could come back tomorrow and finish."

"Thank you, Prior," Charlie said and quickly put away his rag and cleaner. "I'll come back tomorrow after classes."

"Okay. See you then," Prior Anselm called as the door closed behind Charlie.

All the way up to the fourth floor Charlie thought about what he would say to Gus. He played over in his mind how he would walk up to him and ask him why he moved. He hoped that Gus would be in the hall, since entering Saint Peter dorm meant the possibility of running into Dougary and his gang.

As he walked down the empty hall on the fourth floor toward Saint Peter dorm, his heart beat faster and his hands began to sweat. Gus was nowhere in sight. He must be inside the dorm. He first thought about just opening the doors and yelling for Gus but that would surely attract Dougary's attention. He looked around again as he stood in front of the dorm doors to see if he could find a member of Saint Peter whom he could ask to get Gus. There was no one in sight. He took a deep breath and reached for the door handle. His heart pounded in his throat. In the three months since he came to Saint Michael's he had never stopped foot in any dorm except his own and especially not Saint Peter. He listened intently to see if he could hear anyone inside before he slowly opened the door and cautiously entered.

The dorm was a lot like Saint Nicholas, only the colors were different. The braided rug in the center of the room was purple and black. The sofa and the chairs were upholstered in the same plaid pattern of purple and black with a thread of silver. Around the room all the single beds were of different styles. The dorm was nearly deserted except for a small gathering around one cubicle. Through the huddle he caught a glimpse of Gus. He sighed quietly to himself and decided to wait for a safer time to talk to him.

As he turned around to leave the dormitory doors swung open. Charlie froze as Dougary and Travis walked in. The look in their eyes flashed from shock to anger.

"What are you doing in here?" Dougary raised his voice to attract the rest of the dorm's attention. His voice echoed throughout the room. "Hey, Travis," he continued to yell. "What's the punishment for trespassing?"

Charlie took a step back into the dorm. His heart pounded in this throat as he tried to figure a way out of the dorm. Once in the hall he was sure he would be safe. He looked around. Tiny beads of sweat dotted his forehead as the members of Saint Peter dorm surrounded him.

Gus pushed through the circle and looked at Charlie and then at Dougary and Travis.

"I say we teach him a lesson he won't forget soon," he said with a sneer as he looked at Charlie.

Dougary and Travis both gave Gus a shocked look and then

smiled fiendishly to one another. This did not put Charlie at ease. He started to get angry as he felt trapped.

"You had best leave me alone," he ordered boldly.

Dougary laughed and walked over to him. "Oh dear, you know, I think you're right. Hey guys, we best let Charlie go." Charlie could hear the sarcasm in his tone and knew he was being toyed with. "We're so sorry, Charlie." He said and put his arm around Charlie's shoulders. "You are so right. We should let you just go on your merry way."

Suddenly Dougary pushed Charlie into Travis.

"Oh, now you've done it." Travis said as he clenched his teeth. "You crossed the line from trespassing to assault. I have to defend myself." With that Travis gave Charlie a hard push backward. Charlie staggered and then fell on his back on the hard floor.

The circle of members closed in on Charlie as he tried to get to his feet. Hands grabbed at his arms and legs and lifted him off the floor. Charlie struggled to free himself trying to twist and squirm out of their tight grasps but to no avail. Through the mob he caught a glimpse of Father Vicar standing in the shadows of a partition across the room. When their eyes met, Father Vicar pulled back into the shadow. Charlie twisted and struggled more.

"To the bathroom!" a familiar voice yelled. Charlie could have sworn it was Gus.

The mob moved as one out of the dorm and quickly toward the bathrooms. Charlie looked around frantically for anyone who might help him but the hall was deserted. He started to scream out but then someone stuffed a rag in his mouth to muffle the sound. It felt all too familiar and he looked directly into the face of Larry. He turned and looked at Gus in disbelief. Why was he doing this? I thought we were friends. Charlie thought to himself.

"A swirly," Dougary shouted as he opened a door to a stall and flushed the toilet.

Moments later the bathroom cleared and Charlie sat on the floor in a puddle of cold water, alone. His hair dripped cold water onto his white surplice and cassock. He wiped his face and fought back his tears. He felt so humiliated. What had he ever done to deserve this?

Slowly he stood up and opened the door of the stall. He jumped back and tightened his fists as he saw Gus leaning against the wall. When Gus saw him, he stepped forward.

"Just leave me alone, pig boy." Charlie snapped through clenched teeth. His fists were ready for a fight if the need be.

Gus stepped back out of his way. "I'm sorry," he said softly as Charlie walked past him and out of the door.

~§~

Moments later, alone in the nice warm shower, Charlie crumbled to the floor and cried. He wished he were back with his grandmother. Nothing like this had ever happened to him when he was with her. Friends did not do things like that to their friends. "Why? Why?" he cried.

Charlie changed into his dry clothes and walked over to his bed and sat down. He picked up his pen and notebook, then settled back on his bed and began to write. He would send his grandmother a letter and ask her what he should do. She would know.

Howard looked up from his book as he lay on his bed.

"Where've you been?" he asked and sat up. "I thought we were going to talk to Gus?"

Charlie didn't look at Howard but continued to write.

"Forget him. It's a waste of time. He's nothing but a dirty traitor and a jerk and I never want to see him or speak to him again."

Howard recoiled as he looked at Charlie in stunned surprise. "Boy, what's eating you?"

Charlie turned and looked at Howard. He then recounted the events that had taken place in Saint Peter dorm and how Gus had been the instigator of it.

As Howard listened his jaw dropped. He had known Gus since the day Gus came to Saint Michael's. None of this sounded like the mousy little boy he knew.

"Wow, who would've thought?" Howard shook his head. "I guess you just never know about some people. Hey, did you find out any more about the pictures in Prior Anselm's room?"

"No," Charlie sighed. "Not yet, but I will."

PRIOR ANSELM

The late autumn air was a bit cold and the afternoon sky was gray, but Prior Anselm insisted on going outside for a walk. "The fresh air would do you good," he said in answer to Charlie's protests. Actually, it didn't take a lot of convincing to get Charlie out the front doors and onto the front grounds. He was silently eager to get out and see the ponds again.

The two walked slowly across the front lawn toward one of the clusters of trees. The leaves on the trees were completely gone and the flowerbeds were prepared for winter. Prior Anselm sat down on the small bench and faced the pond. He patted the empty space beside him on the bench and urged Charlie to sit down.

Charlie looked around. He was surprised to see Howard walking in the distance with Brother Gregory. Brother Gregory seemed to be excited about something and kept pulling on his robes. Charlie looked closer and gasped. Brother Gregory's habit was wet and muddy. Charlie looked at Howard who seemed to be talking very fast and gesturing frantically with his hands. Charlie quickly looked at the pond and tried not to laugh.

Howard had done it again.

"So, how're you doing in your classes?" Prior Anselm opened the conversation.

"Oh, pretty good." Charlie nodded and watched the fish slowly swim around in the cold water of the pond. "Prior Anselm, can I ask you something?"

"Sure." He nodded and pinched a piece from the slice of bread he pulled from the pocket of his habit. He tossed it into the pond and then watched as the fish darted to the surface of the murky water and in one gulp swallowed the morsel.

"While I was cleaning your room, I looked at the pictures above your chair." Charlie said hesitantly. "Were you a dorm overseer?"

Prior Anselm froze as he started to toss another crumb to the fish. He did not know why he kept those pictures around. He knew that someday someone was bound to ask him about them. They represented some of the worst days of his life at Saint Michael's and yet some of the best. Perhaps, deep down, it was because he truly wanted to talk about them.

"Yes," he finally answered, tossing the crumb. "Yes, I was the prefect of your dorm a long, long time ago."

"You were?" Charlie gasped in wide-eyed shock.

The conversation stalled into silence as Charlie thought about what Prior Anselm just said. He looked around the grounds and then back at the Prior.

"Did you know a boy named Joseph Oswald?" he asked.

The words hit Prior Anselm hard. His whole body suddenly tensed and a sharp pain stabbed him through his chest. Yes, he knew the boy. How could he not? The boy was one of his charges. The one he was most fond of and the reason he had asked to be removed as prefect. He remembered the day he and the then Father Ambrose had climbed out onto the portico but they were too late. He remembered how he looked up at the attic window above as he cradled Joseph's lifeless body in his arms and wept and for a split second, he saw the frightened face of a white-haired boy he had never seen before. Those were the images that had haunted his dreams ever since.

As Charlie looked at Prior Anselm, he became frightened. The Prior turned pale and wasn't breathing. He just sat motionless with his mouth open and his eyes staring blindly ahead.

"Prior Anselm!" Charlie shouted and grabbed the Prior's arm and shook him.

Prior Anselm's chest heaved as he took in a deep breath. The pain in his chest eased and unconsciously he rubbed his left arm. He looked at Charlie, noticing the frightened look in his eyes. He put his arm around him reassuringly and smiled even as tiny beads of sweat dotted his forehead.

"We best go inside." His voice was weak.

"Okay." Charlie agreed and stood up. He helped Prior Anselm to his feet and then the two slowly headed back to the Abbey. Prior Anselm leaned on Charlie's shoulder to steady himself.

"I'm sorry if I upset you, Father Prior," Charlie apologized.

"Oh, rubbish." Prior Anselm shook his head. "You don't need to apologize, Charlie. Why the interest in Joey?"

"It's just that Howard told me the story about the ghost in the attic. He said that some forty years ago a boy was locked in the attic. When his friend came to get him the next morning the boy panicked and his friend fell out the window and died. Since my second week here, I've heard noises, moaning coming from the attic at night. Gus was really upset by it and said it was the ghost of the boy who fell. I don't believe in ghosts. There has to be some other explanation.

"Then on Halloween, Howard and I were jumped and tied to a headstone in the old cemetery. The headstone next to Howard was Joseph's. The dates seemed to fit with the ghost story, and I was just wondering if he was the boy from the story."

"Oh yes." Prior Anselm nodded. "The ghost story. When I first heard that horrible story among the boys, I was quite upset by it. I found out the names of the senior boys who started it and approached the Abbot about disciplining them. The Abbot didn't agree with me, and said to just let it go. He reasoned that once those boys were gone, the story would go with them. However, time has proven him wrong, wouldn't you say?" Prior Anselm stopped and looked at the Abbey building. "When the Abbot passed away and Father Ambrose was appointed, I approached Abbot Ambrose with the recommendation he close the orphanage. He didn't agree with me, so I asked to be removed as prefect and to have no further contact with the children. Abbot Ambrose didn't want to, but he granted my petition." He paused and took a deep breath, then continued walking back to the Abbey.

"Charlie, you're right," he said. "Joseph was the boy that died. He was an orphaned boy who came to us when he was only ten years old. He was so loving and a friend to all the boys, a truly gentle soul. He endeared himself to all the Brothers, always eager to lend a hand. He was a member of Saint Nicholas dorm and helped me with the newer boys who were having trouble adjusting. But there's more to the story. I have something in my room that I'll show you. I'll get it out so on our next visit we can talk about it. Fair enough?"

"Okay." Charlie nodded as they made their way up the staircase in the entry hall. Charlie looked at the Prior again and became concerned. "Are you okay?"

Prior Anselm gripped the handrail and leaned against the wall, appearing to catch his breath.

"I'm just a little tired I guess," he finally said, wiping the sweat from his brow with a handkerchief he took from his pocket. "I'll lay down when I get back to my room."

He looked at Charlie and saw the worry in his eyes. He smiled and patted Charlie on his head playfully. "I'll be okay," he said.

"Okay," Charlie agreed. "I'll see you tomorrow after classes then."

"I'll be here." Prior Anselm said firmly and entered his room. He closed the door without waving good-bye.

Charlie hesitated for a moment outside Prior Anselm's door before he returned to his dorm. He wasn't totally convinced that the Prior was as good as he said but he would talk to him about it tomorrow.

When he entered the dorm Charlie immediately spotted Howard slumped down in one of the overstuffed chairs in the center of the room. His feet were propped up on the coffee table while his elbows rested on the arms of the chair. He held his head between his fists as he stared at the wall across the room. It was obvious he was deep in thought.

"What's the matter?" Charlie asked as he walked over to Howard and sat down in the chair next to him.

"Everything," Howard sighed. "I don't know. Maybe I'm not cut out to be an Altar Boy."

"Don't be so hard on yourself."

"I'm such a klutz." Howard continued without looking at Charlie. "First I break his lamp when I'm making his bed. Then I was helping him at Mass and I get his vestments caught in the door and they tear. I told him I would sew them up for him, but he said he'd just have one of the Brothers in the laundry do it.

Oh, then today was the topper. Brother Gregory wanted to go for a walk outside. So, we went out on the front grounds. I was trying to help him, but he kept pulling away from me. He wanted to look at a fish in one of the ponds. When I took his arm, he pulled away, slipped and fell into the water."

Charlie tried not to laugh.

"He's talking to Abbot Ambrose right now about having someone else visit him," Howard sighed. "I'm a failure. I can't do anything right."

"No, Howard, you are not a failure," Charlie insisted. "Don't worry about it. Abbot Ambrose will take care of things. Besides, wait until I tell you what I found out about Prior Anselm."

Howard gave Charlie a half-interested look. He really wasn't in the mood but he could tell Charlie was dying to tell him.

"Prior Anselm used to be the overseer of our dorm. He knew Joseph and said that he was the boy that fell," Charlie talked excitedly. "He said there is more to the story and he has something to show me tomorrow."

Howard sat up and looked more interested in Charlie's news.

"Did he give you any indication what it is?" he asked.

Charlie slumped down a little in the chair. "No. Actually when I asked him, he started acting weird. He cut short our talk and said he was tired. So, we just came inside."

"That's weird." Howard agreed.

~§~

That night, after he finished writing his grandmother a letter, Charlie lay back in his bed and looked out his window at the night sky. The sky was clear and filled with stars. He wondered if he would hear noises in the attic as he had nearly every night since he came to Saint Michael's.

It seemed as though he had just fallen asleep when the sound of the big bell in the tower tolling caused Charlie to stir. Charlie opened his eyes and sat up in his bed. He listened to the slow, steady tolling and wondered what was going on. He looked around the room but no one appeared to hear it as they slept. He looked at Howard who turned over to face the partition.

"Pssst, Howard," he whispered. "Howard, wake up."

Howard turned back over and barely opened his eyes. "What?" he asked as he yawned?

"What's that noise?" Charlie asked cocking his head to listen.

Howard turned his ear toward the sound. As he listened to the slow, deep pulsing gong, his eyes opened wider.

"How many times has it rung?" Howard asked.

"I don't know, a lot, why?" Charlie answered.

"It's the death toll," Howard answered and yawned again. "One of the Brothers must have died. Go back to sleep."

"What?" Charlie gasped. "Why? Who?"

"It happens, go back to sleep," Howard moaned. "We'll find out in the morning." Howard turned back to face the partition.

"Okay." Charlie said as he slid back down in his bed. He pulled his covers up over his chest and stared at the ceiling. How could he sleep knowing someone just died? His thoughts turned to his grandfather and the night he died. He couldn't remember if he had slept after hearing the news. He looked at Howard. The familiar sound of his soft snores meant he was fast asleep. Charlie turned his head and looked out the window. He began to count the tolls and somewhere after twenty-eight, he drifted off to sleep again.

The sky was still dark outside when the morning bell rang. Charlie sat up and stretched as he yawned. He still felt tired and wished he could stay in bed. He looked around the dorm. Everyone seemed to be as tired as he was. Howard pulled the covers over his head and tried to steal a few more minutes of sleep before his alarm clock rang out.

Still in a groggy haze, Charlie walked over to his closet and grabbed his towel. He headed off to the showers. Perhaps a nice cool shower would wake him up. As he opened the door to the shower room he came face to face with Gus. Suddenly he was wide awake. He smiled at Gus, forgetting his anger over the bathroom incident.

"Hi," he greeted his friend.

Gus's eyes were as cold as the nuggets of coal on a snowman's head. He straightened his back, stuck his nose in the air and pushed Charlie aside, knocking him against the doorpost. Without looking back, he returned to St. Peter's dorm. Charlie shook his head and let the door close.

The shower had its desired effect, Charlie was no longer tired, but he was saddened by his encounter with Gus. Each time he saw Gus, his hopes of being able to talk to him were crushed. He shrugged his shoulders and he headed back to his dorm.

As he entered the hallway, he noticed two boys from Saint Sebastian dorm staring at him. He ignored them and walked. When he realized the boys by the sinks stopped brushing their teeth and were also staring at him, he became a bit self-conscious. He glanced at his reflection in the mirror and ran his hand over his hair, making sure he looked all right. He looked over his shoulder at the boys and continued on his way back to his dorm.

"Hey, Howard," Charlie called as he walked into the dorm.

The dorm suddenly became silent. All heads turned to look at Charlie. He noticed their stares and began to grow angry.

"What?" he snapped at them.

No one said a word. They just stood like statues staring at him.

"Sheesh!" Charlie said, shaking his head. He walked over to his closet. "What's going on, Howard?"

Howard quickly straightened his surplice before closing his closet door. He turned and faced Charlie. Charlie didn't like the look in Howard's eyes. He had never seen him look that way before. He began grow anxious.

"What is it?" Charlie insisted.

"Charlie, you need to hurry up and get dressed. Abbot Ambrose wants to see you in Father Emmanuel's office right away." Howard's voice was soft and somber.

Charlie threw his towel into his closet and grabbed his clothes. He grabbed his jeans and pulled them on all the while his mind racing, trying to figure out what it could be. Was it about his grandmother? Maybe his parents had finally come for him? That must be it, he thought to himself.

Howard noticed that Charlie's hands were trembling as he tried to button his cassock. "Here, let me help you," he said and took over the task. "It's going to be okay. I'm here for you."

Charlie looked at Howard and smiled. "Don't worry. I'll ask them if you can come too."

Howard gave him a curious look. "There," he said as he straightened Charlie's surplice. "Go."

Charlie hurried to Father Emmanuel's office. He wondered how he would react at seeing his parents. He wondered what they looked like after all these years. Would he recognize them? Would they recognize him? He couldn't stop smiling as he knocked on the door.

"Come in," Father Emmanuel invited as he opened the door.

Charlie walked into the office. He'd been there before. Right beside the door, Father Emmanuel's oak desk sat with its edge against the wall creating a walkway into the rest of the room. Behind the desk, running the full length of the wall, was a huge bookcase like the one in Abbot Ambrose's office. The shelves weren't as crowed with books though. Instead, plants, family photographs of his brothers, sisters, nieces and nephews, a stereo and a stack of record albums were mixed in with an armful of books. Under the window on the north wall were two comfortable, swivel-rocking chairs. Between them stood a small table with a lamp and another plant. A door on the east wall led to Father Emmanuel's bedroom and private bathroom. More photographs hung on the west wall. These pictures however were black and white and of old buildings. Charlie never asked Father Emmanuel about them and none of the other boys ever mentioned what they were.

Abbot Ambrose rose from one of the chairs under the window. He smiled at Charlie and reached out his hands to greet him. He embraced Charlie in a fatherly hug.

"How are you this morning, son?" Abbot Ambrose asked.

"Fine, Father Abbot," he answered politely.

"That's good to hear. Please, have a seat." Abbot Ambrose invited Charlie to sit in the chair beside him. Father Emmanuel sat down in his chair behind his desk. He tried to avoid eye contact with Charlie, which made Charlie uneasy.

"Do you know why we've asked you here?" Abbot Ambrose said once he and Charlie were settled in their seats.

"Not really but I was thinking it must be about my parents?" Charlie asked and hoped.

"No, son, it's not that." Abbot Ambrose shook his head.

Charlie's eyes widened as he noticed for the first time that Abbot Ambrose's eyes were red and wet with tears. He looked over at Father Emmanuel who quickly looked away. His heart beat faster as his thoughts suddenly turned to his grandmother.

"Charlie, last night Prior Anselm passed away," Abbot Ambrose spoke gently.

Charlie shook his head. He was confused for a moment and was not sure he heard correctly. He looked at Abbot Ambrose intently.

"Prior Anselm died?" he repeated slowly.

"Yes, son." Abbot Anselm nodded. "He had a heart attack last night."

Suddenly Charlie remembered the tolling of the bell. It wasn't another dream. It had actually happened. He rocked back in his chair, feeling all of his strength drain out of him. He couldn't move, couldn't speak. Prior Anselm was dead? Another person in his life he cared about was gone. He wanted to cry but couldn't. He was numb. He looked at Abbot Ambrose and then at Father Emmanuel. They were both looking back at him with tears in their eyes.

"Are you okay?" Father Emmanuel asked.

Charlie opened his mouth to speak but nothing came out. All at once he choked and the tears began to flow. Abbot Ambrose reached over to him and took him in his arms. Charlie held him tightly and buried his face in the Abbot's robes. The tears streamed down his cheeks and his whole body trembled. His thoughts flashed to his grandfather, to the day he was taken away from his grandmother, and to Prior Anselm. All of the pain that was bottled up inside him began to pour out.

Abbot Ambrose felt a bit of relief as he held Charlie in his arms. From his conversations with Charlie's grandmother over the past months he knew Charlie was holding back and it worried him. Now, as he consoled Charlie, he felt that everything was going to be all right.

Charlie's tears subsided. He loosened his hold on Abbot Ambrose. Father Emmanuel pulled a handkerchief from his pocket and held it out. Charlie didn't notice and wiped his tears on his sleeves and stepped back.

"It's going to be okay," Abbot Ambrose tried to reassure him. "Today we have suspended classes so the Brothers will be available to the boys that need someone to talk to. I'm here for you, Charlie."

"Thank you, Abbot Ambrose." Charlie's voice quivered as he spoke.

"There's something else, too." Abbot Ambrose looked at Father Emmanuel who handed him a framed photograph. "We found this in Prior Anselm's office it had this note attached to it, 'For Charlie.' I thought you should have it since Prior Anselm appears to have wanted you to."

Charlie took the picture and looked at it as he sat down. He stared at faces of the boys in the photograph, all assembled neatly together. A sign in front of them read in gothic type, "Saint Nicholas' Dorm". He looked at the thin, dark haired monk and smiled. It was Prior Anselm when he was young and the prefect.

"Thank you," he said softly and held the picture to his chest.

"Are you okay, Charlie? Do you want to stay in here for a bit?" Father Emmanuel asked.

"No." He shook his head. "I think I'd like to go back to my dorm."

"Okay," Abbot Ambrose nodded and put his hand on Charlie's back as they walked to the door. "But if you need me, just ask Father Emmanuel or come down to my office."

"Thank you again." Charlie nodded and headed back to his dorm.

Howard and Rick were waiting in the dorm's center lounge area. When Charlie opened the door, they both jumped to their feet. Howard immediately ran to him.

"You okay, Charlie?" he asked and looked him over.

"Yeah." Charlie nodded.

"Hey, I'm sorry. You can take over Brother Gregory for me if you want," he offered.

"No. You'll be fine."

"What's that?" Howard asked and pointed to the framed photograph in Charlie's arms.

Charlie looked at the photograph again and sighed. "It's a picture of Prior Anselm and the guys from when he was the dorm prefect."

"Really?" Rick said rushing over to them. "Can I see it?"

Before Charlie could answer Rick took the picture from him and began studying it. Howard looked at Rick then back at Charlie. He shook his head.

Rick turned the picture over, looking at its tattered back. He frowned and scrunched his nose in a puzzled, disappointed look.

"This is it?" he said finally looking at Howard and Charlie. "What a stupid thing to leave someone."

"What did you expect, you moron. He was a monk not a millionaire," Howard snapped at Rick and reached for the picture but Rick pulled it away.

Howard turned to Charlie. "You wanna go for a walk?"

"Sure," Charlie nodded.

Howard and Charlie walked away leaving Rick behind. As they reached the door, Rick hurried over to them.

"I'm sorry," he apologized.

Just then the door opened in front of them. Gus stood with his back touching the door, ready to run if anyone tried to do to him what he had done to Charlie.

Howard stepped in front of Charlie and puffed out his chest. "What do you want, Nazi?"

Gus' eyes were filled with tears. He knew he deserved that comment but it still hurt.

"I just heard the news and I wanted to come by and tell Charlie that I'm sorry," Gus said sheepishly.

"Don't waste your breath." Howard snapped. "Traitor."

"I'm not a traitor," Gus defended himself. "I just couldn't stay here anymore. That's all."

"Well, no one is keeping you here now. So why don't you run back to Dougary and his freaks," Rick snapped. "You're not welcome here anymore."

Gus looked at his one-time friends as his vision blurred because of his tears. He tried to speak but the words stuck in his throat. He turned around and disappeared out the door.

"Can you believe the nerve of that guy?" Howard said as he turned back around. "Coming in here like we were still friends and all?"

"Well, I think he knows how we feel now." Rick nodded in agreement. "I don't think he'll be coming back any time soon."

Charlie felt his throat tighten as his eyes fill with tears. He felt sorry for Gus and yet he was still very hurt by him. He missed his friend. He took his picture back from Rick and retreated to the security of his cubicle and bed.

"He's really taking it hard," Howard said to Rick in a hushed whisper.

"I know," Rick agreed. "Who would've thought he'd get

so attached so quickly? I mean, I'm not that close to old Father what's-his-nose."

"Father Mathias, Rick," Howard said disgustedly. "I'm glad we're not all like you. Cold to the heart, that's what you are."

"I am not," Rick snapped in an offended tone.

Howard shook his head and went back to his cubicle. He stopped when he reached the foot of his bed.

Charlie sat on his bed, his back against the headboard, staring at the picture. He seemed to have recovered from his last wave of emotion. Howard cautiously sat down on the edge of his own bed across from him.

"You okay, Charlie?" he asked.

"Yeah, I guess," he answered. "Why do you suppose he gave me this? I mean, is Rick, right? Who wants a picture of all of these guys? I don't know any of them except Prior Anselm."

"Can I look?" Howard asked.

"Sure." Charlie handed him the picture then sat back against the headboard again.

Howard studied the picture for a few moments. "You don't suppose this is what he was going to show you, I mean about the ghost story, do you?"

"I don't know," Charlie answered staring at the ceiling. "He did say that Joseph Oswald was the boy that died and that he was a member of Saint Nicholas dorm."

"Do you think that maybe one of these guys is him?" Howard looked at the faces in the picture in earnest.

Charlie looked at Howard. He started to answer but something caught his eye. Something was sticking out of the bottom of the frame. It appeared to be a corner from a piece of paper or an envelope. He turned and sat on the edge of his bed.

"Howard, turn the picture over," he instructed.

Howard turned the picture upside down and gave Charlie a funny look.

"No, silly." Charlie stood up and took the picture from him and turned it around to the back then sat down next to Howard. "Look," he said as he slid the back off the frame. A thin envelope fell to the floor. Charlie handed the picture and frame back to Howard and picked up the envelope.

"What is it? What does it say?" Howard asked as Charlie took a folded-up piece of yellowed paper out of the envelope and unfolded it. His eyes scanned the paper quickly. He looked up at Howard in shock.

"Come on, read it," Howard urged, anxious to hear what it said.

Charlie looked at the paper again. "It says:

> 'My dear Joey,
>
> I'm so sorry that I sent you up there. I should have gone myself. I knew Jeffrey was frightened but I never expected this to happen. It's all my fault. I should have been the one, not you.
>
> 'Please rest in peace knowing that Franklyn and the other boys from Saint Peter who did this to Jeffrey and ultimately you were punished. Of course, not severely enough for what they did but they were punished just the same. In fact, Franklyn is no longer here. He's been adopted. Oh, please don't think he is being rewarded. His future is going to be one of hard labor. His adoptive parents, Maxwell and Helga VonDuggan, are poor farmers from town. They needed help with their land and the Abbot

offered them Franklyn. They know what he has done, and Mr. VonDuggan thinks the hard work will straighten him out. We shall see.

'Oh, Joey, I know you would have forgiven them for what they did and even me for sending you up there. That was the sort of kind soul you were. As a priest I suppose I can forgive them, too, but I can never forgive myself. I am so sorry. Father Anselm'"

Howard sat and stared blindly at the floor, in shock at what he had just heard. Charlie folded the piece of paper up and tucked it back inside the envelope. He sighed and looked at Howard.

"So, that is it," he said softly.

"Yeah." Howard breathed. He looked at Charlie, suddenly full of excitement. "You don't suppose this Franklyn kid is any relation to Dougary do you? I mean, VonDuggan and Duggan are very close to being the same name. I've heard of a lot of German immigrants who dropped the Von from their names after the Second World War, you don't suppose?"

"I don't know," Charlie admitted. "They could have."

Howard looked at the photograph in his lap. Slowly he picked it up and turned it over.

"Charlie," he said in a surprised tone. "Look, there is writing on the back of the picture. It's kind of faded and hard to see." He squinted.

"Let me see it," Charlie said, and took the photograph. He stared intently at the writing and then flipped it over to look at the faces of the boys. He did this several times and then froze.

"It's him," he said. "Right there. That's Joseph." Charlie pointed at the picture.

Howard looked at the handsome young man standing next to a young Prior Anselm. He felt a shiver run up his spine and he looked away.

"This is too creepy," he shuddered. "Maybe we shouldn't be looking at this. I mean, before it was just a story but now it's really awful."

"I know." Charlie flipped the picture over again and tried to read more of the names. He stared at it in silence for a long time then suddenly he flipped it back and looked at the faces again. He turned it over and counted the names in the fourth row and then turned it back around. "That's really strange."

"What's strange?" Howard looked over Charlie's shoulder at the picture.

"This boy here," he said as he pointed to a small boy in the fourth row barely visible behind an older boy. "Has the same last name as Joseph. I think it says his name is Kermy Oswald?"

"Let me take a look at that," Howard said, and squinted as he tried to read the name on the back. "It's Kenny Oswald," he said positively.

"So, do you think Joseph had a brother?" Charlie asked.

"It's possible," Howard answered. "But it's hard to tell from this picture. I wonder if one of Prior Anselm's other photos would show him better?"

"But who knows where they will end up?" Charlie sighed. "I wish he were still here. I can't believe it."

~§~

Prior Anselm's funeral was a big event for the Abbey. Charlie could not believe the fuss they were making as he looked around the Abbey church. There were Bishops and the Archbishop, priests and nuns from all over. Even some of Prior

Anselm's relatives were there. Charlie recognized one of the Prior's brothers from a photograph the Prior had shown him only days before he died.

Slowly, Abbot Ambrose walked around the casket draped in a white cloth with a large spray of flowers covering its top. He swung the censer, or thurible as Steve corrected Rick before the Mass, back and forth as he walked, causing a thick cloud of incense to rise toward the ceiling.

The spicy scent of carnations and the heavy sweet scent of the incense began to overwhelm Charlie as he stood at the foot of Prior Anselm's casket. The gold ornate candleholder became heavier in his hands. He glanced to his right at Howard standing a few feet from him holding the matching candlestick holder. Howard tried to give Charlie a reassuring smile but the odors were getting to him as well.

Once Abbot Ambrose took his place between Charlie and Howard, he handed the thurible back to Rick who grimaced as a thick cloud of white smoke assaulted his face. Abbot Ambrose nodded to Randy, who stood at the head of the casket holding the processional cross, a long pole with a golden crucifix on its top. Slowly Randy turned around, facing the back of the church. The pallbearers took their places beside the casket and slowly turned it around. Once everyone was ready, Randy began to walk slowly. Charlie, Howard and the Abbot followed the casket and the procession out of the Abbey church to the cemetery began.

Charlie was relieved to get outside to the fresh air even if it was biting cold. When the graveside service was over, Abbot Ambrose asked Charlie to stay with him. Steve took the candlestick back to the sacristy. Charlie followed the Abbot back to the Abbey. He stood beside him while he greeted the guests in the seminarian's large refectory.

"Charlie," Abbot Ambrose said as a short thin elderly man approached them. "I'd like you to meet Prior Ambrose's brother, Frederick."

Charlie smiled and shook Frederick's hand. To Charlie's surprise, Frederick had a strong grip and his hand was still rough from years of farming.

"I've heard so much about you, Charlie. Thank you for bringing my brother so much happiness. I haven't heard him as excited or happy in a very, very long time." Frederick smiled.

Charlie was speechless. He just smiled and nodded.

After shaking too many hands to count, the line of guests came to an end. Charlie rubbed the cramping out of his fingers.

"Thank you, Charlie." Abbot Ambrose smiled and put his hand on Charlie's shoulder. "The Sisters have prepared a buffet for everyone. Why don't you go and get yourself something to eat?"

Charlie nodded again and went to join Howard. The seminarian's refectory was across the hall and bigger than theirs. Everything about it seemed larger, the furniture, the plates, even the food appeared bigger. But then again, Charlie was hungry. He didn't have anything to eat all morning. He was too nervous about the funeral at breakfast to eat. He quickly grabbed a plate and helped himself.

Howard and Charlie stood in a corner and held their plates with their finger sandwiches of sliced ham and cheese, potato salad, coleslaw, flavored gelatin salads. They ate and watched the crowd. Rick joined them after unsuccessfully trying to include himself in Abbot Ambrose's conversation with the Archbishop.

"Can you believe the turn out?" he said as he looked around.

"This is hardly a baseball game, Rick." Howard shook his

head. "Turn out, indeed."

"I only meant that there are a lot of people here. Who would've thought a monk would know so many important people?"

"Prior Anselm would be embarrassed by all of the fuss." Charlie said plainly. "He liked things simply."

"So, who do you think the next Prior's going to be?" Rick asked. "I bet it will be either Father Hugh or Father Paschal." He motioned toward the two monks who had joined the Abbot and the Archbishop. "But the guys in Saint Peter are betting it'll be Father Vicar."

"Oh, you're such a moron," Howard snapped. "Prior Anselm isn't five minutes in the ground and you're already betting on his successor. You're sick."

"Hey, life goes on," Rick said as Howard walked away. Rick looked at Charlie. "What's his problem?"

"Oh, shut up, Rick," Charlie said, and shook his head. "Just shut up."

Rick looked at Charlie with a shocked expression. He started to say something but then stopped himself. He turned around and walked away.

CHRISTMAS

With all of the commotion about Prior Anselm's funeral and then the rush to cram for mid-term exams, the Christmas season seemed to sneak up on everyone. The weather outside had become very cold and some of the older boys in the science class were even predicting snow. Charlie didn't believe them since whenever they made predictions in the past, they never come true. Still, he liked to think they were right. Snow would make it feel more like Christmas, especially since this would be his first without his grandmother. He wondered how she would be spending the day as he sat in his World Cultures class daydreaming instead of finishing his exam.

Howard glanced over at Charlie. He noticed that Charlie seemed distracted by something because he was staring at the chalkboard in the front of the room. He looked at Brother Simon, who was too busy with his head down grading papers to notice. He looked back at Charlie and pretended to cough. Brother Simon looked up just as Howard ducked his head down. Brother Simon surveyed the classroom, his eyes squinting and his lips pursed. Satisfied that no one was cheating, he returned to grading the stack of papers on his desk. Howard glanced at Charlie again. His signal worked. Charlie was writing again.

The bell sounded just as Howard put down his pencil. Brother Simon told everyone to leave their tests face up on their desks, and they were dismissed. As they filed out of the room, he reminded them that he was sure they all failed miserably, and not to get themselves too excited over their holiday. Charlie and Howard headed back to their dorm.

"So, what happened in there?" Howard asked as they mounted the stairs.

"Oh, nothing." Charlie shrugged, feeling a bit depressed. "I was just thinking about my grandmother. This will be her first Christmas without me, you know?"

"She'll be all right. Don't worry about her," Howard tried to reassure Charlie. He knew the other thing that worried Charlie more was that this would be his first Christmas without her.

"I hope you're right, Howard," Charlie tried to sound positive.

"Grown-ups are stronger than you think. They can handle everything." Howard threw his arm around Charlie's shoulders and gave him a reassuring hug.

"Hey, Charlie, see any ghosts lately?" The familiar drone of Dougary's voice echoed up the stairs.

Charlie and Howard stopped immediately and turned around. Just as they suspected, chumming around with Dougary and his gang was none other than Gus. They both knew Gus had spilled the beans about their sleuthing.

"Forget it, Charlie." Howard said and tugged on Charlie's arm. "They just want to make trouble for you. Besides, they're going home for the holidays so we'll have two whole weeks of peace. Too bad Rick's not going home this year. We'd really have a blast then."

"Hey, I think our toilets need to be cleaned again." Travis yelled and then laughed. "You want to give us a hand, Charlie, or should I say your head?"

Howard tightened his grip on Charlie's arm and quickened their pace up the stairs as the echoes of laughter raced after them.

"You know, soon everyone will know about our secret research project," Howard said as they cleared the fourth floor and started down the hall toward their dorm.

"I know." Charlie nodded. "You don't think we'll get into trouble, do you? I mean with the Abbot?"

"No." Howard shook his head. "It'll just be that much harder to find people who'll be willing to talk about it, that's all."

"Well, if we can locate some more of Prior Anselm's old photographs, we won't need any more talking to solve this thing. We just need to match up the faces with the photograph I have and when we find an extra, that will be our Jeffrey." Charlie made it sound so easy.

"But we still need to find out who this Kenny Oswald is," Howard reminded Charlie. "And for that we will need more than photographs."

"True." Charlie nodded.

As the two entered their dorm, Charlie froze and looked on in awe. In the center of the room stood a twelve-foot Douglas fir tree, trimmed and ready to decorate. Boxes and boxes labeled "Christmas" were stacked all about. The chairs were placed across from the tree and a decorative fireplace made of plywood and fake bricks stood where the chairs once sat. There were red furry stockings with white bands piled next to the fireplace. Each stocking bore the name of one of the boys in the dorm.

Charlie was surprised to see his name on one.

"After dinner tonight, we all get to decorate the tree. It's our annual tradition to gather around and sing carols and drink eggnog while we decorate for Christmas. It's a lot of fun."

Charlie walked with Howard over to their cubicle. "Howard," he started to ask, "Just what happens here on Christmas? I mean, we have no parents to give us gifts so what do we do?"

Howard smiled. "Tonight, we'll draw names and then we set out to make that person a gift. We have five days before Christmas so that should give us plenty of time. Then on Christmas Eve, we put our gifts under the tree before we go to midnight Mass."

"I see." Charlie nodded and tried to hide his growing fear. Make something for someone else, how and with what? This was not good news for Charlie. The only thing he knew how to do was draw and even that was not good enough for a gift.

All through dinner he tried to figure out what he could make. He was so distracted by his thoughts that the boy next to him had to nudge him three times before Charlie would pass him the pepper shaker. Unable to figure out what to do, Charlie gave up and finished his dinner.

The dorm was filled with excitement as two of the older boys climbed ladders and hung tinsel garlands and mesh paper bells from the ceiling. Next, Father Emmanuel climbed the ladder, which Rick said would never support the weight, and placed a miniature Saint Nicholas doll on top of the tree. After he came down off the ladder, Howard turned to Rick and said, "See, he's not as big as you think."

Music played and the boys all sang Christmas carols while they decorated their tree. The gold, green and silver glass ball ornaments sparkled like glitter around the tree lights. Father

Emmanuel brought out the last box and the boys quieted down. Carefully he opened the white box revealing twelve antique German glass ornaments. After the last one was hung, Father Emmanuel closed the empty box. The boys all gathered around and marveled at the tree. It was the most beautiful tree Charlie had ever seen.

"Now we have come to the last event of the evening." Father Emmanuel announced. "The drawing of names for our gift exchange."

Charlie suddenly felt ill. He was so caught up in the moment he had forgotten all about the drawing. Now there was no escaping it.

One of the boys stepped forward with an old tattered Santa Claus hat in his hands. He held it out to Father Emmanuel who took it and looked inside. He stuck his hand inside and mixed up the pieces of paper.

"Is everyone ready?" he asked with a jolly laugh.

"Yes." They all shouted eagerly.

"Then we'll start this year with our newest member, Charlie. You get to draw first."

Charlie stood frozen in his place beside Howard. He stared at the hat as though he were afraid of it.

"Go on, Charlie." Howard prodded him.

Slowly Charlie stepped forward. Father Emmanuel smiled and held out the hat.

"Now, just draw one name and don't tell anyone who you drew. But, if you draw your own name, you have to put it back and draw again." Father Emmanuel instructed.

Charlie reached into the hat. He felt the tiny papers inside, and carefully drew out one of them. He looked at the name on the paper, and sighed in relief. He tucked the paper into his pocket and went back to stand next to Howard.

"Who'd you get?" Howard whispered excitedly.

"I can't tell you," Charlie said without looking at him.

One by one each of the boys stepped forward and then it was Howard's turn.

"I just hope I don't get Rick again," he muttered and left Charlie's side. In a flash he was back grinning from ear to ear.

"Who did you get?" Charlie asked.

"I can't tell you, remember?" Howard answered smugly and took another look at his paper.

Charlie tried to sneak a peek, but Howard quickly stuck the paper in his mouth and chewed it up. Charlie, not willing to be outdone, did the same. The two laughed at each other and went to bed.

That night Charlie found it hard to sleep. He kept thinking about what he was going to make for his gift. He looked over at Howard, who was sound asleep. He was glad he had drawn his best friend's name but that made it even more difficult. Now the gift had to be really good because he cared what Howard thought. Finally, sleep found Charlie and his worries disappeared even if just for the night.

The days seemed to fly by for Charlie with Dougary and his thugs gone, but they were all but peaceful. He had two days left before Christmas and he still hadn't come up with an idea for Howard's gift.

After breakfast was finished, Charlie stayed behind to help the Brothers clean up. At least that was what he told Howard and Rick. Actually, he just wanted a chance to talk to Sister Margaret Mary in the kitchen. The two met when Charlie was helping Prior Anselm.

Sister Margaret was a kind old woman and reminded Charlie of his grandmother. She was short in stature with a round figure was just like his grandmother's. Charlie imagined that had his grandmother been a nun, she would have looked a lot like Sister Margaret.

At his first opportunity, Charlie took a cart of dishes back to the kitchen. He found Sister Margaret Mary in the bakery, busy kneading bread dough in a cloud of flour dust. She smiled warmly as Charlie walked in.

"Hi there, Chuck." She always called him Chuck which, coming from her, he didn't mind.

"Hello Sister," Charlie greeted. "It always smells so good in here. What are you baking today?"

"I'm making raised bread rolls for tonight's dinner," she said as she threw the mound of dough into a large metal bowl and covered it with a damp cloth. She then emptied out another bowl of dough onto the floured table and began all over again.

"What's on your mind, Chuck?"

"We drew names the other night and we're supposed to make something for that person for Christmas. I'm stumped. I don't know what I could possibly make that would be good enough," he confessed.

"I see." Sister Margaret Mary nodded. "Whose name did you draw? Maybe I can help?"

"I drew Howard's," he whispered and looked around to be sure no one else heard him.

"Howie Miller?" she laughed. "Oh my, he's a piece of cake."

"You know Howard?" Charlie was surprised.

"Honey, I know all of my boys," she laughed. "I've been here for nearly fifty years and I could tell you the names and about all of my boys."

"So, what do you think Howard would like?"

"Howie has a sweet tooth." She paused momentarily as she kneaded the dough. "I suspect a good batch of gingerbread cookies, stained-glass sugar cookies and a bunch of sweet rolls would sure put a smile on his face."

"But I have to make the gift and I don't know anything about baking."

"I see." Sister Margaret Mary nodded knowingly. "I guess you'll have to learn then. What do you say we get together this afternoon, after lunch, and begin your lesson? I could sure use another pair of hands."

Charlie smiled. Finally, he knew what he was going to do and with her help it would be a snap. "That sounds great."

It was nearly dinnertime when Charlie finally made it back to the dorm after his lesson with Sister Margaret Mary. Together they made hundreds of different Christmas cookies and breads. Charlie was so excited he thought he was going to spill the beans to Howard when they bumped into each other in their cubicle. He quickly sat down on his bed and pulled out his pad to write a letter to his grandmother.

That night as he lay awake in his bed, Charlie thought about his conversation that morning with Sister Margaret Mary. Then it hit him, if she knew all of the boys, perhaps she would know if Joseph Oswald had a brother. He would ask her in the morning. He turned over and drifted off to sleep.

The next morning Charlie slipped away and down to the kitchens. Sister Claire and Brother Columban greeted him as they cleaned up after breakfast. Sister Margaret Mary was busy in the bakery, putting away the leftover maple bars and doughnuts from that morning's breakfast.

"Good morning, Chuck," she greeted over her shoulder as she sealed the container and shut the drawer.

"Hi, Sister," Charlie returned. "What are we making today?"

"I thought we could make stained glass sugar cookies and

then some gingerbread men. How does that sound?"

"Great." Charlie said as he donned his apron and rolled up his sleeves.

"First we'll need that sack of flour over there." Sister Margaret Mary pointed to a large cloth sack in the corner. "I'll get the sugar and eggs."

"Sister, yesterday you mentioned you know all of the boys here," Charlie said as he heaved the twenty-pound bag of flour onto the kneading table. A cloud of white dust bellowed up into his face and dusted his auburn hair. He coughed and fanned the air to clear it.

"Yes," she answered and began scooping out cups of flour.

"Do you remember a boy named Joseph Oswald?"

Sister Margaret Mary froze as she dumped a cup of flour on the table, missing the large mixing bowl completely. She looked over at Charlie with a shocked look on her face.

"Why do you ask?" she asked and studied his face.

"Prior Anselm gave me an old photograph, and in the photo is Joseph but also another boy named Oswald."

"Oh yes, Kenneth." She nodded as she remembered. "He was very close to his brother and after Joseph died in that tragic fall, Kenneth was never the same."

Charlie listened and tried hard not to react to the news. He held the sack of flour open as Sister Margaret Mary emptied the mixing bowl back into the sack. He could not wait to tell Howard.

"Whatever happened to him?" Charlie asked.

"Oh, Kenneth became a monk here," she answered and began once again to scoop out cups of flour. "One, two, three."

Charlie didn't press the subject any further. Even though Sister Margaret Mary was very patient and kind, he heard she also had a very bad temper. If he made her lose count again, he feared he would see it for himself.

The morning passed quickly as they made batch after batch of cookies. The bakery smelled wonderful, just like his grandmother's in the weeks before Christmas. He couldn't wait to tell her about the stained-glass sugar cookies. How the tiny bits of candy would melt and make a candy glass windowpane. Those were the most fun. He also enjoyed decorating the gingerbread men with candies and icing. He was having such wonderful fun.

"You can take the afternoon off," Sister Margaret Mary said as Charlie washed his hands. "I have enough help. You can pick up your package this afternoon. I'll have it wrapped and ready to put under the tree for you."

"Thank you." Charlie beamed. He thought for a moment as he dried his hands. "Ah, Sister, could I ask another favor?"

Sister Margaret Mary turned around. Her thoughts raced ahead as she tried to anticipate what Charlie was about to ask. Was it more about the tragedy? Did he know about Jeffrey? What?

"Could I have a few more cookies and cakes to give to Gus? I know he's not talking to me and Howard but I still would like to give him something," Charlie asked nervously.

Sister Margaret Mary smiled. "Of course, you may. I'll have them both ready for you."

"Thank you so much." Charlie smiled, wrapped his arms around her neck, and gave her a hug.

"Oh my." She smiled and hugged him back. A tear came to her eyes. It had been years since she felt a child's arms around her. Her mind flashed back to Joseph. He was a sensitive and thoughtful young boy. Occasionally he would help her clean up the kitchen at the end of the day staying late into the evening. They were the best of friends, she being a young nun only seven years older than he was.

"You're welcome to come back anytime you like," she said as Charlie headed for the door.

He paused and looked back. "I'd like that." He nodded, then hurried off.

He took the stairs two at a time to get back to his dorm. He was anxious to tell Howard that Kenny became a monk. When he reached their cubicle, Howard wasn't there. Charlie looked around. He noticed Rick was in his cubicle listening to some old records on his stereo.

"Hey, Rick," he called. "Have you seen Howard?"

Rick looked up. "He's helping Brother Gregory out in the woodshop, but he said for you not to come out there. Guess he and Brother Gregory are finally getting along."

"That's great." Charlie smiled. He knew it would eventually happen if Howard just gave it half a chance. He turned around and headed downstairs to check his mail slot for a letter from his grandmother. He had forgotten to check it earlier that morning, and hoped he'd finally hear from her. It had been two weeks since her last letter and he hated to admit it, but he was a bit worried.

On the wall between the first floor and the basement where the stairs turned at the landing, hung a large wooden box with several compartments. Each compartment was labeled with the name of one of the boys. Charlie's name was in red as were all the boys from Saint Nicholas' dorm. He quickly looked in his box and to his surprise there was a letter and a bright red envelope with his name on it and the return address of his grandmother. He tucked them into his pocket and raced back to his cubicle to read it in private. He was just about to open the door to the dorm when the lunch bell rang out. Reluctantly he turned around and headed back down the stairs.

Howard was waiting with the rest of the members of their dorm as Charlie took his place in line.

"So, you and Brother Gregory are doing better?" he asked.

"What? Oh yeah."

Howard's distracted answer was short and Charlie knew it meant that he didn't want to talk about it. However, Charlie was too curious to let it drop.

"So, you two have been working in the woodshop? I didn't know you were interested in that sort of thing."

"Well, Brother Gregory is really good at making things and he's showing me how. It's actually pretty fun." Howard answered and looked impatiently at the line ahead of him. "Come on," he groaned looking at the doors. "Open."

"I have some more news about Joseph Oswald and Kenny Oswald," Charlie whispered.

Howard's ears perked up and he looked at Charlie. "And?"

"They were brothers," Charlie whispered. "In fact, Kenny became a monk."

"He did?" Howard looked surprised and then his expression changed as he thought. "I don't know of any monk named Kenneth. No, I'm certain of it, there isn't any. There must be a mistake."

Charlie slumped as his excitement waned. He had thought he was so close to having the ghost story figured out. Father Emmanuel walked up as the doors of the refectory opened. The boys fell silent as they filed inside.

After the prayer, Charlie sat down and continued to think about what Howard had said. He couldn't believe he'd come so close to solving the mystery only to end up back at the start. He looked at Howard.

"Howard, are you sure about there being no monk named Kenneth?"

"Yes." Howard sighed. "I'm positive."

"What're you two talking about?" Rick asked as he leaned across the table and grabbed the salt shaker.

"Charlie found out that Joseph Oswald had a brother here who became a monk," Howard whispered.

"Oh, you guys aren't still talking about that are you?" Rick frowned.

"Yes," Charlie spoke up. "And I'm not going to stop until I find out the whole story about what happened."

"So, what's the name of this brother of Joseph's?" Rick asked, not really interested, but just wanting to be part of the conversation.

"His name's Kenneth," Charlie answered.

"But I've already told Charlie that there is no monk named Kenneth," Howard said, with his mouth full.

"That's not surprising." Rick shrugged. "When you become a monk, you change your first name."

Charlie looked up at the sound of the news. He was back on the trail after all.

"So, all we need to do is find out which monk has the last name of Oswald," he said out loud. The enthusiasm in his voice was obvious to them all.

"What we need is a list of the monks' names," he continued. "Do you know if there is such a thing?"

"I suppose the switchboard operator would have a list," Rick offered. "If not, I'm sure he'd know who would have the name Oswald."

"That's it, then." Charlie said with a broad smile. "After lunch, do you want to go with me to see the operator?"

Howard cocked his head. "I'm sorry, Charlie but I already have something I need to finish. It's important or I would."

"I'll go with you," Rick jumped in.

Charlie looked at him surprised. "But I thought you said we were wasting our time."

"Well, yeah," Rick admitted sheepishly. "But this is getting interesting. Can I go with you?"

"Sure." Charlie nodded. "We'll meet in the hall after lunch."

"Great." Rick smiled and started to eat his lunch faster. He was more excited about being part of Howard and Charlie's clique than about the ghost hunt. Since Gus had left the dorm, he didn't have anyone to pal around with and quite honestly, he was a bit jealous of Howard and Charlie. He would never admit it out loud, but he did miss Gus.

After lunch Howard slipped away without a word. Charlie and Rick met by the foot of the stairs. Charlie brought Rick up to date on all the things he had found out over the last couple months as they headed for the monastery wing.

The switchboard was located just inside the door of the monastery wing on the first floor. Charlie in all of his times visiting the monks had never been to the switchboard. He was surprised when he opened the monastery wing's door in the entry hall to see another large room inside. To the left wing backed chairs and coffee tables were set up into comfortable sitting areas for visitors. To the right a reception counter stretched out. Behind it were two oak desks. On one set a large console with lighted buttons and a telephone dial. A monk sat behind the desk with his back to Charlie and Rick. Immediately Charlie recognized the monk.

"Hi, Brother Tobias," he greeted.

Brother Tobias turned around and smiled as he stood up. "Well, well, what a nice surprise."

"I thought you were the mechanic." Rick looked at him, confused.

"We all take turns at the switchboard," Brother Tobias answered and looked over his shoulder at the flashing lights on the console. "It's pretty quiet today but some days it can be hectic. So, what are you two up to?"

"We were wondering if there is a list of all of the monks here at the Abbey," Charlie answered.

Brother Tobias thought for a moment and then gave them a curious look. "What do you need a list for?"

"We're looking to see if there's a monk here with the last name of Oswald. He's the brother of the boy that was killed a long time ago," Rick answered.

A sudden jolt like that of electricity stabbed Brother Tobias in the back. His whole body stiffened for a moment as he struggled to remain composed. His hands began to tremble and his forehead began to sweat. He covered his mouth for a moment and tried to think.

"I'm afraid there isn't a list," he said, and hoped they wouldn't pursue the matter.

"Shoot," Charlie said disappointedly.

"Would you know of any monk named Oswald?" Rick asked.

Brother Tobias thought for a moment. "Oswald," he repeated and shook his head. "I'm afraid I don't recall anyone with that last name. You know, some of the monks were sent to our Priory in Idaho. Maybe this Brother is there?"

Charlie sighed out loud and frowned. "Thanks anyway, Brother Tobias."

"I'm sorry," he apologized as the console behind him let out a loud buzzing sound. He quickly returned to his desk and answered the caller.

"Come on, Rick. Let's go." Charlie's voice was definitely disappointed.

Rick continued to stare at Brother Tobias' back as they walked toward the door. Once in the entry hall again Rick grabbed Charlie's arm and halted him.

"Did you notice that?" he asked.

"Notice what?" Charlie tugged his arm free of Rick's grasp.

"The way Brother Tobias reacted when you brought up the dead boy's name."

"No," Charlie confessed.

"Oh, come on, get with it. If you are going to be a detective you need to be more observant." Rick shook his head and let out a sigh of disgust. "His hands trembled and the look in his eyes was like he was about to panic or run."

"Oh, that." Charlie shrugged as though it were no big deal. "He always acts like that. When Howard and I saw him in the garage he was acting like that."

"Well, I think he knows more than he's letting on," Rick said refusing to give up.

On his way back to the dorm, Charlie stopped by the kitchen to pick up his packages from Sister Margaret Mary. She was sitting at the kitchen table with Sister Claire, Brother Columban, and two other workers that had stopped in, still dressed in their dirty overalls. Sister Margaret Mary smiled when she saw Charlie coming.

"I suppose you came back for your packages." She beamed. "I have them all ready for you in the bakery." She rose from her seat and met him at the bakery door.

"I really appreciate this," Charlie said, still distracted by his conversation with Brother Tobias and Rick's comments.

"Oh my, looks like someone is troubled about something," she said as she placed the packages on the table. "Do you want to talk about it?"

"I'm just confused is all." Charlie answered. "You remember you said that Kenny Oswald became a monk?"

"Yes," she nodded.

"Well, this afternoon Rick and I asked Brother Tobias if there were any monks here with the last name of Oswald. He said there weren't any. Are you sure he became a monk?"

Sister Margaret Mary looked very confused. She scratched her forehead and frowned.

"Chuck, I'm positive," she answered. "I just can't understand why he would say such a thing."

"Why?" Charlie asked curiously.

"Oh, nothing." Sister Margaret Mary shrugged, still deep in thought.

It was obvious to Charlie that she was not going to tell him what she was thinking. Now he was more confused than before.

That evening, at dinner, the refectory was decorated with green cedar garlands, red bows and a large tree decorated in silver and gold glass bulb ornaments. White linen tablecloths covered each table. A decorative tapestry runner in the dorm's color and stitched with Christmas scenes ran the entire length of the table. Arrangements of unlit white candles surrounded by pine-sprigs and cones sprinkled with glitter were placed in the center of each long table. At each setting, gold-plated spoons, knives, and forks replaced the usual silverware. Crystal goblets replaced the plastic drinking glasses and cloth napkins the paper ones.

Charlie stood at his chair in awe. Everything was so beautiful. He was finally excited about Christmas. He smiled and looked at Howard who seemed to be just as awestruck as him. After the prayer was said and everyone was seated, the signal came that it was okay to speak.

"Is it like this every Christmas?" Charlie asked Howard.

"Yes," Rick answered before Howard could speak.

"I think I'm gonna like it here." Charlie beamed.

"So, what did you guys find out at the switchboard today?" Howard asked.

"Nothing," Rick again answered as Charlie frowned.

"Brother Tobias was there and we asked him, but he said there wasn't anyone named Oswald here. Maybe at the Priory in Idaho there could be," Charlie added, his mood sinking to a miserable pout.

"Well, I know who he is," Howard said proudly, grinning like the cat that swallowed the proverbial canary.

Charlie and Rick both looked at him in surprise.

"How did you find out when Sister Margaret Mary wouldn't tell?" Charlie whispered loud enough for Rick to hear too as the serving Brother set their dinner in front of them.

"I have my sources too," Howard continued to grin.

"Well who is it?"

"You talked to him this afternoon." Howard smiled, obviously enjoying toying with them.

Charlie looked at Rick. "Brother Tobias?" they said at the same time.

"Brother Tobias Oswald, to be exact," Howard answered. "This afternoon I was talking to Brother Gregory about our ghost hunt."

Charlie frowned at Howard. He hated their mystery investigation being called a ghost hunt.

Howard continued, "Brother Gregory was the prefect of Saint Thomas dorm back then. He said that he remembers after Joseph's fall—and get this it was on All Saints' Day—Kenny became so upset he couldn't be consoled. He cried every night so they had to move him out of Saint Nicholas dorm. They converted the large broom closet into a bedroom for him, and as time went on, he appeared to settle down. He was then placed in Saint Thomas dorm."

"Wow," Charlie breathed, totally enthralled by the story. Now it made sense why Brother Tobias had been in the cemetery on Halloween night.

"Brother Gregory said that shortly after Kenny came to Saint Thomas dorm, a couple wanted to adopt him. He would have none of it. He told them he couldn't leave his brother here alone. So the couple, thinking his brother was alive, said they would adopt him too. But after Brother Gregory explained that Joseph had died, they wanted nothing to do with Kenny and left. Kenny did that to every couple that asked to adopt him until no one asked anymore. He entered the monastery against the better judgment of Brother Gregory. He thought and still does that Kenny, Brother Tobias, should leave the Abbey and get on with his life elsewhere."

Rick and Charlie listened with open-mouth shock at the news. Neither one even looked at the food on their plates.

"So, why do you suppose he lied to us this afternoon?" Charlie asked Howard.

Howard shrugged. "How should I know? Maybe he doesn't want us snooping about asking questions about his past. Or, maybe he thinks we're out to cause him trouble?"

"Or maybe he's the 'ghost in the attic,' the one moaning or *crying* every night," Rick added in a whisper. He sat back in his chair and looked smugly at both Howard and Charlie. "So that's it. Case closed. Mystery solved. Brother Tobias is the one crying in the attic."

Howard looked at Rick in disgust. "No, I don't think so. For one thing, why would Brother Tobias go to the attic to cry? Why not go out to the cemetery instead. Charlie, what was the name of the white-haired boy? Remember the letter we found in

Prior Anselm's picture?"

Charlie nodded. "Jeffrey, I think. I still have it in my nightstand."

"What do we know about him?"

"All it said was that he became a monk too." Charlie answered.

"What's his last name?" Rick asked in his usual condescending tone.

"I don't know. The letter didn't say," Charlie admitted.

"Well, then we're at a dead end," Rick scoffed.

"Maybe not," Howard spoke up. "We know he was a member of Saint Nicholas dorm. All we need to do is find where they put the rest of Prior Anselm's pictures and then we will find our Jeffrey."

"Good idea." Charlie beamed.

The rest of the meal passed quietly as they ate and thought about the things they discovered. After the dismissal the three hurried to Howard and Charlie's cubicle to have a look at that letter and photograph again.

"I don't believe this." Howard shook his head.

"Who would've taken it?" Charlie asked in disbelief as he sat down on his bed and stared at the empty drawer in his nightstand.

"Three guesses and the first two don't count," Howard sighed. "It had to have been Jeffrey. He must've found out about our snooping around from either Brother Tobias or Brother Gregory."

"But how did he know about the photograph?" Rick asked sarcastically.

"He may have known all along," Charlie said. "Anyone who visited Prior Anselm's room would've seen it hanging on the wall."

"That's true," Rick had to agree. "Well, there's nothing we can do about it tonight. See you later." He turned around and headed over to his own cubicle.

"Don't worry about it, Charlie," Howard tried to console him. "We'll figure out a way to get it back."

"It's okay." Charlie shrugged and closed the drawer. "It's not as if I knew any of the boys in the picture anyway. Maybe Jeffrey, whoever he is, wanted it more."

"Yeah." Howard nodded. "Well I have something I need to do right now. I'll see you later."

Before Charlie could say another word, Howard was gone. He quickly dispelled any more thoughts about the missing photograph and letter, and turned to his more pressing matter. He stood up and looked around to be sure no one was watching. Then he bent down, lifted up the bedspread, and pulled the festively wrapped packages from under his bed. Sister Margaret Mary had done a good job of wrapping them. Bright ribbons and curling bows held the paper in place. He glanced, over his shoulder, then hurriedly placed the packages under the tree.

Charlie stood in front of the tree and looked at all the gifts that had been placed under it. He thought about his grandmother and the Christmases they shared together. He began to feel homesick, when he suddenly remembered the letters in his pocket. He pulled out the red envelope and letter, and sat down in one of the overstuffed chairs. He ripped open the red envelope and pulled out a card. He smiled at the drawing of a mother deer and her fawn curled up beneath a snow-covered tree. Above them, in the night sky, glitter stars sparkled. Inside the message read:

Charlie,

With warm wishes
to you during this holiday season.

Merry Christmas.
Love, Grandma

He smiled and then turned his attention to the letter. He opened it and took out the single page letter.

> *Dear Charlie,*
> *Thank-you for the lovely card and candle. They are both beautiful. They won't let me light the candle here at the home, but that is okay. I'll always have it to remind me of you.*
> *Charlie, I don't want to alarm you but I must tell you. A man came by the other day with your Uncle Chester. He was asking me a lot of questions about that key, but I did not tell him anything. Charlie, he may show up there. Don't listen to him. It is very important. No matter what, do not give him or anyone else the key. I can't tell you any more just yet, except that it is very important. I'm talking with your Aunt Bernice to see if she will bring me down for a visit. I'll let you know.*
> *I love you, Grandma.*
> *P.S.*
> *I've sent a little gift for you to Abbot Ambrose. Tell him "Hello" from me.*

Charlie sat and stared at the letter. It would be good to see his grandmother again. It seemed like it had been forever since he was with her on Tam O'Shanter Drive. So much had happened since then. He had so much to tell her. But would his aunt really bring her? And what was so important about the key and who was this strange man? He shook his head and folded up the letter, then stuffed it back into its envelope.

Midnight came slowly. Charlie, Howard and Rick had to meet early with the other Altar Boys to prepare for the Midnight Mass. It was Charlie's turn to bear the thurible. Even though he liked the smell of frankincense, it was too strong. He had to keep swinging the thurible at the end of the golden chain to keep the smoke from overwhelming him. Howard and Rick were assigned as candle bearers. The three would lead the procession with the Abbot behind them into the Abbey church.

The Mass had an added feature that night. First the Abbot blessed the manger scene while the monks' choir sang. Charlie jumped when the trumpets sounded and the pipe organ began to play. It was all very beautiful but he couldn't wait until it was over. Even though he was able to put the thurible in the sacristy after the blessing of the manger, he could still smell the strong incense and his head ached. He wished now he'd taken a nap as the others had. He was too excited over hearing from his grandmother and finding Kenny to be able to sleep.

When the Mass had finally ended, the Altar Boys made sure all the candles were extinguished and everything was securely put away and cleaned up. Only then could they go to bed. It was nearly three in the morning when Charlie's head finally hit his pillow.

It had seemed as though he had just shut his eyes when the morning bell rang and Charlie was awakened. Even though he was tired, he was excited too. He glanced over at Howard's bed only to see it was empty. He jumped from his bed and joined the rest of the boys around the tree.

There were more gifts under the tree than when they had gone to bed. Someone had doubled the amount, if not tripled it while they slept. There were candy canes hanging on branches of the trees, and the stockings that hung on the decorative fireplace were filled so full that they were placed on the floor under the tree. Charlie could not believe his eyes.

"Come over here Charlie," Howard said, and made room for him on the sofa next to him. "Sit with me."

Charlie hurried over and sat down. "Where did all of this come from?"

"Santa Claus, of course." Howard nudged him and smiled. "The Brothers all pitch in and give us each extra little things. Sometimes it's clothes and sometimes it's things that have been given to them by the town's people."

"That's so nice of them," Charlie said.

Howard looked at Charlie and smiled.

"What's keeping Father Emmanuel?" Rick asked impatiently.

"He'll be here," Howard assured Rick and then leaned closer to Charlie. "We have to wait until Father Emmanuel arrives to hand out the presents. He really gets into it and dresses up like Saint Nicholas. Wait and see. It's really funny."

Just then the doors of the dormitory burst open and sure enough, in walked Father Emmanuel dressed in a long red velvet robe with white fur cuffs and a long walking stick. Over his shoulder was flung a bag filled with even more gifts.

The dorm was filled with excitement as Father Emmanuel handed out the gifts. Soon the floor was littered with paper and ribbons as the boys tore open their gifts. Then as Charlie watched, Father Emmanuel handed Howard the gift Charlie had made for him. Howard read the tiny card and saw it was from Charlie.

"You drew my name?" he said with a big smile. "I don't believe it. Father Emmanuel, could you hand Charlie that one there." He pointed to a large package on the other side of the tree.

Father Emmanuel handed it to Charlie with a cheerful, "Ho, ho, ho." He sounded more like Santa Claus than Saint Nicholas but no one seemed to mind the mixing of the two.

Charlie read the tag and looked at Howard. "You had my name?"

"Yep." He grinned.

They both tore into their gifts at once. Charlie sat back and looked at his, a wooden checkerboard, complete with wooden checkers. He turned to Howard with tears in his eyes.

"You made this for me?" he said in disbelief.

"Well, Brother Gregory helped me a lot, but yes," Howard admitted, then looked inside his box at all of the goodies. "Wow! You baked these?" he said as he bit into one of the gingerbread men.

"Sister Margaret Mary helped me," he admitted. "She thought up the idea. I hope it's okay."

"Okay," he repeated with his mouth full. "These are wonderful. I hope you draw my name next year."

"And, Charlie, here is one more for you," Father Emmanuel said as he handed Charlie a small package.

Charlie looked at it, confused at first, and then he remembered his grandmother's card. The little package was from her. He recognized the wrapping paper. Carefully, he removed the ribbon and paper; he wanted to save it as a keepsake from her.

"It's from my grandmother." Charlie smiled. "You have to meet her, Howard. She's so neat."

Howard nodded silently and leaned a bit closer to get a better look as Charlie removed the top of the little box. Inside it was another box, only this one was covered in velvet. Charlie took the box and opened it. A golden medallion sparkled in the lights of the Christmas tree.

"A Saint Christopher medal." He said and smiled. He carefully took it out of the box.

"That's so cool." Howard smiled, happy for his best friend. "Put it on."

Charlie quickly took the chain from around his neck and added the medallion to it. "How does it look?"

"Great." Howard beamed. "But what is with that key?"

Charlie quickly grabbed it and looked around to see if anyone else had noticed. They were all too busy with their own gifts. "Nothing." He shrugged and tucked it under his nightshirt.

"Hey, do you want a cookie?" Howard offered, changing the subject.

"What's this?" Father Emmanuel chuckled as he picked up the last package that was tucked deep under the tree. "Gus?" he read the name on the tag out loud. "Charlie?" He turned to look at him.

"What?" Rick gasped indignantly.

Charlie quickly grabbed the package from Father Emmanuel and gave him a sheepish look. "I just thought I should."

Father Emmanuel smiled. "That's very thoughtful of you. Do you want me to take it to him?"

Charlie remembered the last time he had entered Saint Peter dorm. He quickly handed the package to Father Emmanuel. "Yes, please," he said with a nervous smile.

"I don't believe you did that," Rick snapped at Charlie and then took his things back to his cubicle.

"Don't listen to him," Howard said, and put a reassuring arm around Charlie's shoulders. "You did okay."

That evening Charlie and Howard sat on Charlie's bed and played checkers over and again. Charlie was still in awe at how wonderful the checkerboard was with its dark red-brown wood squares and the lighter oak squares surrounded by a boarder of same dark red-brown wood. The checkers were made from matching wood, dark red-brown and oak. It was the best present a friend had ever given him; in fact, the only gift from a friend.

Charlie looked at the Saint Christopher medal that hung from the chain around his neck. He picked it up and looked at it closely. The image was of a man wading through a river with a small child on his shoulders. Charlie turned it over and stared at the back.

Howard was watching Charlie curiously.

"So, what is it with the key?" he asked. "You've been protecting it since the day you came here. What's it to?"

Charlie looked at Howard. He was torn between telling him about the key and keeping silent. Surely his grandmother didn't mean to keep it a secret from his best friend. He thought a moment longer and looked at the key.

"I don't know," he answered. "The day I came here my grandmother gave it to me and told me to guard it. She wouldn't tell me what it's for or anything. Yesterday I received a letter from her saying that some man came to see her with my Uncle Chester. He was asking about the key."

"Wow," Howard breathed. "It must be important."

"I guess." Charlie shrugged. "But I don't know why. Grandma told me that no matter what I wasn't to let anyone have it." He looked at the medal again. "Hey, Howard," he said with puzzled look on his face. "Look at this."

Howard leaned forward and looked at the back of the medal as Charlie held it out. On the back was a small engraving of an address but without the city and state.

"That's a strange thing to have engraved on a medal," he said, and sat back. "Do you know where it is?"

Charlie thought for a moment then shook his head. "No."

"Boy, another mystery to solve." Howard shook his head. "You do have an interesting life."

Charlie looked at Howard with a forced frown.

"You'll have to write your grandmother and ask her where she got it. Maybe it is the address of the original owner or the shop she bought it from."

"Yeah." Charlie thought to himself and nodded. "I'll ask her."

The lights in the dorm turned off and they were suddenly plunged into darkness. Charlie leaned over and turned on the dim light on his nightstand.

"Guess that means it's time for bed." Howard said and stood up.

Charlie quickly put the checkers back in the small wooden box and put the game under his bed. He then crawled under the covers and lay down. He reached up and turned out the light.

"Hey, Howard," he said as he stared at the ceiling. "Thank you for making this the best Christmas I've ever had."

Howard looked at Charlie in the darkness but could only see his silhouette. He smiled proudly to himself. It was a good Christmas for him too. "You're welcome," he whispered. "I'm glad you're here."

He turned over and faced the partition. Soon he was asleep.

GUS

The morning sun shone through Charlie's window and its warmth felt good against his face. Outside, the mid-January weather had turned bitterly cold. Snow covered the grounds and the tall pine trees. It was picture-perfect, except for the occasional snapping and crashing as tree limbs broke under the added weight.

Howard walked into the cubicle just as Charlie crawled under his bed. He stared at him in wonder, and scratched his head.

"Charlie you're not still looking for that letter from your grandmother, are you?" he sighed.

"Yes, I am," The muffled answer came from under the bed.

"Well come on, we're going to be late for Brother Simon's class. I don't want work crew in this weather. You can look for it later."

"All right," Charlie sighed disgustedly and climbed out from under his bed. He stood up and wiped the dust from his robes. "First the picture and letter that Prior Anselm gave me, and now a letter from my grandmother. I can't believe someone would take it."

"Well, don't worry about it now. Come on or we're going to be late." Howard turned around and headed for the dormitory doors.

Charlie grabbed his books from the top of his bed and hurried to catch up.

"I still can't believe we passed Brother Simon's exam." Howard shook his head as they quickly headed for the stairs. "I'm not complaining, mind you."

"I know," Charlie agreed. "I thought for sure I was going to flunk. But what I don't understand is how Rick failed. He's supposed to be the smart one."

"Guess his brown nosing didn't pay off." Howard smiled fiendishly.

"Well, I still feel sorry for him," Charlie admitted. "But it's good to see him not so cocky. He's not such a bad guy after all."

The two hurried down the stairs to the basement. The hall was still buzzing with boys rushing to their classes. Howard and Charlie slipped into Brother Simon's classroom and quickly took their seats. The room was silent. Brother Simon sat behind his desk taking roll. His steely eyes seemed to look right through each of the boys as though he could read their minds. Howard and Charlie didn't dare to even look at one another. They could tell that something was bothering Brother Simon. Once the bell rang, Brother Simon stood with his thick World Cultures book opened in one hand and his long pointer stick in the other.

"Open your books to chapter ten," he ordered. "Master Miller, read until I tell you to stop."

Howard opened his book and began to read silently. Instantly the pointer stick slapped down on his desk narrowly missing his hands. Howard jumped and nearly dropped his book.

"I'm not in the mood for your jokes this morning. Out loud!" Brother Simon snapped in his usual monotone.

Howard began to read out loud while he nervously kept an eye on Brother Simon and his stick. As Howard read, Brother Simon paced and watched to make sure each student was paying close attention to what they were reading.

"Master Miller, stop. Master Kugele, read," came the next order.

Without skipping a beat, Gus picked up where Howard left off. His voice trembled as he read and he began to stutter which brought the wrath of Brother Simon upon him. The pointer slapped down hard on Gus's desk, bringing Gus to tears.

"Read, MacCready," thundered Brother Simon as he glared at Gus.

As Charlie read, he could not help but feel sorry for Gus. His outburst of tears not only brought out Brother Simon's anger but would surely cause Dougary and his vultures to begin tormenting him. Life in Saint Peter dorm would no longer be as peaceful for Gus.

"Master Duggan, read."

Charlie sighed and wiped his forehead; relieved to be finished reading out loud.

"MacCready, read," snapped Brother Simon.

Charlie panicked. He didn't anticipate having to read again and lost his place. He started to read where he had left off only to have Brother Simon bring down his pointer hard across Charlie's book. He pulled his hands away just in time.

"You get an F for the day, Master MacCready." Brother Simon said through clenched teeth.

"But—" Howard started to defend Charlie.

Brother Simon's mouth curled into a fiendish smile. "And an F for you too, Master Miller."

"Then I don't need to stay here," Howard snapped back, and slammed his book closed. He stood up to leave. "I don't know what your problem is, but you don't need to take it out on us."

"Take your seat, Master Miller," Brother Simon's voice thundered. "Or you'll be spending every minute of your weekend in work crew shoveling snow until your hands bleed."

Charlie looked at Howard and motioned silently with his eyes for him to do as he was told. He didn't want Howard getting into any more trouble because of him. Howard's temper slowly waned. Reluctantly he slipped back into his chair.

"Master Fulton, read," Brother Simon called out.

Austin began reading and Brother Simon continued to pace up and down the aisles.

The bell rang and signaled the end of the class just as Rick began to read. Charlie was never as happy to hear the bell as he was at that moment. He closed his book and grabbed his things and stood up with the rest of the boys and started for the door.

"What's with Brother Simon today?" Howard asked in a whisper as he and Rick gathered their things.

"I don't know and frankly I don't care," he answered with a note of anger in his voice. "I still can't believe he gave me an F for the first semester."

"Where's Charlie?" Howard looked around, then spotted him just about to leave the classroom.

"Masters MacCready, Miller, Walters and Gustav," Brother Simon's voice thundered over the din.

Charlie froze. One more step and he would've been in the hall, safe.

"I want to see the four of you at my desk, now," he ordered.

The four slowly gathered in front of Brother Simon's desk as the room finished clearing. Howard looked at the door only to see Dougary and his goons snickering at them from the hallway. He glared at them and turned back to Brother Simon.

The circles under Brother Simon's eyes appeared darker than usual. His cheeks were more drawn. He folded his thin arms over his chest and looked down his long, crooked nose at them.

"It has been brought to my attention that the four of you fancy yourselves as some sort of detective squad. Seems you have been nosing around in places you ought not. A bit too much free time on your hands, ah? Well, no more! You are each to hand in a ten-page report by this weekend on the ancient Roman Empire. We'll see just how much free time you have after that."

"But—" Howard started to protest, but the words stuck in his throat as Brother Simon glared down harder at him. "Yes, Brother," he said and ducked his head.

"That will be all." Brother Simon dismissed them with the wave of the back of his hand.

Silently the four walked into the hall.

"What am I going to do?" Gus began to cry again. "I can't write ten pages in three days, not with having to make Dougary's bed and—" the words stuck in his throat.

"What?" Charlie gasped and halted him with a tug on his arm. Howard and Rick were just as aghast.

"Nothing." Gus shrugged. "Since when do you guys care about me?"

"Since the day we met," Charlie answered. "We're friends, remember?"

Gus looked at them all and the tears fell from his eyes. "I didn't think you guys had time for me anymore. I mean now that you're Altar Boys."

"What?" Howard looked at Charlie and Rick in disbelief then back at Gus.

"Well, you're the one who moved out of our dorm," Rick snapped at Gus.

"Rick!" Charlie glared at him. Rick shrank back a bit.

"I know I did, and I'm sorry," Gus admitted. "It was all my fault. I was just a bit jealous is all. You three were named as Altar Boys and it appeared you didn't have time for me. I mean, I tried to congratulate you, Rick, but you just snubbed me."

Rick opened his mouth as though to protest but caught the look in Charlie's eyes and closed it.

"I don't believe you, Rick. Gus was the one Abbot Ambrose talked to the night before he made the announcements. Gus was his first choice over you," Charlie informed them. Gus just looked at Charlie in shock. He didn't know that anyone else knew. "It was Gus's idea for Abbot Ambrose to name you because you helped him with his costume."

"It was?" Howard gasped and looked at Gus in surprise.

"Yes," Gus admitted. "I thought I could handle it because we were all friends, but when you ignored me, Rick, it hurt. I'm ashamed to say it but I regretted my choice. So, I asked Abbot Ambrose to move me out of Saint Nicholas dorm." Gus continued. "I feel really awful about how I've acted."

"You have nothing to be sorry for," Charlie assured him and looked at Rick.

Rick was speechless. He thought back and remembered the day when he was sitting next to Gus in the refectory and Gus kept telling him to relax. How when his name was called, he did snub Gus. A wave of guilt washed over him.

"Gus, I'm sorry," he apologized. "I really mean it."

"Okay." Gus nodded and wiped the tears from his puffy cheeks.

"Well, it's in the past," Charlie said and put his arm around Gus' shoulders as they started to walk down the hall again.

"There's something else," Gus said, and stopped.

"Something else?" Howard cocked his head and looked at him.

"I told Dougary and his friends all about the ghost in the attic and how you're trying to find out the real story behind it. I'm afraid it must've been one of them who told Brother Simon. Oh, this is all my fault," he moaned.

"I don't care." Charlie shrugged. "They can't do anything to us. We're friends again."

"That's right, Gus," Howard added. "So, are you going to talk to Abbot Ambrose about moving back to your old cubicle? After all, now that Dougary saw you cry he'll have it in for you."

"I was going to talk to Abbot Ambrose at lunch," Gus said as they entered Sister Regina's Reading class.

"Good." Rick nodded approvingly.

The rest of the morning seemed routine and uneventful. Sister Regina, a tall, thin nun with black horn-rimmed glasses and a crooked smile, was her normal pleasant self. She had a soft spot in her heart for the boys that were orphaned, which prompted some to accuse her of favoritism. Charlie really liked her.

Brother Blaise's Math class was the last class before lunch. Brother Blaise, a young portly monk who resembled Father Emmanuel so much so that some boys thought they were real brothers, lectured in his usual monotone voice, which nearly put Howard to sleep. So far, the classes seemed the same as the semester before.

"Too long and too boring," Howard said to which Charlie and Gus agreed as they all headed to the refectory for lunch.

"So, are you going to ask Abbot Ambrose after lunch about coming back to Saint Nicholas'?" Howard asked as a way of reminder to Gus.

"Yeah," Gus nodded. As he caught sight of Dougary, Travis and Larry standing in the Saint Peter line he felt a knot in his stomach. When they saw him, Dougary began whispering wildly into their ears.

"Hey cry baby," Dougary called so that everyone could hear. "Need your diaper changed?"

Larry and Travis then began to fake cry and suck their thumbs. The small gathering of Saint Peter dorm members all joined in. Gus' face turned red as he walked over to his place in line among them. The boys nearest him began to push at him.

"Just knock it off, Dougary," Charlie snapped at them. "Leave him alone."

"Oh, I'm sorry," Dougary mimicked fear by trembling exaggeratedly. "I'm so scared. We better not tease Gus, guys, or Charlie will sick his ghost friends on us."

The fake crying gave way to laughter and fake trembling. Gus struggled to stay in line as the other boys kept pushing him away. He accidentally bumped into Larry, who turned around and gave Gus a violent shove that knocked him to the floor.

Howard quickly grabbed Larry, even though he was nearly a head shorter than the bully, and gave him a hard push. Larry lost his balance and hit the wall behind him with a loud bang.

"Back off, Larry," Howard growled.

Rick quickly helped Gus to his feet and dusted off his robes.

"You're sitting with us," he said and put a protective arm around Gus' shoulders.

Gus smiled to himself at Rick's gesture. After the way he had acted over the past two months, he was really surprised to see who his true friends were. He took off his purple surplice and wadded it into a ball then threw it at Dougary.

"Hypocrite," he cursed. "Someday you'll get what's

coming to you."

The surplice hit Dougary in the face and he caught it before it could hit the floor. He wadded it back up and started to throw it when Abbot Ambrose rounded the corner of the hall. Immediately he caught sight of Dougary.

"Don't you dare, Master Duggan!" his deep voice echoed down the hall.

Dougary felt a sudden rush of adrenaline and froze. There was only one person that he truly feared and that was the Abbot. Slowly he dropped his attacking stance and stood straight in line.

"Hand me that surplice, please." Abbot Ambrose held out his hand. "Gus, I believe this is yours," he said and handed Gus his surplice. "I will see you after lunch," he added plainly then went into the refectory.

Soon afterward the prefects arrived and they all filed silently into the refectory for lunch.

Lunch, like the morning's classes, seemed to drag on for Gus who sat two chairs down from Dougary and across from Travis. Travis kept kicking Gus' legs under the table until finally Gus wrapped them around the legs of his chair. He tried to eat his lunch but the knot in his stomach felt bigger as he thought about the look in the Abbot's eyes.

Across the room, Howard and Charlie were having the same trouble eating. Howard was still angry with Dougary, and Charlie was finding it hard to eat thinking about what Gus was going through sitting at the table with his tormentors. Rick, however, had no trouble eating his lunch of corned beef and cabbage. After finishing his, he eyed Howard's plate hungrily. Howard shoved his plate at Rick and continued to fume.

"How can you eat?" Howard asked angrily. "Don't you even care about Gus?"

"Yes, I care," Rick answered with his mouth full. "But starving to death isn't going to help anyone. Besides, I didn't eat breakfast this morning."

Charlie nodded as he remembered. Rick was too nervous about Brother Simon's class to eat his breakfast. He smiled to himself almost pleased to know there was someone that had that effect on Rick.

After lunch was over, Rick hurried off to the dorm and left Howard and Charlie standing in the corridor outside the refectory to wait for Gus. Gus seemed to be taking a long time talking with Abbot Ambrose. The hall was completely deserted except for Howard and Charlie. Howard began to pace while Charlie leaned against the wall.

"What's taking him so long?" Howard griped.

"I don't know. Do you think the Abbot will let him move back?"

"Why shouldn't he? He's the one who let him move out. It's only fair to let him move back. Especially with the way Dougary and his creeps have been treating him and not to mention how they will continue to treat him if he doesn't." Howard answered as he paced.

"Do people move between dorms a lot?" Charlie asked.

"No, not usually," Howard answered. "They want us to bond with the other members of our dorms and be like a family, since we residents have none. Usually the moves happen when one of the students doesn't come back in the fall or when new students come."

Charlie looked at the refectory doors and frowned. That didn't sound promising for Gus. Just then the doors opened and Gus walked into the hall.

"Well, it's about time," Howard sighed. "What took you so long?"

"I had to explain why I had asked to move and why I now want to move back. Abbot Ambrose had a lot of questions." Gus answered as the three headed up the stairs.

"Well?" Charlie probed.

"I told him that I had asked to move because I was jealous of Rick and that I regretted saying that he should appoint Rick to the Altar Boys. He then lectured me about how jealously is a terrible thing and one of the things God hates. He said that when we do things out of jealousy, we tend to regret them."

"And?" Charlie prodded.

"He then asked me why I wanted to move back. I told him that we have all made up and that we are now friends again."

Howard stepped in front of Gus and faced him as they stopped on the landing between the third and fourth floors. He looked directly into Gus' eyes and with an almost exasperated tone asked bluntly.

"So, do you get to move or not?"

Gus looked at Howard and then a Charlie. His eyes filled with tears and he looked at the floor.

"No."

"What?" Howard shouted in surprise. His voice echoed up and down the stairwell.

Charlie looked at Howard whose eyes were bulging and whose face had turned an angry red. He could tell that Howard was close to losing his temper.

"Why wouldn't he let you?" Charlie asked Gus.

"He said that I need to learn that when I make a decision I can't just run from the consequences. He said something about it could be my penance for succumbing to my feelings of envy and jealousy," Gus replied.

"But what about Dougary and his jerk friends?" Howard jumped in. "Doesn't he know about them?"

"I tried to tell him, to get him to understand, but he wouldn't listen." The tears started to fall again. "They're going to kill me."

"No, they aren't," Charlie tried to sound convincing but failed miserably.

"Dry your eyes," Howard ordered. "You don't need to be caught crying again. We need to get to class."

As they headed back down the stairs to their homeroom, Charlie and Howard tried to get Gus's mind off his dorm troubles by filling him in on the progress they made in their not-so-secret investigation. Gus couldn't believe his ears when he heard that Brother Tobias was Joseph's brother. His mouth dropped open and then he began to get angry.

"He lied to me," Gus said with indignation. "He just played me for a fool. Told me those things because he figured I was gullible enough to believe him."

Howard bit his tongue to keep from laughing out loud.

Charlie snickered. "But Gus, you did believe him." He barely had the words out before he broke into laughter, which was more than Howard could take and he burst into hysterical laughter himself.

Gus looked at them and then he too started to laugh. He had fallen for the story. He didn't feel too dumb since more than half of Saint Nicholas dorm believed in the story also.

"Well, the next time we hear the thing in the attic, we're going to catch him," Gus said with a fearless tone in his voice.

Howard looked at Charlie surprised by Gus' display of courage.

~§~

Three weeks had passed since Charlie, Howard, Rick and

Gus had patched up their friendship. Life in Saint Peter dorm was pure torture for Gus. Each night, he had to check his bed thoroughly before climbing in. The first night he found that his bed was short sheeted, but not before he stuck his feet through the sheet, tearing it in two. Then, on another occasion, he climbed into bed only to have the frame fall apart and crash to the floor. Father Vicar scolded him and made him sleep on the floor for the rest of the week for having made noise after lights out. It was getting to the point that Gus was not sleeping very well, if at all, at night and his eyes were starting to show it. Fear of having another rubber spider dropped on him or of having shaving cream put in his hand and then having his nose tickled or the worst, having water dumped on him so the others would think he wet the bed, kept him awake.

Adding to Gus's stress, Brother Simon was more cross with all of them than usual. He continued to focus his hostility on Charlie, Howard, Rick and him. Gus was too tired most of the time to care, but being so tired also meant that he cried more often which prompted more teasing and harassment. It was a vicious circle.

"Come on, Gus," Charlie coaxed. "I asked Sister Margaret Mary for these just for you." He waved a plate of pastries and cookies under Gus' nose. "You have to eat something."

"I can't." Gus pushed them away and slumped back on the sofa. Life in the refectory was not any better. Sitting by Dougary, Travis, Larry and Austin was stressful enough and their intense dislike of him was obvious. Every meal, Gus found it harder to eat. He even quit eating out of fear. It started out as teasing. Dougary said he put spit in Gus's food, but the day Gus found a dead bug on his plate was the last straw. He began to lose weight as a result, and the sparkle in his eyes had faded.

Charlie looked at Howard and Rick who sat on the arms of

the overstuffed chair in Saint Nicholas dorm. They shrugged their shoulders. He turned back to Gus.

"You haven't eaten for weeks," Charlie sighed. "Please, for me? Just one?" he begged but Gus only shook his head.

"Just leave them on the table," Howard told Charlie.

Charlie set the plate down on the coffee table-trunk. "This is nuts. I'm going to see the Abbot," he said and stood up. "You guys coming with me?"

Howard and Rick just looked at each other as Charlie quickly disappeared out the door.

Abbot Ambrose was in his office on the first floor when Charlie knocked. His voice sounded preoccupied when he invited Charlie in. He looked up from behind a pile of papers and books and an opened Bible on his desk. It was obvious he was researching something, possibly a sermon.

"Yes, Charlie." He smiled. "What can I do for you?"

"Abbot Ambrose, I'm sorry to bother you," Charlie apologized as he closed the office door behind him.

Abbot Ambrose looked over the top of his glasses at Charlie and smiled.

"It's okay, son," he said. "I could use a break. What's on your mind?" he asked and leaned back in his chair.

"Gus, Father," he answered then quickly added, "I know you have your reasons and I don't profess to know more than you, it's just that he's miserable. He's constantly tormented by Dougary and his cronies—" Charlie froze as the Abbott's eyes widened at the description. "I'm sorry, friends," he apologized.

Abbot Ambrose smile gave way to a laugh. "Don't be silly. You had it right the first time."

His laugh put Charlie more at ease but he was still nervous as he continued.

"They're making life miserable for Gus in the dorm and in

the refectory. Gus won't eat now and I know he's not sleeping."

"I've noticed," admitted Abbot Ambrose in a voice that sounded troubled.

"What I would like to ask, for Gus' sake, would you please allow him to move back to Saint Nicholas dorm. If someone has to be in Saint Peter, then move me instead. I can handle Dougary and his friends."

"I'm sure you could, Charlie," Abbot Ambrose smiled proudly at Charlie's self-sacrificing spirit. "But—"

"Please, Abbot Ambrose," Charlie interrupted. "I'm just worried about Gus. He doesn't look good or act like he's happy anymore."

"Okay, okay." Abbot Ambrose nodded and smiled raising his hands in a surrendering gesture. "Gus should know what a good friend he has in you. He can move back immediately."

"Oh thank you, thank you so much." Charlie gushed and grinned from ear to ear. "I'll get my things packed."

"No." Abbot Ambrose halted Charlie before he could leave.

Charlie turned around at the door and looked back at the Abbot.

"No, Charlie," he repeated. "You're to stay in Saint Nicholas dorm where you belong. Besides, Gus will need you there."

"Thank you, Father Abbot." Charlie smiled and nodded respectfully. "I'll let you get back to your work. I'm sorry for interrupting you," he said, then slipped out the door.

That evening at dinner in the refectory, Gus took his place across from Charlie. At first, he was cautious when his food was served but soon, he relaxed and began to eat slowly. Charlie looked up at the head table and saw Abbot Ambrose watching Gus with a deeply concerned look in his eyes. He does care,

Charlie thought to himself.

THE NEW PRIOR

The night air was cool as it blew through the slightly open window. Charlie sat in his bed and leaned against the window sill. He looked out at the night. Outside, the deep blue sky was clear and speckled with twinkling stars. Charlie sighed out loud as he thought about his grandmother. It had been weeks since he heard from her. When he asked her about the address on the medal, she told him she would tell him later. It was not safe to write it in a letter. Perhaps when they saw each other, but so far she had not been successful in her attempts to convince his Aunt Bernice to bring her. He began to wonder if he would ever see her again.

Just then a loud thump shook the ceiling above him. He jumped and looked up. Ghosts don't bump into things, do they, he thought to himself. Then came low moaning sounds like someone was in pain. He quickly jumped out of his bed and nudged Howard.

Howard opened his eyes and started to speak but saw Charlie motion for him to be quiet. They listened to the sounds above them for a moment and then tiptoed across the room toward the door.

"What are you guys doing?" Gus asked in a whisper as he climbed out of his bed.

"The ghost," Howard answered and pointed toward the ceiling.

Gus listened for a moment and then threw his covers off himself. He grabbed his robe from the end of his bed and put it on as he hurried over to them.

"I'm going with you," he said through pursed lips.

"Are you sure?" Howard asked.

"Yes," Gus answered firmly.

"Okay then, we have to be quiet," Charlie reminded them.

Quietly, the three of them crept into the hallway and toward the fire doors to the stairwell. Slowly Howard reached for the door.

"You guys didn't wake me up," a voice said behind them.

All three jumped and gasped. They covered their mouths quickly to stifle their yells as they spun around. Their hearts pounded in their chests and suddenly they were out of breath and panting.

"Dang it, Rick," Howard cursed in a forceful whisper and punched him in the arm. "Don't sneak up on people."

"But you didn't wake me up," Rick protested as he rubbed his arm.

"Will you keep your voice down," Charlie snapped at Rick. "You want us all to get caught?"

Just then they heard a noise on the other side of the fire doors. It sounded as though the attic door shut with a slam.

Gus glanced down the hall toward the opposite end and noticed Dougary leaving the bathrooms. He was not sure if Dougary had spotted them but he didn't appear to have as he continued back to his dorm. Gus turned back to the others, just as Howard cracked open the door.

Howard peered through the crack caught a glimpse of someone slipping into the monastery wing. He quickly threw open the door and rushed after him. Charlie, Gus and Rick followed close behind. Once inside the monastery wing, they spotted the figure as he rounded the corner at the end of the hall. Charlie and Howard raced after him. As they reached the corner, a door at the far end of the adjoining hall closed. Lights switched on under a couple doors along the hall. Charlie and Howard quickly retreated back to the others, and then back to their dorm.

The next morning was Saturday. After breakfast, the four huddled outside, in a corner of the field away from the rest of the boys. The air was cold against their faces and their breath rose in a fog in front of them. Gus shivered and folded his arms tightly across his chest even though the sun felt warm.

"I can't believe it's this cold and Easter is only two weeks away." Gus fought hard to keep his teeth from chattering.

"So, whose room was that?" Rick asked.

"It wasn't a room," Howard answered. "It was a stairwell."

"Did you see who it was?" Rick turned to Charlie.

"No." he shook his head. "I only saw his back but it was a monk."

"Well that narrows it down," Rick said sarcastically.

"Stop it, Rick." Howard snapped. "If it weren't for you sneaking up on us, we might have caught whoever it was."

"Did anyone see anything else last night?" Charlie asked, grasping at straws.

"Well," Gus hesitated. "Last night, just when we heard the noises in the stairwell, I did notice Dougary at the other end of the hall. He was coming out of the restrooms. I don't think he saw us, though. He just walked back to his dorm."

Charlie looked at Howard. As their eyes met, it was as

though they were reading each other's thoughts. They both turned back to Gus.

"You said it was when we heard the noises?" Charlie asked. "Are you sure?"

"Yes." Gus nodded his head and shivered. "Why?"

Charlie looked at Howard, who nodded. "Because there is another entrance to the attic above one of the stalls in the restroom."

"Ah-ha!" Rick gasped. "So, you did go to the attic that day we were confined to our dorm." He looked at Howard and Charlie.

"Oh, get over it." Howard brushed him off.

"But Dougary couldn't have been the one making the noises," Gus spoke up. "What about the monk?"

Charlie looked at Gus and his shoulders slumped. "That's right," he had to admit.

"No, he couldn't have made the noises but he could have tipped off the one who was," Howard spoke up.

"But that would mean whoever is doing this is doing it to scare us deliberately," Rick scoffed. "Why would they do that?"

"Who knows?" Charlie shrugged.

"Well, I don't care. Whoever is doing it needs to be stopped," Howard spoke up indignantly.

"But which one of the monks would team up with the likes of Dougary?" Rick protested. "This isn't making any sense at all. This is just a waste of time. I'm cold and going back inside."

"That's fine, Rick," Howard called after him. "Who needs you anyway?"

"That wasn't very nice," Gus told Howard.

Howard looked at Gus in surprise. Never had he spoken up in defense of anyone before. "No, you're right," he admitted. "But sometimes Rick makes me so angry."

"Yeah." Gus looked over his shoulder as Rick disappeared into the Abbey building. "I know what you mean, but he's still my friend."

"Ours, too," Charlie assured him. "So, what's the plan?"

"For starters, we need to catch whoever it is in the act." Howard said. "After lights out, two of us will sneak out of the dorm and spend the night in the attic. Since we don't know when he'll strike next, we'll have to be there every night. Charlie and I will go tonight. Then, if we can convince Rick, Gus, you and he will take the next. We'll trade off."

"Bu-but," Gus started to protest.

"It'll be okay," Howard assured him.

"Hey, have you seen any of the Brothers today?" Charlie changed the subject as he looked around. "Usually there's one or two of them walking around."

"They're all in prayer today," Howard answered. "They are deciding on the new Prior."

"Oh, I hope it's not Father Vicar." Gus shook his head.

"Who do you think it's going to be?" Charlie asked them.

"From the rumors I've heard, some think that Brother Blaise or Father Mathias will get it. But I personally hope it's Brother Benedict. He's so nice," Gus answered.

"It doesn't matter to me who gets it." Howard shrugged. "They don't do anything for us anyway."

"What do you mean?" Charlie asked.

"The Prior's duties are focused on the monastery, keeping things running smoothly," Howard explained. "The only one who has any direct impact on us is Abbot Ambrose because he's the one the prefects report to. Whoever is named won't change anything for us."

"How soon will we know?" Charlie asked. This was all new to him and Howard seemed to know a lot about it.

"It depends on the Brothers. The last time they decided on a Prior was years before I came here. I'm told they only took an hour but from what Father Emmanuel said back then, that was the fastest assignment in their history. So, no one really knows."

"Oh no, here comes Dougary and his bullies," Gus said and stepped behind Howard. "Let's get out of here."

"Stay calm, Gus," Charlie said.

"So, what are you girls doing?" Dougary asked and walked directly over to Charlie. Travis and Austin turned their attention to Howard and Gus.

"We aren't girls, dog breath," Howard sneered.

"My pardon." Dougary grinned, then glared at him. "So Charlie, I hear your grandmother sent you a medal with strange writing on the back for Christmas. Mind if I look at it?"

Charlie gave Howard a disappointed look but Howard shrugged. Charlie noticed Gus looked at the ground, and tried to hide behind Howard. He knew, however, that Gus couldn't have told them because he hadn't told Gus. He lost the letter from his grandmother before classes resumed after the holidays. He turned back to Dougary.

"So, who said I got a medal?" he asked. "Unless you're the one who stole my letter."

Dougary put his hand over his heart and dropped his jaw. "Why Charlie, I am offended. Why would you say such a terrible thing like that? I was only trying to be your friend."

"No, you aren't," Charlie answered him. "You don't fool me."

"Did you hear that, guys?" Dougary asked in a mock-offended tone and looked at his friends. They grunted and nodded their heads.

"Look, Charlie." Dougary tried to put his arm around Charlie's shoulders but Charlie pulled away. "I'll get that medal one way or another. Mark my words, you little mama's boy. Come on guys, let's go."

Howard moved over to Charlie's side as they all watched Dougary, Travis, Larry and Austin walk away.

"What's with them?" Howard asked. "What's the sudden interest in your medal?"

"I don't know." Charlie shook his head. "My grandmother said not to let anyone touch it. I sure wish she'd hurry up and tell me what it's all about."

"Why don't you ask her?" Gus spoke up.

"I have several times but she said it was too dangerous to write in a letter and that was the last I've heard from her. She hasn't written me back." Charlie looked at them. "I'm getting very worried."

"I'm sure there's a logical explanation." Gus tried to encourage Charlie while he searched his memories about something that he had seen once. "You'll hear from her soon. I'm sure." He shook the thoughts from his mind, unable to remember clearly.

"I hope you're right," Charlie said but his tone said he didn't believe him.

"Hey, let's go up to the attic and get a place set up for our stake out tonight." Howard changed the subject.

"You go ahead." Charlie shrugged. "I just want to be alone for a while."

"Okay." Howard nodded. "You coming?" He turned to Gus.

"Sure," he answered and the two headed off for the attic.

Charlie looked around the baseball field, at the boys laughing and playing ball. He didn't feel like joining them so he headed off for the kitchens. Perhaps a cup of milk and a talk with Sister Margaret Mary would cheer him up.

As he approached the back door to the student wing of the Abbey, he glanced down the path toward the cemetery. He was surprised to see Dougary talking to a man that Charlie had never seen before. The man stood taller than Dougary and looked angry about something. He waved his thick arms around and shook his finger at Dougary, thumping his chest a couple of times as he ranted. Charlie crept into a shadow of a shrub and continued to watch the scene with interest. He wished he were closer so he could hear what was being said. Finally, the man looked around and then retreated into the woods. Dougary stood for a moment and then turned around to return to the Abbey. Charlie crept deeper into the shrub so he was completely concealed.

"So, what did your dad want?" Travis asked as he, Larry and Austin joined Dougary.

"He's just upset that it's taking so long," Dougary answered. "So, did you guys see where that MacCready dweeb went?"

They looked around and shrugged.

"Come on," he sighed and lead his goons away.

Cautiously Charlie emerged from the shrub and brushed himself off. What were they up to, he wondered as he continued on his way to the kitchen.

The kitchen smelled of baking bread and roast beef. Charlie's mouth watered with anticipation for lunch as he headed for the bakery. Just as Charlie expected, Sister Margaret Mary was there, sitting on a stool and sipping a cup of coffee while reading the newspaper, waiting for her bread to finish baking. She looked up at him as he entered the room and smiled.

"Chuck." She beamed. "What a pleasant surprise. How are you?"

"I'm okay," Charlie sighed, and sat down on a stool he

pulled out from under the kneading table.

"Uh-oh," Sister Margaret Mary said as she folded her newspaper. "I say we need a cup of cold milk and some cookies. I want to hear all about it." She disappeared and a moment later returned to the bakery with a glass of cold milk, a napkin and a plate. She handed Charlie the glass and napkin then turned around and opened the cookie drawer. She quickly selected an assortment of cookies and closed the drawer.

"There, that's much better." She smiled as she settled back on her stool. She picked up her coffee cup and took a sip. "So, what's troubling you?"

Charlie looked at the plate of cookies. They all looked so good but he was not very hungry. His mind was spinning.

"I just saw Dougary and his dad talking a few minutes ago," he said as he swirled the milk in his glass. "After he left, I overheard Dougary and his goons talking about me." He looked up at Sister Margaret Mary. "Did Dougary's father ever go to school here?"

Sister Margaret Mary pulled her head back as though she was stung by his question. She thought for a moment. "Why yes, I believe so," she answered. "Franklyn was adopted by the VonDuggans on a farm just outside of town. When they passed away, he inherited their land and sold it for a pretty penny. He dropped the Von from his name for whatever reason. Anyway, I'm surprised he'd show up here. Abbot Ambrose has strictly forbidden it. If he were caught, I'm not sure what would happen."

"I knew it!" Charlie smiled knowingly. "Prior Anselm gave me a photograph and behind it was a letter about what had happened that night. How Franklyn and his buddies had locked the boy named Jeffrey in the attic. I knew it was Dougary's dad."

"Well, I must say," Sister Margaret Mary sighed. "You're quite the detective aren't you."

Charlie looked at her and was not sure if he should smile or not, so he shrugged his shoulders.

"Is there anything else bothering you?" she asked and cocked her head as she studied his eyes.

"Yes," he admitted. "There're a couple things. Someone stole the photograph and letter that Prior Anselm gave me, and a letter that my grandmother sent me. They were in my nightstand in the dorm. It wouldn't be so bad except that shortly after that, she quit writing. I'm worried about her."

"Have you written her?" Sister Margaret Mary asked and sipped her coffee again.

"Oh yes." Charlie looked at her, his eyes filled with tears. "Nearly every day. Do you think something has happened to her? I mean, the last time I heard from her she told me some man came by with my uncle, and they were asking a bunch of questions. She warned me that someone might show up here looking for me. You don't think he would have hurt her, do you?"

"Oh no, Chuck." She shook her head. She reached out and took his hand. "I'm sure she is fine."

"I hope so," he sighed. "It's just that she's so old and my uncle is so mean."

Sister Margaret Mary glanced over at the black telephone that hung on the wall next to the door. She thought to herself for a moment, weighing in her mind whether or not to suggest it. Finally, she nodded.

"I have an idea," she said. "I'm sure Father Abbot wouldn't mind. What do you say we just give your grandmother a call? You do have her telephone number, don't you?"

Charlie's eyes lit up. "Yes, I do. Can I?" he asked, unable

to hide his excitement.

"Of course, you can dear," she nodded. "I'll leave you alone for a few moments, so you can talk in private."

"Thank you so much." Charlie beamed. He followed her over to the door with his eyes fixed on the phone.

"Now, don't forget to dial a nine so your call won't go through the switchboard. We don't want to disturb the Brothers today. They have a lot on their minds selecting the new Prior and all. I'll be in the other room," she instructed before she left.

Charlie nervously picked up the receiver and dialed his grandmother's telephone number. He had only called her once before but purposely memorized her phone number in case the opportunity came again. The telephone rang on the other end of the line. Charlie silently counted the rings, two, three...

"Hello?" came the familiar sweet voice of his grandmother.

"Grandma, it's me, Charlie," he said excitedly.

"Charlie, dear, it's so good to hear you. How are you? Everything is okay isn't it?"

"Yes, grandma," he answered. "I'm fine. I was just worried about you. I was wondering why you haven't written in so long."

"Why Charlie, I have. I write you every week. In fact, I just sent you a letter two days ago. You should have received it today."

"But I didn't," Charlie replied, near tears. "Are you sure?"

"Yes, honey," his grandmother's voice was definite. "Could someone there be taking them?"

Dougary's face flashed in his mind. Unconsciously Charlie's jaws tightened and he glared at the wall.

"I'll check into it," he said. "Grandma, remember the man who came to see you with Uncle Chester?"

"Yes, dear."

"Do you remember his name or what did he look like?" Charlie asked.

"Oh my, it's been so long ago, his name escapes me at the moment," she said as she thought. "He was about the same height as your uncle, though, but heavier. His had a square jaw and looked stern, sort of gruff. Why do you ask, Charlie? What's this all about?"

"I was just wondering is all," Charlie answered, and tried not to sound too interested. "Do you know when you will be able to come to see me?"

"I wish I did. But I don't. I just about had your Aunt Bernice talked into it when your Uncle Chester put the stop to it. He showed up the very day that we were going to come up there. I haven't given up, Charlie. I just have to be more careful."

"I can't wait to see you again," Charlie sighed and fumbled with his Saint Christopher medal. "And finally find out what the key and medal mean. Why won't you tell me?"

"It's for your safety that you don't know just yet, Charlie," she said. "You have to trust me. I could not keep those things lying about, not since your Uncle Chester gained control of all of my money and everything else. Remember, honey, do not give the key to anyone. Don't let it out of your sight for a moment. It's very important. Once it is safe, I'll explain. Charlie, there's someone coming, I have to go. Thank you for calling. I love you."

"I love you, too, Grandma."

The line went dead before he could finish his sentence. He hung up the receiver more confused than before he made the call. Slowly he walked back to his stool and sat down.

"That was quick," Sister Margaret Mary said as she walked back into the bakery. She took her seat on her stool at the table and looked at Charlie. "Oh, that doesn't look like the face of a happy boy. Bad news?"

"Sort of," Charlie answered. "Grandma has been writing me and someone must be stealing the letters."

"Oh dear, that doesn't sound good." She shook her head again. "Shall you tell Abbot Ambrose?"

"I don't know," Charlie sighed as he thought. "No," he said firmly. "I think I've got a plan."

"Well, that's my little detective," she smiled. "Speaking of which, I heard that you figured out who Kenny is."

"Actually, it was Howard who found out," Charlie admitted and sank as he sat on his stool.

Sister Margaret Mary straightened her back and looked at him cautiously. "I don't know, Chuck. You boys have really upset Brother Tobias."

"I'm sorry. I never meant to upset anyone," Charlie apologized. "It's just that someone is making noises in the attic at night. I don't know if they're trying to scare us or if it's Brother Tobias still upset about his brother."

A tear came to Sister Margaret Mary's eyes as she remembered that night years ago. "He's not doing it," she spoke confidently. "It has to be someone else."

"But why?" Charlie asked.

"I don't know, but I do know that it is not Brother Tobias," she repeated.

Suddenly the oven timer went off and Sister Margaret Mary jumped. She quickly turned it off and opened the large oven doors. Inside were twelve loaf pans in a line, each with a golden-brown loaf of fresh bead. It smelled so wonderful, like his grandmother's kitchen. Slowly Charlie stood up.

"I guess I should be going now. Thank you for the phone call and the milk and cookies."

"Oh, don't mention it," she smiled absentmindedly. "Why don't you take the rest of those cookies with you? I'm sure Howard would love to help you eat them. Tell him hello for me, will you?"

"I will." Charlie smiled as he looked back from the door. "I'll see you later."

Charlie hurried back to his dorm. He had just enough time to change into his robes before the lunch bell. The halls were quiet; suddenly he remembered the meeting the monks were in to decide on the new Prior. He hoped it wouldn't be Father Vicar. There was something about him that made Charlie feel uneasy. Perhaps it was the way he looked at Abbot Ambrose. Charlie hurried by Saint Peter dorm and down the hall to Saint Nicholas.

Inside the dorm he quickly found Howard, Gus and Rick. They were dressed and ready for lunch.

"So, where have you been?" Rick asked in his usual bossy tone.

"I was talking to Sister Margaret Mary, if it is any of your business," Charlie bit back. Rick gave him a look as though he were insulted and stormed out of the dorm.

"You have to hurry if you don't want to be late for lunch," Gus urged. "I think they've decided on the new Prior."

Charlie looked at Gus as he took off his shirt and tossed it into his locker. "You do?"

"We saw Abbot Ambrose in the hall a few minutes ago," Howard spoke up.

The hall outside the refectory was unusually quiet as Charlie, Howard and Gus descended the last few steps to the main floor. Rick looked up as the three took their place in line.

"Boy, why is everyone so quiet?" Howard asked as he looked around. Even Dougary and his gang were behaving themselves for a change.

"Abbot Ambrose is inside," Rick whispered in answer.

"So?" Howard replied. "He's always inside before every meal."

Rick glared at Howard, still angry with Charlie because of his comment upstairs. "Just keep quiet," he said through clenched teeth. "Unless you want to get us all in trouble."

"Okay," Howard said and held up his hands in surrender. "Geesh!"

Charlie smiled at the bantering as he glanced around the hall. His smile faded as he spotted Dougary. Dougary stood leaning against the wall staring back at him. Charlie glared back. He wondered if it was Dougary's father who went to see his grandmother with his uncle. Why were they so interested in the key? What was Dougary's sudden interest in the Saint Christopher medal? It did not make sense. Dougary finally looked away, so Charlie turned back to Howard and Gus.

The refectory doors opened and much to everyone's surprise, the Abbot himself motioned for the boys to file in. Howard gave Charlie a quick curious glance before their line began to move. It seemed strange that the prefects didn't come out to take their places at the front of the lines as they did before every meal since Charlie came to Saint Michael's. Instead, they stood quietly behind their chairs at the head table.

After the prayer came the usual clap of the wooden block that signaled it was okay to talk, but no one did. Charlie looked around. Even the four prefects at the head table weren't talking. Then he noticed that Father Emmanuel was not eating. In fact, he was not looking up from his plate as he moved his food around. Charlie looked at Father Vicar. It was obvious he was angry by the way that he chewed on a chunk of stew meat. Charlie leaned over to Howard and gently nudged him in the ribs to get his attention.

"What's going on?" he whispered.

Howard looked around. "I don't know. It's kind of weird."

The rest of the meal passed in silence, and then Abbot Ambrose rose to his feet. His expression was very serious as he walked around to the front of the table. He looked across the room as though taking a quick mental roll call of everyone. With a deep breath he leaned back against the table.

"As you all know, the members of the Abbey have been in prayer and in a meeting this morning to select the new Prior," he announced. "We have reached a decision and unfortunately it will mean some changes for one of our dorms."

An excited murmuring rose from the Saint Peter table. Father Vicar looked up at his boys and glared bitterly at them. Charlie smiled and gave a sigh of relief. It was evident Father Vicar had lost out on being the new Prior. Abbot Ambrose held up a quieting hand and the room fell silent again.

"Father Emmanuel has been named as our new Prior. Brother Simon will, for the time being, oversee Saint Nicholas dorm."

A gasp rose from the boys at the Saint Nicholas table while Dougary and his group burst into laughter. Charlie looked at Father Emmanuel who had finally looked up. His eyes were red and damp with tears.

"That will be enough!" Abbot Ambrose's voice thundered. "Masters Duggan, Bleckinger, Hertz and Fulton, I will see you after the meal." He turned to the members of Saint Nicholas table. "After lunch I would like you boys to meet in your dorm. Father Emmanuel would like to speak with you and I will be bringing Brother Simon over to get reacquainted." He turned back to the whole assembly.

"Change is never easy for any of us but it is a part of life.

We all have to change in order to grow. You have already been through tremendous changes in your young lives and there will be many more to come, I can promise you that. So, as difficult as it is for you now, in a while it will eventually work itself out. You will see. That's all for now."

Abbot Ambrose looked around at the room full of sullen faces and sighed. He understood how hard it was for them but it was unavoidable.

After the prayer the members of Saint Nicholas dorm filed out into the hallway and headed back to their dorm.

"I don't believe this is happening." Howard said in a disgusted tone as they started up the stairs. "How could they do this to us?"

"It's not personal, Howard," Rick snapped. "This is a big honor for Father Emmanuel to be chosen Prior; that's second in line over all the monks. Only the Abbot is higher."

"Big woo," Howard quipped. Inside his heart was breaking. Ever since his first day at Saint Michael's, Father Emmanuel had been his prefect. He looked up to him like a son did his father. Now it was as though he had lost his father all over again. He felt lost, alone and afraid of what would happen to him.

Charlie sensed Howard's sadness and put his arm around his shoulders. "It's going to be okay, Howard. We're still here, and as Altar Boys we can see Father Emmanuel whenever we want, remember?"

"Yeah," Howard nodded.

Even though what he said was true, Charlie knew life in Saint Nicholas dorm was not going to be the same with Brother Simon as prefect. The thought of their World Cultures teacher being their prefect was enough to scare even the bravest of boys, and Charlie was far from the bravest.

Everyone gathered around the lounge area in the center of the dorm. Some of the older boys brought in some chairs from the common area so everyone who wanted to sit could. Silently, they waited for Father Emmanuel. To the amazement of the younger members of the dorm, some of the older boys were actually crying. Charlie was among those that were surprised. He would miss Father Emmanuel but he was not as attached to him as Howard and Gus were. Perhaps given time, he would have been, and then he too would be shedding tears.

The doors opened and Father Emmanuel bounded into the dorm with a big smile on his lips. His puffy cheeks were their usual rosy pink and even his eyes twinkled a bit. Charlie wasn't fooled. He knew Father Emmanuel had shed a few tears.

"Oh, what's with all of the sullen faces?" he said in his usual jolly tone. "Did someone die and no one told me?" he teased.

A few of the boys forced a smile but no one felt much like laughing at Father Emmanuel's jokes. Father Emmanuel sensed he had lost his audience and his face took on a more serious look as he sat down in one of the empty chairs.

"I know this isn't easy for any of you," he began. "It's not going to be easy for me, either. In addition to my duties as Prior I'll be working on a project for the Abbot. So I'll be very busy. Not much time to visit my old friends here. But I want you to know that my door will always be open to all of you."

"It's not fair," blurted one of the older boys in the back.

Father Emmanuel looked in his direction and smiled sympathetically. "You'll learn, Todd and all of you, sometimes life isn't fair. Believe me, this is as much a surprise to me as it is to you. I never expected this, never."

"But you accepted it," Another boy spoke up. There was a touch of anger in his voice.

"Yes." Father Emmanuel nodded. "I did. As you grow up you will come to realize that as adults, we all have to do things we don't want to at times. And being a monk only adds to that list. I took a vow of obedience and I take my vows very seriously. So when the Abbot asked me if I would assume the role as Prior which my fellow Brothers had decided on, I couldn't refuse. It would have been selfish of me to have turned him and them down."

"So, that's it?" Howard spoke up. "You're leaving and we're getting a new prefect just like that." He snapped his fingers. "We have no say? What we feel doesn't matter? It's that easy for you?"

Father Emmanuel looked at Howard and a tear fell from his eyes. "No, it's not easy for me. You all mean so much to me. I couldn't love you more if you were my own sons. This is tearing me apart inside."

As Father Emmanuel began to sob, Howard forgot about himself and felt sorry for Father Emmanuel.

"We'll be okay," he said for everyone.

Father Emmanuel tried to smile but the tears continued to fall. As one, the boys surrounded him and gave him a hug. Slowly he regained his composure and took a deep breath.

"Be good to Brother Simon," he instructed. "Make me proud."

Just then the doors opened and Abbot Ambrose escorted Brother Simon into the dorm. Slowly the boys returned to their seats. Father Emmanuel dried his cheeks and quickly slipped away before the Abbot could see that he had been crying.

"Hello, boys," Abbot Ambrose greeted everyone. He couldn't help but notice that several of the boys had teary eyes and some even damp cheeks. "You all know Brother Simon," he began. "Something you might not know about him is that he used to be a member of Saint Nicholas dorm years ago."

"Many years ago," Brother Simon quickly added, dryly.

Abbot Ambrose smiled. "Yes. Before I let you get acquainted, I want you all to know, the assignment of Father Emmanuel to Prior was one reached by the entire assembly of Brothers. He will serve the Brothers well, and I know he will never forget you boys. So, when you see him around, be sure to say hello." He looked at all their faces and nodded, understanding their feelings. He turned around and left them.

Once the doors closed and the Abbot was gone, Brother Simon took a deep breath and folded his arms under his robes. He looked down his long, crocked nose as he made a little inspection of each member of the dorm. Slowly he began to pace.

"I am quite well aware of how lax Father Emmanuel has been with tending to his duties here," he began coldly. "I promise you I will not be making that same mistake. I find that young boys tend to thrive when they have boundaries and guidelines. So, from now on we will have a set of rules of behavior that will be strictly adhered to. Beginning with, no more crying!" He raised his voice and looked directly at Gus.

"You are young men not a bunch of little girls. Is that clear?" He stopped pacing as he waited for their answer. "I see," he said, and straightened his back even further, giving him a more ominous presence.

"On your feet, all of you. Form a line," he ordered. "Now!"

The boys jumped to their feet and quickly did as they were instructed. Charlie took his place between Howard and Gus who was shaking noticeably. He feared that at any moment Gus would burst into tears. It was obvious to him that life in Saint Nicholas dorm would never be the same.

"When I ask a question, I expect an answer immediately!"

he barked.

"Yes," came the less than enthusiastic reply.

"Yes, Brother Simon," he corrected them sternly and resumed his pacing. "Every morning after breakfast we will have dorm inspections. Each of you is to stand at the foot of his bed while I make my rounds. Any unmade bed, any dust under a bed or on a nightstand or any locker out of order will earn the transgressor an hour of work crew for each infraction. And since the common area of the dorm is everyone's responsibility to keep clean, any infraction there will result in the entire dorm having work crew. Cleanliness is next to Godliness. God does not make messes, and does not tolerate them either. And neither do I. Is that clear?"

"Yes, Brother Simon," came the clear and united response.

"Additionally, there will be no rough housing, loud talk, loud music or any disturbances coming from or in this dormitory. If you feel the need to do any of these things, do so outside and away from the Abbey. Violators of this will earn themselves two hours of work crew." He paused and looked directly at Charlie and Howard. "Anyone caught out of bed after lights out will find themselves working three hours of work crew for each occurrence."

"But, Brother Simon, what if we have to go to the bathroom?" a voice at the other end of the line spoke up.

Brother Simon turned and glared at the one who asked. "That will be an hour of work crew for speaking without raising your hand first," he snapped. "You are to use the restroom facilities before you go to bed. If you have a problem in that area, you may do well to reconsider having anything to drink an hour or two before lights out."

The boys' mouths dropped open but no sound was uttered as they listened in disbelief. Brother Simon, however, turned his attention back Howard and Charlie.

"Is that clear?" he asked.

"Yes, Brother Simon," they shouted.

Brother Simon smiled, pleased with himself, as he continued to glare at Charlie.

Charlie stared blankly, defiantly back at him. He was not going to allow Brother Simon to bully him.

"That will be all for now." Brother Simon said as he turned away. "You are all dismissed."

No one moved until the dormitory doors closed and Brother Simon was gone. Then all at once the boys let out a groan and started talking to each other.

"I can't believe this is happening," Gus sighed and shook his head.

"Oh my God," Howard spoke in shock. "Are we in for it or what?"

"Seems your little ghost hunting days are over," Rick said smugly as he walked over to the three.

Charlie glared at Rick. "Why don't you go soak your head?"

"I thought that was your job," he returned sharply.

"Back off, Rick," Howard warned. "I'm not afraid of a little work crew." He added as he doubled up his fists and stepped between the two of them.

Rick tried to puff up his skinny chest to look more intimidating, but gave up and left.

"What am I going to do?" Gus sighed and looked at Charlie. "You know whenever I get upset, I cry. I can't help it. It just happens."

"Well, you're going to have to learn to hold it in," Howard answered flatly.

"But what if I can't?" Gus protested. "I'll die if I have work crew."

"No, you won't," Charlie tried to reassure him.

"And how am I going to keep from having to use the bathroom during the night?" Gus fretted some more. "I have to have water."

"We'll help you," Howard answered. "Don't worry about it. He's not going to hurt any of us. Abbot Ambrose won't let him."

"I hope you're right," Gus answered. "So, what are you guys going to do about the attic?"

"I don't know yet." Charlie looked at Howard. "Maybe we should hold off until things settle down more. Besides, I talked to Sister Margaret Mary and she said that the noise is definitely not Brother Tobias."

"Then who could it be?" Howard asked.

"Maybe it's Jeffrey?" Charlie shrugged. "I don't know."

"No, I don't think it's him." Howard shook his head. "He's afraid of the dark, remember? And I'm sure he would not step foot in the attic again after what happened to him."

"That was forty years ago," Charlie reminded him. "Surely by now he's grown out of his fear of the dark."

"I don't know," Gus' voice quivered. "Some people may never grow out of it." He was thinking more about himself than Jeffrey. He hated the dark and especially the attic.

"Whatever the case," Charlie said. "I don't think it's him."

"Why?" Howard asked.

"I just have this feeling," he admitted. "I don't think Jeffrey would do that." He glanced over his shoulder at the doors.

"Well, I guess we'll never know." Howard sighed. "It's not worth losing a Saturday afternoon over."

Charlie gave Howard a disappointed look. "I suppose you're right," he said but deep down he knew he wouldn't let it go. He would find out who was behind the noises in the attic.

THE STAKE OUT

Charlie raced back to his cubicle after breakfast. It had been nearly six weeks since Brother Simon began his dorm inspections. So far Charlie managed to escape the dreaded work crew. Howard had also escaped but Gus had not fared as well. Twice he received work crew. Once because he forgot to tuck in the sheets; when Brother Simon came for inspections, there were wrinkles in the bedspread. The other time was for being out of bed after lights out. He had slipped up and had a drink of water before turning in. Sure enough, Brother Simon was on the prowl, and caught Gus leaving the restroom. Since then, Howard and Charlie reassured Gus, they would help him avoid any further infractions of the rules.

As Charlie and Howard looked under their beds for any dust, they heard Rick's voice. He was in the next cubicle talking with Gus. Howard glanced at Charlie and the two quickly jumped to their feet.

"Just what are you doing?" Charlie asked as he looked at Rick.

"Nothing, just talking with Gus," he answered as he looked

up at Charlie.

"Get off his bed, now," Charlie ordered and grabbed Rick's arm pulling him to his feet. "I don't believe you. Are you trying to get Gus into trouble?"

Gus looked at Charlie. "That's right. How could I be so stupid?" He quickly finished putting his nightstand in order.

"Inspections are any minute, Gus," Charlie said as he straightened Gus' bedspread again. "You have to be more careful."

"I'm sorry," Gus apologized and helped smooth out the wrinkles. "I guess I wasn't thinking."

"And you, Rick." Charlie turned to him. "I thought you were Gus' friend. What is the matter with you?"

"Nothing!" snapped Rick. "I was just talking to my friend is all. I didn't mean any harm."

"Yeah, well, with friends like you, who needs enemies?" Howard said as he walked up.

Charlie frowned at Rick. "You know how Brother Simon is. You have to keep on your toes at all times."

The dormitory doors opened and Brother Simon, clipboard in one hand, white glove on the other stepped inside. He blew the whistle that hung from a string tied to the clipboard. The boys quickly took their places at the foot of their beds.

Rick gasped as he hurried back to his bed. His once made bed was in shambles. His pillow was on the floor and the bedspread was pulled back. He panicked and quickly tried to remake his bed.

"Did you not hear the whistle?" the familiar stern voice asked from behind him.

Rick spun around and looked at Brother Simon. His mouth dropped open. "Yes, but I was—someone messed up—I was just trying—" he stammered.

"Take your place and not another word," Brother Simon ordered.

Rick took his place at the foot of his unmade bed and glared across the room at Howard. Brother Simon stepped inside Rick's cubicle and took up his pen.

"One hour for the unmade bed," he counted off. "One hour for the litter on the floor."

"But that's not fair," Rick protested. "The pillow's part of the bed."

Brother Simon turned his glare on Rick. "Then it should have been on the bed. One hour for back-talking."

Rick's mouth dropped open and he quickly turned around. Tears filled his eyes and he fought hard to hold them back lest he get another hour for crying. He glared at Howard and clenched his teeth.

Charlie looked at Howard in shock. He knew that Howard was behind Rick's unmade bed. Part of him actually felt sorry for Rick but another part fought hard to keep from laughing out loud.

Howard bit his tongue to keep from showing any reaction to Rick's ordeal. He knew that even the slightest smile would bring the wrath of Brother Simon down hard upon him.

The rest of the inspection went without incident. As soon as Brother Simon left, Rick rushed over to Howard.

"I know you're behind this," he hissed. "I won't forget this and I will get even!" He shook his fist in Howard's face. "Just you watch yourself."

"Now, Rick," Charlie spoke up. "Please, don't—"

"And you, too, MacCready. You aren't fooling me. I know you aren't as nice as everyone thinks. Just you wait." He turned around and stormed back to his cubicle to finish making his bed before class began.

"Howard," Gus said sheepishly. "Tell me you didn't do that."

Howard looked at Gus. "Don't defend him," he said. "Gus, he was trying to get you in trouble."

"I know," Gus sighed. "But we don't need to fight among ourselves. I mean, we have enough to handle dealing with Brother Simon and those jerks in Saint Peter dorm and the ghost in the attic keeping us up all night. We should be helping each other, not trying to get each other into trouble."

Howard nodded his head. "You're right," he admitted. "I'm sorry. Next time, I'll just let you get work crew." He said and walked off.

"That's not what I meant." Gus grabbed his books and hurried after him.

Charlie picked up his books and the letter he had written to himself. He looked at the address and smiled. "I'll find out who is taking my mail," he said to himself and headed for the mailbox on his way to class.

"Another letter to your grandmother?" Howard asked as he waited for Charlie outside their homeroom door.

"No." Charlie shook his head. "It's a little test. Somebody's been taking my mail. A few weeks ago, I talked to my grandmother. She said that she's been writing me every week, but I haven't received any of her letters. So, I've written myself a letter. I should get it back in a couple days. If I don't, then I know someone here has been taking my mail. If I do, then it has to be someone at her end."

"What a great idea," Howard answered. "You're so smart."

"Well, let's just see if it works first," Charlie said as he took his seat. "I have to stake out the mail slots for the next couple days."

"Speaking of stake out, what about the attic?" Howard

asked.

Charlie looked at him in surprise. "I thought you were through with that?"

"Well, I was but the noise every night is getting on my nerves," Howard said. "Did you hear him last night?"

Charlie nodded. He did hear it. In fact, every night since the day Brother Simon became their dorm prefect, the wailing seemed to have become louder.

"So?" Howard asked.

"So what?" Charlie shrugged.

"Are we going to stake out the attic?" Howard whispered.

"No," Charlie answered. "We are not. It's too risky, remember?"

"I know, I know." Howard rolled his eyes. "But I really think it's time we put our plan into action. We need to stake out the attic tonight. I've been keeping track and the ghost has been at it every night around one o'clock in the morning. Brother Simon is sure to be in bed by then so we'll be safe."

"Howard, I don't think that is such a good idea. Not with the enemy you made with Rick this morning. If he catches wind of our plans, we're in big trouble. He'll tell Brother Simon for sure."

Howard thought for a moment. It was true. Rick did have it out for them. "Okay," he relented.

The bell rang and Howard and Charlie both opened their books.

~§~

The dormitory was dark except for the light from the moon that shone through the windows. Charlie lay quietly listening to the night. He looked over at the clock on Howard's nightstand.

One o'clock, it said. Suddenly there was a thud from the attic. The ghost had returned right on time to begin his moaning yet again. Charlie waited but the noises didn't begin. He looked over at Howard, who was fast asleep.

The morning bell rang and Charlie opened his eyes. When did he fall asleep? He rolled over and looked at Howard's clock again, six o'clock? He climbed out of his bed and quickly showered.

"Did you hear it last night?" Howard asked as Charlie dressed.

"No," he admitted. "I mean, I heard him up there but then I must have fallen asleep. Was he loud?"

"I'll say." Howard shook his head. "I thought for sure he was going to wake Brother Simon this time. Charlie, we have to do something. One of us has to stake out the attic and find out who is doing this once and for all."

Charlie looked at Howard as he finished buttoning his cassock. He knew that Howard was right; but three hours of work crew on a Saturday afternoon for being out of bed, he was not sure that Howard could survive it.

"Look, Howard, Rick still has it out for you. You can't risk it."

"Oh, who cares about Rick?" Howard scoffed and threw his surplice over his head. "I don't," he answered as he stuck his arms through the sleeves.

"Well, what about spending your Saturday afternoon in the orchards with the Brothers?" Charlie reminded him.

"I can live with that," Howard fired back without hesitation.

"Can you?" Charlie asked and looked at him suspiciously.

Howard turned back to his locker and ran a comb through his hair. Charlie was right. Saturdays were not much fun spent working all afternoon. Even when the weather was nice out it was still work.

"Howard, I'll do it alone," Charlie whispered. "But you have to keep an eye out for Rick. If he hears about this then we're in big trouble."

Howard looked at Charlie. He nodded and smiled. "Deal," he agreed.

It wasn't until after inspection that Charlie remembered his letter. He quickly grabbed his books and hurried down the stairs. He made it just in time to see Brother John sort the mail into the many slots. He watched with anticipation. "It has to be here," he whispered to himself as he crouched out of the sight of the boys that huddled around the monk. Charlie searched the crowd. Sure enough, there were Dougary and his brood. Charlie looked at his mail slot. It was there, the letter. Now all he had to do was watch.

Brother John finished his sorting and headed up the stairs as the crowd gathered around the mailboxes. For a moment Charlie's view was blocked as Brother John paused on the steps as though he just remembered he had forgotten something, but then he continued on his way. When Charlie looked at his mail slot, the letter was gone. Dougary and his three goons were still huddled in front the boxes. He watched them.

"What are you doing back here?" Howard asked as he and Gus walked up behind Charlie.

Charlie jumped and let out a yell that echoed up and down the hallway. He spun around. His heart pounded in his chest.

"Don't sneak up on me like that I was watching the mail slots." He gasped for air. "My letter showed up today and someone took it. I think it was Dougary or one of his goons," he whispered.

"Well, didn't you see?" Howard asked.

"No," Charlie sighed and gave him a disgusted look. "Brother John was blocking my view."

"What's this all about?" Gus asked as he looked at the two of them.

"Someone's been stealing Charlie's mail, remember?" Howard answered. "Hey," he said as he remembered that Gus was once a member of Saint Peter dorm. "You wouldn't happen to know if one of Dougary's gang is stealing Charlie's mail, would you?"

Gus thought for a moment. There was something he had seen. He tried harder to remember. Then suddenly it came back to him. He recalled an incident once when he had walked up on all of them, and they suddenly quit talking. He thought that Dougary had given Austin something but he wasn't sure. What he did know was that Austin acted strangely, as though he was hiding something behind his back. He told them what he remembered.

"That's it then," Howard said confidently. "They are stealing your mail."

Charlie shook his head. "We can't be certain. We need more proof."

"Just go to the Abbot and tell him. He'll search their dorm and find the missing mail," Howard said as the three headed for their class.

"They wouldn't keep that sort of thing lying around." Charlie shook his head again. "No, we have to be more creative." A grin spread across his lips as a plan began to form in his mind. "I'm getting an idea. But I'll need Rick's help."

"Oh, that'll take some doing," Gus said. "He's not exactly speaking with the two of you, you know."

"But he *is* speaking to you." Charlie smiled.

Gus looked at Charlie and then at Howard. He didn't like

the look in their eyes. This was going to be tricky, his getting Rick's help for them without Rick knowing.

"When is Rick going home for the weekend again?" Charlie asked as they took their seats in Brother Simon's World Cultures class.

"I think this weekend," Gus said after he thought for a moment.

"Good because I need him to buy me something. We'll talk later," Charlie said, just as the bell rang to begin class.

That afternoon, Charlie met with Howard and Gus in their dorm and went over his plan. Gus agreed to ask Rick if he would pick up the needed things, but added it wouldn't be easy.

"Rick will want to know why I want the stuff, and what is in it for him." Gus told them.

"Tell Rick that you're planning to booby trap Howard's nightstand with it to pay him back for what he did to him." Charlie smiled, pleased with how quickly he had thought up a cover.

Howard looked at Charlie. "Hey, let's not give him any ideas now."

"That's perfect," Gus agreed. "He'll buy that. I'll talk to him after dinner."

Charlie handed over the last bit of money his grandmother had given him just before her letters stopped. He was saving it for the day when he would be allowed to go to town, but that didn't seem likely to happen in the near future. Steve had told him that eighth graders were not allowed to leave the hilltop, even if they were Altar Boys.

Gus reported back to Charlie and Howard just before lights out that evening. "Mission accomplished. Rick agreed to do it."

"Well, I just hope he doesn't get the idea to actually booby trap my nightstand thanks to your plan," Howard said as he climbed into his bed.

"He won't," Charlie tried to assure him. However, he wasn't totally sure himself. He climbed into his bed and turned to look out the window. It didn't take long for him to fall asleep.

The rest of the week seemed to drag by for Charlie. He couldn't wait until the weekend was over, and Rick was back with the things he'd asked for. Every day that passed meant another day without any word from his grandmother. He just knew that Dougary was behind the missing letters, and he was anxious to prove it.

Finally, the weekend came and went. After classes Charlie, Howard, and Gus headed back to their dorm. Gus was dreading the final exams that were coming up in a few weeks, especially after Brother Simon told them all that they were sure to fail his test. He decided he better use his afternoon studying. Charlie and Howard paid no attention to Brother Simon's taunts. They were beat. They decided to spend the afternoon napping instead.

Rick checked to make sure that Charlie and Howard were asleep before he quietly tiptoed over to Gus's cubicle. He hid the small brown paper sack under his surplice just in case someone should see him.

"Pssst, Gus," he whispered as he stood at the foot of Gus' bed.

Gus turned around in his chair as he sat at his old desk. Since he didn't have a bunkmate, he was permitted to put a desk in his cubicle.

"What?" he asked.

"I have the stuff you asked for," Rick said quietly.

With everything that had gone on in class that day, Gus had forgotten about the things he had asked Rick to buy. He quickly stood up.

"Charlie," he called.

"What?" Rick looked at Gus in shock and tried to quiet him.

"What?" Charlie said as he walked around the partition still rubbing the sleep from his eyes.

"Rick has the stuff you asked for," Gus said.

"Wait a minute. I thought you said this was for you?" Rick said, and threw the paper sack on Gus' bed.

Gus' mouth dropped open. He had done it again. He had blown the secret. He looked at Charlie, and then at Rick, and could not think of a way out of his mess.

"Rick," Charlie spoke up. "It's not Gus's fault. I asked him if he would do it. Someone has been stealing my mail and I wanted the stuff to set a trap for that person."

Rick looked at Charlie and then at Gus. His lips were pursed in anger as all his thoughts of getting even with Howard disappeared.

"Fine," he said in a huff and turned his back on them.

"Rick," Howard spoke up. He had been lying on his bed, listening to what was happening on the other side of the partition.

Rick turned around and folded his arms over his chest defiantly.

Howard jumped to his feet and walked over to him. "I just wanted to apologize for trashing your bed and getting you in trouble. I'll go to Brother Simon and tell him that I did it if it'll make us all friends again."

"You would do that?" Rick challenged him warily.

"Yes, I would. I will," Howard said matter-of-factly and nodded his head.

"Then do it. Right now." Rick ordered smugly.

Charlie watched Howard head for the door. He turned to Rick, who appeared to be gloating, thinking of the trouble

Howard would be in.

"Rick!" he shouted. "What's the matter with you? Howard, come back here," he called.

Howard stopped and turned around. He returned to the group.

"What do you mean, what's the matter with me?" Rick became indignant. "He's the one responsible for my having work crew. Why shouldn't he get into trouble?"

"Because, it's not the right thing to do," Charlie answered. "What about forgive and forget? Turn the other cheek? He apologized. Isn't that enough?"

"No!" Rick snapped. "I want him to pay. I want revenge—" The word echoed in the dorm like a resounding bell. Rick froze. He looked at the floor and thought about what Charlie said. "I suppose you are right," he mumbled.

"Thank you," Charlie smiled. "Friends?" He held out his hand to Rick.

Rick sheepishly took it. "Friends," he said and nodded. He then shook Howard's hand and Gus's just for good measure.

"So, would you like to help me find out who is stealing my mail?" Charlie asked.

"Why not?" Rick shrugged. "I've already bought the stuff you asked for." He smiled playfully. Actually, he liked being included again in their sleuthing, but he would never admit it.

The four huddled around as Charlie explained his idea in a hushed whisper.

"Great idea." Rick nodded.

"Thanks. Now, I figure tonight after dinner I'll put it all together and then drop it in the mail downstairs. That should mean we should stake out the mail slots two days from now."

"Good." Howard nodded. "We'll be ready."

That night after dinner Charlie hurried back to his bed. He

looked around to be sure no one was lurking about as he pulled out the brown paper sack from under his mattress. He carefully took out his writing tablet and an envelope. He addressed the envelope to himself and then put as the return address his grandmother's address. After placing the stamp on it, he set it aside.

He picked up the paper sack and carefully emptied its contents onto the tablet on his lap. There was a single sheet of blue carbon paper, two small bottles of glitter and a bag of foil confetti. Charlie carefully lined up the carbon paper with a sheet of his stationary from his tablet. Then he folded the papers into a tight pocket in which he poured some glitter and confetti. Carefully he stuffed the pocket into the envelope and sealed it.

Howard walked up just as Charlie prepared to leave to mail his trap. He grinned fiendishly. "I sure hope this works."

"It has to," Charlie said. "Once Dougary pulls open the pocket, it will pop and shower him with the confetti and glitter. Then the carbon paper will get ink all over his hands, and we'll know it was him."

"He's gonna be so mad." Howard continued to grin. "You know, he'll probably get work crew for making a mess in the hall but he can't say anything because then he'll have to tell that he opened your mail."

"Either way." Charlie smiled proudly. "I win. It can't fail."

Charlie slipped the envelope into the outgoing mailbox and then met up with Gus for a game of checkers before lights out.

~§~

"I am so tired." Howard yawned as he and Charlie walked down the stairs after inspection two days later. "That noise in the attic last night was louder than I've ever heard it. It actually kept me awake."

"Me to," Charlie agreed and tried not to yawn but to no avail.

"When are you going to stake it out?" Howard whispered.

"Soon," Charlie said. "Brother Simon isn't doing his rounds as often during the night, so I may be able to sneak out."

"Good!" Howard breathed. "I don't know how much more of this I can take."

Gus was waiting in place at the foot of the stairs as Howard took his place beside him. They had a clear view of Charlie's mail slot. Charlie and Rick hid where they could get a view from above.

Right on time, Brother John showed up with his mailbag, followed closely by Dougary and his gang. They kept pleading with Brother John to let them do the mail sorting but Brother John flatly refused. They stayed back and waited and watched.

Brother John's hands moved quickly as he dispensed the mail. Charlie didn't see that his letter had arrived. He watched as Brother John placed the larger mail on the shelf above the slots. He secretly wished that one day he would receive such a package. Rick gently nudged him in the side and brought his mind back to the present.

As Brother John left a swarm of boys flooded the stairwell. Rick stretched his neck to try to see around the boys but gave up with a sigh.

"I can't see a thing," he said bitterly.

"Neither can I," Charlie admitted. "Maybe Howard and Gus are able to see."

As the boys began to thin out and headed for their classes, Rick let out a gasp.

"It's gone!"

Charlie looked and smiled fiendishly. "Now, all we have

to do is watch Dougary. He'll open it eventually."

The two proceeded down the stairs to their class. At the foot of the stairs Howard and Gus stepped forward.

"I'm sorry, we didn't see a thing," Gus admitted.

"Neither did we," Rick shrugged.

"That's okay. The trap is set, we just have to wait, that's all," Charlie assured them.

As the four walked into Brother Simon's World Cultures class, Charlie felt great. He looked Dougary in the eyes and smirked. He barely even glanced at Larry, Travis and Austin as he walked in front of them to take his seat. No longer was he tired. He caught his second wind.

"What's his problem?" Dougary whispered as he leaned toward Larry.

Larry shrugged. "I don't have a clue." He looked at Charlie and wiped the tiny beads of sweat from his forehead.

Brother Simon was unusually agitated during class. During his lecture he kept looking at Charlie and Howard with his usual glare. But there was something unusual about his appearance. The circles under his eyes were darker, as though he hadn't slept in a long time, Charlie thought to himself. He wondered if Howard had noticed too. He glanced at Howard.

Howard's head was beginning to bob as his eyes slowly shut. Charlie quickly looked at Brother Simon. Too late, he had noticed Howard too. Slowly he folded his arms over his chest as he continued to lecture and watch Howard.

Charlie looked back at Howard. Howard was gone. His eyes were shut. His head was bowed. His breathing was slow. Charlie looked back at Brother Simon.

"Master Miller!" his voice thundered. "Are you sleeping in my class?"

Howard instantly sat up straight in his chair. His eyes wide open and alert behind his black rimmed glasses.

"Just checking my eye lids for pin holes, Brother," Howard retorted.

The class burst into laughter to which Brother Simon fumed even more.

"Silence!" he shouted. "I will see you after class, Master Miller."

The bell rang and signaled the end of the class. Charlie took his time gathering his books. He looked up at Howard who walked up to Brother Simon's desk. Brother Simon had taken his seat.

"So, what is the idea sleeping in class? And I'm not in the mood for your jokes." Brother Simon began.

"I'm sorry, Brother," Howard apologized. "I just couldn't sleep last night. You see there is this ghost in the attic that keeps making noise at night. Last—"

Brother Simon slapped his hands on the top of his desk with a loud bang that caused Howard to jump back.

"There is no such thing!" he said angrily. "I am aware of the rumors and stories. They are about as funny as your jokes. I suggest you do more sleeping at night and less snooping about. Now, get out of here!"

Howard nodded and quickly left the room, followed closely by Charlie. Brother Simon wiped the sweat from his forehead and tried to calm his shaking hands. His teeth were clenched tight as he watched the boys leave his classroom.

"I can't believe you didn't get work crew," Charlie said, shaking his head as they hurried to their next class. "I thought you were in for it for sure."

"I know," Howard agreed. "I was sweating it. But did you see Brother Simon's reaction when I mentioned the ghost?"

"Couldn't miss it." Charlie nodded. "Do you think he heard

it too?"

Howard shrugged. "Don't know. I must have struck some nerve with him though. Just wish I knew what it was that did it."

Their conversation died as they entered Sister Regina's classroom and met up with Rick and Gus.

"That was a good one, Howard," Rick said and chuckled lightly to himself. "Checking your eyelids for pin holes, where did you come up with that?"

"Don't know." Howard shook his head. He placed his books on his desk and sat down in his chair.

"So, how long do you think before Dougary opens your letter?" Gus asked and changed the subject.

"I don't know," Charlie admitted. "But one thing, when he does, we will know about it."

The four laughed at the thought and took their seats as Sister Regina walked into the room.

For the rest of the day, Charlie kept an ear open to see if anyone was talking about his letter. There was nothing. Not even a faint whisper. All through dinner, Charlie stared at Dougary and his goons. They laughed and jabbed each other and were as obnoxious as always.

After dinner Charlie returned to his dorm, to his cubicle, to his bed. He didn't feel too much like talking with anyone. His perfect trap had failed.

Howard walked over to his bed and sat down. He knew that Charlie was depressed over not finding out who had taken his letter.

"Don't worry about it," he said, trying to sound lighthearted. "Just because he didn't open it right away doesn't mean anything. Maybe he's waiting until lights out so he can open it privately." Howard began to chuckle. "Just think about the look on Dougary's face when a shower of confetti erupts from the pocket all over him and the floor. I just hope Dougary doesn't notice the carbon paper and goes to bed with ink on his hands. So much for his white sheets. It could still work," he tried to sound encouraging.

"I don't care anymore," Charlie sighed and stared up at the ceiling. It was a lie but he didn't want to talk about the letter anymore. "Do you think our visitor will be back tonight?" he changed the subject.

Howard looked up at the ceiling and shrugged. "He's been here every night for the last six months, why should tonight be any different?"

"True," Charlie agreed.

"So, are you going to stake it out?" Howard whispered.

Charlie didn't answer. He didn't want Howard to be involved in case he was caught; but that was what he was thinking about. Tonight, would be the night he would do it. First, he would have to wait until everyone was asleep and then for Brother Simon to make his rounds. That usually happened at ten forty-five. Then he would slip out of the dorm and up to the attic quietly.

It didn't take long for the sounds of sleep to fill the dorm. Charlie was wide awake as he lay in his bed. Like clockwork, Brother Simon arrived on time to make his rounds. Charlie closed his eyes and pretended to be asleep as Brother Simon passed by. Once he heard the sound of the dormitory doors close, he opened his eyes. He glanced over at Howard who was already fast asleep. By morning, he would have solved the mystery about the ghost in the attic, and would tell Howard all about it.

Charlie lay awake in his bed and stared up at the ceiling. He wondered which of the monks he would see up there. Did he know him already? At midnight, Charlie quietly crept from his bed. Quietly he put his ear to the door and listened before he opened them and slipped out into the hall. The light in Brother Simon's room was out. He gave a silent sigh of relief and headed for the attic.

Charlie crouched behind a stack of boxes across from the dormer window. The attic was dark except for the light of the moon that shone in through the half-moon windows. With no clock in sight, time seemed to pass slowly. Charlie began to tire while waiting.

Suddenly there was a creaking sound from the monastery wing. Charlie was wide awake. From his hiding place he couldn't see but he heard the sound of footsteps drawing closer. Charlie pulled back into the shadows more.

Brother Simon carefully made his way around the darkened dorm. He kept the beam of his flashlight low and toward the floor. The flashlight emitted just enough light for him to keep from bumping into the partitions and beds. He clenched his teeth as he inspected each bed. He swung the flashlight beam quickly over Charlie's bed and then over Howard's, then froze. He turned back to Charlie's bed shining the light on it.

"Master Miller," he spoke in a hushed voice. "Howard, wake up!"

Howard turned over and opened his eyes. "Wha—?"

"Where's Master MacCready?" Brother Simon asked.

"Who?" Howard asked still half-asleep. He glanced over at Charlie's empty bed. "I don't know. Maybe he went to the restroom."

Just then the faint sounds of moaning drifted down from

the attic above Charlie's bed. Brother Simon shone the light at the ceiling and Howard saw the color drain from the monk's pale face.

"What's that?" Brother Simon asked.

"That's the ghost in the attic," Howard answered with a groan, still half asleep.

"There's no such thing," Brother Simon snapped. "I bet that is your little friend's idea of a joke."

Howard suddenly remembered the stake out and sat up in his bed, wide awake.

~§~

Charlie stared across the attic at the figure of a man dressed in the robes of a monk. The hood attached to his scapular was pulled up over his head, hiding his face from view. Even so, he was still too big to be Brother Tobias, Charlie thought as he studied the figure. Perhaps it's Jeffrey. Suddenly Charlie felt pangs of sympathy for the man. It wasn't his fault. It was an accident. Slowly he stood up. Cautiously he approached the hooded monk from behind.

"Excuse me," Charlie said softly so as not to scare the monk.

The man suddenly quit his crying and spun around, standing straight up. The moonlight flashed across his face. Charlie took a step back. He recognized the round face, the dark piercing eyes.

"I know who you are! You aren't supposed to be here," Charlie snapped at the monk. "If Abbot Ambrose finds out you're in for big trouble."

The man lunged at Charlie and grabbed his arms. He spun Charlie around, trapping him in the dormer.

"Well, he's not going to find out, is he?" the man said, and removed his hood.

"You don't scare me, Mr. Duggan. I know all about you and what you did to Jeffrey," Charlie said boldly. "And I will tell the Abbot you have been up here." Charlie faked as though he were going to run toward the right of Franklyn but darted left.

Franklyn bought the trick and Charlie slipped past him. But Franklyn's long arms grabbed Charlie. He lifted him off the floor and threw him back into the dormer. Charlie flew through the air and landed hard on the floor next to the window. His foot kicked the glass and the window shattered, showering bits of glass below.

Brother Simon was just about to leave when the crying stopped. He cocked his head and listened. Howard did the same. The heavy sound of something hitting the floor brought Howard to his feet.

"He's up there with Jeffrey," Howard admitted as he grabbed for his robe.

"What?" Brother Simon asked, and looked at Howard.

"Jeffrey, the boy in the attic forty years ago," Howard explained. "We found out he became a monk. We think he's the one making the noises in the attic."

Brother Simon was just about to say something when there came another loud thud, then the sound of shattering glass. Brother Simon's face grew even paler as he saw the rain of broken glass pass by Charlie's window.

"Oh my God," he shouted as he started out of the dorm. "Master Miller, get the Abbot. Hurry!" he shouted as he left the dorm.

Gus and Rick were to their feet and met Howard at the doors.

"What is going on?" Rick asked.

"Where's Charlie?" Gus added.

"He's in the attic. I think Jeffrey may be trying to throw him out of the window. We have to get the Abbot." Howard said quickly as he headed for the monastery wing followed closely by Rick and Gus.

~§~

Charlie moved quickly away from the shattered window. The cold night air blew in and he shivered. His thin robe and pajamas were not warm enough against the night air.

"I should've known you would be just like your father, a little rat!" Franklyn sneered.

"You don't know my father," Charlie fired back at him. "He would never have anything to do with the likes of someone like you."

"Oh, I know him," Franklyn laughed smugly. "In fact, I'll never forget him, Patrick MacCready. His parents died when he was just a kid. He was here when I came to the Seminary. We were both members of Saint Peter dormitory, and friends. That is, until he ratted me out about locking Jeffrey up here overnight. Never mind that he went along with Hertz and me in tormenting the fool kid all night, but I got the blame for the whole thing.

"But that doesn't matter now," he said as he stepped closer to Charlie. "Because now I get my revenge."

"That's enough," a deep voice said from the shadows.

Franklyn lunged. Charlie pulled away and lost his balance. He screamed as he began to fall backwards out of the window.

Then something or someone grabbed his legs and stopped his fall. The back of his head hit the brick wall hard. He was still.

Franklyn had grabbed Charlie's ankles and held them against the floor. Charlie was now hanging upside down out of the window from his knees. Franklyn looked over his shoulder at the monk in the shadows.

"Don't take another step, Jeffrey or I'll drop him," he yelled.

Charlie's mind was a blur. His head hurt and his ears pounded with each beat of his heart. In the moonlight he could see the roof of the portico three stories below. Fear swept through him. He could feel that someone had a tight grip around his ankles, pressing them to the attic floor, but he was still frightened. At any moment the person, whether it was Franklyn or the voice in the shadows, could release his grip and he would plummet to his death, just as Joseph had.

"You don't want to do that," Jeffrey said nervously. His mind flashed back to that morning forty years ago. He was so frightened. He didn't mean to hurt Joseph but his fear had blinded him. He couldn't remember what he thought but when it was over, he crept over to the broken window and looked down. There he saw Father Anselm cradling Joseph's bloody body while looking up at him. He pulled himself away from the window in shock.

"It was your fault that boy died, not mine," Franklyn snapped at him.

"Yes. It was my fault," he admitted. "And I have had to live with that guilt ever since. If you hurt that boy now, you will have to live with that for the rest of your life. You don't really want that, do you?"

"But his father ruined my life," Franklyn choked, as he remembered the years of slaving for the VonDuggans on their farm.

"But you were adopted," Jeffrey reminded him. "You had a family, a home."

"No!" Franklyn yelled. "We were not a family. They didn't love me. They just wanted a slave, someone to help them with their farm. Mrs. VonDuggan never loved me like the mother I always wanted. She wouldn't even let me call her mom. I worked hard for them, from sun up to sunset, every day. And for what? To get to eat the scraps left over after they ate. To sleep on the floor of a tiny room in their basement with only a blanket. I didn't have any friends. I wished it would've been me that died that day."

"But you married and have a son," Jeffrey reminded him.

"Oh yes." Franklyn laughed. "An arranged marriage to a girl I hardly knew. She doesn't love me, just the money I inherited when the VonDuggans died. She doesn't even love the boy. That's why she travels all of the time. She only loves to spend that money."

"But why do this?" Jeffrey asked. "The boy didn't hurt you."

"His father did, that's why." Franklyn snapped.

Charlie gasped as he felt the grip on his ankles loosen for a moment. Tears began to fill his eyes as his fear was gripping him tighter, but he forced them back. He wished his mother and father were there to save him. He silently began to pray.

"I want to hurt him like he hurt me. I want him to suffer," Franklyn hissed.

"His father is dead, Franklyn. You can't hurt him." Jeffrey shook his head.

"His father is not dead!" Franklyn yelled. "You're lying!"

"No. I'm not lying," Jeffrey answered nervously. He feared at any moment that Franklyn would let go of Charlie's legs and history would repeat itself right before him. "I spoke to his uncle the day I picked him up from his grandmother's. Patrick and his wife are both dead," he said as he stepped out of the shadows.

Franklyn looked at Jeffrey, and suddenly his eyes focused on the monk standing before him, at the thin gaunt features of his face, at his white hair. They were no longer boys.

Franklyn turned toward the window and leaned forward.

"Give me your hand," he said to Charlie as he took a hand from Charlie's ankle and reached for him.

Charlie panicked and gave a yell as he felt himself slip. He looked up and saw the hand reaching out to him and he grabbed it. With a swift yank, Charlie was safely back in the attic. Franklyn looked at Charlie and waved his hand as though shooing him away.

Brother Simon smiled and held out his hands to Charlie. Charlie ran the few steps to him and hugged him. Brother Simon hugged him back.

"I was so scared," Charlie admitted. "But I didn't cry."

"It's okay, Charlie." Brother Simon hugged him and sighed with relief. "Thank God you're safe."

"Yes, thank heaven," Abbot Ambrose breathed a sigh of relief as he stepped from the shadows with two policemen behind him.

Charlie looked over to him and eased his hold on Brother Simon. Brother Simon immediately straightened his back and tucked his hands under his robes. Abbot Ambrose smiled at him knowingly, and then turned to Franklyn.

"As for you," he said coldly. "I told you never to come back here. I was hoping you would put all that happened behind you. Now, it's out of my hands. What you did tonight was nothing short of attempted murder."

The policemen immediately took Franklyn into custody.

Franklyn didn't resist or say another word. Obediently he walked between them to the waiting police car outside.

"Let's get out of here," Abbot Ambrose said. "I'll have Brother Gregory board up that window tomorrow morning. And we'll have Brother James look at your head, you're bleeding, son."

Brother Simon quietly escorted Charlie to Brother James's room. Even though he was tired, Brother James graciously washed and treated the cut and bump on the back of Charlie's head.

"You'll be fine," he said as they left his room.

Charlie suddenly felt nervous as he walked in front of Brother Simon. Not only was he caught out of bed but also in the attic. He feared what his punishment would be. How many hours of work crew would that all add up to? He glanced over his shoulder at Brother Simon.

Brother Simon had returned to his cold stern self. His face was expressionless, void of all the emotion he'd shown just moments ago.

"Go straight to bed, Charlie," he said as they returned to the student wing. "We'll talk in the morning."

"Yes, Brother," Charlie said sheepishly.

As Charlie opened the door Howard, Gus and Rick rushed to him. Howard threw his arms around his best friend and hugged him.

"You're okay," he said. "I was so scared when I saw the glass fall. What happened?"

Just then Brother Simon walked into the dorm. Gus, Rick, and Howard all gasped.

"It's time for bed, boys. You can talk in the morning," he said and nodded to them.

They did not have to be told twice. They quickly returned

to their beds. Charlie lay in his bed and turned toward the window. Quietly he began to cry as the reality of what had just happened to him slowly sank in.

JEFFREY

A cool spring breeze blew through the trees as Brother Simon walked with Charlie through the monastery garden. The morning sun cast long shadows from the statues that lined the path. The well-tended flowerbeds in full bloom with their brilliant colored flowers and green lawns were even more beautiful than the front grounds.

"How are you this morning?" Brother Simon asked as they walked.

Charlie took a deep breath of fresh air and thought about what had happened the night before; about what Franklyn said to him about his father. He was so confused.

"I'm okay, I guess," he answered. "My head is a little sore, though."

"Yes, I imagine it is." Brother Simon nodded. For some reason he felt nervous around Charlie, much the same way he feels around Brother Tobias. "Charlie, do you remember what was said last night?" he asked.

"Well, I'm a bit confused about some of the things that Mr. Duggan said," Charlie began slowly. "He said he and my father were dorm mates. He said that my father was one of the boys that locked Jeffrey in the attic. He called my father a rat because my father told on him. He's lying."

Brother Simon took a deep breath and held it as he debated on whether or not to say what he was thinking.

"Charlie," he said in a kind voice. "How much do you know of your father?"

Charlie stopped for a moment. It seemed strange but he never really thought about what he actually knew of his father. In his absence, he imagined his father was a great man; a fearless man who was strong and brave yet who was gentle and kind and loved by all. He never really stopped to think of his father being a boy like him.

"To tell you the truth," he said and started walking along the path again. "I don't really know anything about him. My grandparents never talked about him, or my mom, for that matter. My grandma says it's safer that way if I didn't know too much."

"Charlie," he hesitated. "Franklyn was telling you the truth. Your father and he were friends and they did lock Jeffrey in the attic that night."

"No!" Charlie shouted and stopped walking. "It's not true!" He covered his ears with has shaking hands.

Brother Simon turned around to face him on the path. He looked at the monastery in the distance and then up at the leaf covered tree branches over his head. He looked at the boy in front of him; a boy who was about the same age as he was that night so many years ago.

"It is true, Charlie," he spoke softly, taking Charlie's hands from covering his ears. "I know because, I'm Jeffrey."

Charlie looked at Brother Simon in shock. His eyes filled with tears. "No. He couldn't have been so mean," Charlie choked and shook his head.

"No, he wasn't mean or cruel," Brother Simon agreed. "He was just a typical boy. He never meant to hurt me, or anyone else for that matter. We actually became friends after the incident. He looked out for me. He was a good person, Charlie."

Charlie thought about what Brother Simon said. It was good to finally hear about his father, but the news was hard at the same time. He looked at the flowerbeds and tried to understand.

"But did he really tell on Franklyn, I mean, Mr. Duggan?" Charlie asked. His voice was a mere whisper.

"Yes," he nodded. "But it wasn't totally as cold as it seems. The prefect of Saint Peter turned the three boys over to the Abbot. The Abbot talked to all of them, but only your father and a boy named Ted Collins would admit to it, and were truly sorry. Franklyn and another boy showed no signs of remorse, and even blamed the Abbot for not locking the attic doors. He brought his troubles on himself."

Charlie listened quietly. His thoughts kept going over every detail about his father.

"Do you have any pictures of him?" he asked. "Of my father?"

Brother Simon thought for a moment. His mind flashed back to what Abbot Ambrose had instructed him to do, about the trunk in the attic.

"I'm afraid I don't," he answered and frowned a bit more than his usual frown.

"I thought not." Charlie nodded.

They resumed their walking along the path. The scent of roses filled the air as they passed by the rose garden corner. Brother Simon rubbed his hands together nervously.

"Charlie," he said with a slight quiver in his voice. "I heard about your ghost hunt."

Charlie didn't look at Brother Simon. He felt a bit embarrassed by it all now.

"So, I suppose you're going to tell Howard and the boys about—" he paused and looked at Charlie.

Charlie looked at Brother Simon. With everything that happened, he hadn't thought about what he would actually tell the guys.

"I guess it'll come out sooner or later." Brother Simon shrugged and started walking again.

Charlie followed him quietly. His thoughts now turned to what to do about the things he'd learned. His whole purpose was to prove to Howard, Gus and Rick that there was no ghost in the attic. He had to tell them something.

"There's one other thing," Brother Simon said as their walk in the garden neared its end. "I just want you to know, the reason I'm so strict with you boys is because I don't want what happened to me, the teasing and the jokes, to happen to any of you. Boys are cruel. Any sign of weakness and they will use it against you. That's all," he said and walked away.

Charlie stood for a moment in shock. He had always thought of Brother Simon as cold and heartless but this changed everything. He headed back to Saint Nicholas' dorm.

Just as he turned the corner in the stairwell, he ran into Dougary and his gang. Dougary's eyes instantly narrowed in an angry glare.

"You have a lot of nerve showing your face around here," he hissed. "Or are you just stupid?"

Charlie rolled his eyes and quietly sighed. Of all the people in the school, Dougary was the last person he wanted to run into today.

"You won't get away with it. My father has money and

good lawyers. He'll get out of jail, just you watch. In the meantime, you'll pay for what you did. You won't know how or when, but I'll get even with you."

"Yeah, Abbot's pet," Larry spoke up. "You may have him fooled but not us. You're toast."

"I'm actually looking forward to rearranging your face," Travis said and held up his fist. "You don't know who you're messing with."

Charlie looked at Austin expecting him to add to the threats, but Austin looked away. His hands were shoved deep into his jeans pockets and his shoulders were raised as though he were trying not to be seen. Charlie turned back to Dougary.

"You don't scare me," he said and walked past them.

Dougary seethed even more. He spun around and watched Charlie ascend the stairs. "You should be!" he yelled and waved his fist at him.

The hall was quiet on the fourth floor as Charlie headed toward his dorm. Surely by now everyone had heard some bits of news about what happened, he thought. Maybe that was why there was no one around? Charlie really didn't mind. It felt nice to have it quiet. He could think better that way.

He opened the door to Saint Nicholas and walked into the dorm. He glanced at Rick's cubicle. He was already gone for the weekend. Good, he thought to himself. He spotted Gus reading a comic book in one of the overstuffed chairs. He didn't look up as Charlie passed by him.

Howard sat up on his bed as Charlie lay down on his. He looked at Charlie, who appeared to be ignoring him.

"Well?" Howard said and waited for Charlie to fill in the blanks.

Charlie looked at Howard. "Well, what?"

"Oh, come on Charlie," Howard sighed disgustedly. "You

know perfectly well what. What happened up there last night?"

Charlie was just about to speak when Steve walked up. Howard and Charlie both looked at him in surprise.

"Can it," Steve said anticipating their comments. "I just came in here to tell you that Father Abbot wants to see you, Charlie. He's out on the front grounds. You shouldn't keep him waiting."

"Okay." Charlie nodded and stood up. "We'll talk later."

Charlie hurried out of the dorm after Steve. He was grateful to Steve for interrupting them. He still hadn't made up his mind what to tell them about what happened the night before. His mind was still trying to sort out everything he heard and what Brother Simon just told him that morning.

As he walked out the front door of the Abbey, he spotted Abbot Ambrose immediately. He was seated on a bench under a weeping cherry tree that was filled with cherry blossoms. He hurried over the lawn toward the garden oasis. His mind was too numb to think what the Abbot wanted to see to him about, and he was too numb to be nervous.

Abbot Ambrose looked up and smiled as Charlie walked up.

"Charlie, thank you for coming. Please sit down," he invited, patting the bench beside him.

Charlie sat down next to the Abbot.

"Charlie, I've been informed about Howard and your antics," he began as he stared at the pond in front of them. "It was bound to happen sooner or later. I mean that one of the boys would start asking questions about what happened to Joseph. But never did I ever think it would result in what happened last night. Charlie, it can be a dangerous thing digging into other peoples' pasts. Not everyone wants to be reminded about the things they did when they were young." He turned and looked at Charlie. "Are you okay, son?"

Charlie looked up. "I'm okay, I guess," he said, and shrugged his shoulders.

"That's good." Abbot Ambrose nodded. "You don't have to worry about Mr. Duggan coming around here again. The police told me this morning that he was committed to the state mental hospital. It will be quite a while before he's released."

"How did he get up here without anyone noticing?" Charlie asked.

"From what the police have pieced together, he would follow the road up the hill, staying near the forest's edge so he could hide quickly if someone drove by. As a matter of fact, he was in the forest on the day you arrived. He immediately recognized you as being Patrick's son, and it only took talking with Master Duggan to confirm it. That's when he hatched his plan. Every night after lights out, Master Duggan would slip down the stairs to the back door and let his father in. Mr. Duggan stole one of the Brother's habits from the laundry to disguise himself with so that he wouldn't be spotted in the Abbey. From there it was just up to the attic to put his sick plan into action.

"I am so sorry you had to go through all of that and I'm sorry you had to learn about your father that way," Abbot Ambrose sighed and looked over at Charlie again. "It was a very difficult time for all of us, but you have to know this, your father was a good man. He had a kind heart, Charlie. He never meant any harm to Jeffrey. He had no way of knowing that this stunt of theirs would turn out the way it did.

"He spent the rest of his days with us watching over Kenny and Jeffrey. And only after they both joined the monastery did he set out to make a life for himself."

"As for Jeffrey and Kenny, they have tried to put the whole incident behind them. They have tried to move on. It was Master

Duggan who had scared Gus with the ghost story. He prompted Gus to talk to Brother Tobias about it. Brother Tobias reinforced the story to keep from having to answer a lot of questions about what had happened. When Brother Simon heard about it, he had words with Brother Tobias in the garage. That is what you almost witnessed on the day you and Howard used the tunnel to meet with him."

Charlie looked up at Abbot Ambrose in shock. His mouth dropped open.

Abbot Ambrose laughed and put his arm around Charlie's shoulders and gave him a hug. "Who do you think gave Howard the map of the tunnel?" he laughed.

"You did?" Charlie asked, shocked that Abbot Ambrose had known all along.

"Yes, son," he nodded. "I figured that it would help you get settled here. I had no idea it would turn out like this."

Charlie looked at the fish swimming in the pond and thought about Howard, Gus and Rick.

"What's on your mind, son?" Abbot Ambrose asked as he noticed the change in Charlie.

"I was just thinking about what to do," he said. "Howard, Gus and Rick want to know what happened last night."

"You haven't already told them?"

"No." Charlie shook his head.

"Why? Is there something wrong?"

Charlie looked at the Abbot for a moment and then back at the pond. The late morning sun shimmered across the ripples. He could see the rocks covered with algae on the bottom in the clear water.

"It is just that it was different when we found out that Brother Tobias was Kenny," Charlie began. "Sure, he was upset with us but we don't have that many dealings with him. But knowing that Brother Simon is Jeffrey and he's our prefect," Charlie paused as he thought about it. "It's just different. I'm afraid if they knew it would soon be all over the school and people would treat him differently."

"I see what you mean." Abbot Ambrose nodded thoughtfully. "So, do you have to tell them?"

Charlie looked at the Abbot. "I have to tell them something."

Abbot Ambrose nodded. "I suppose you're right. Well, you do have a problem but I'm sure you'll do the right thing when the time comes."

"Excuse me, Father Abbot," a novice interrupted them as he walked up.

Charlie looked at the young man and thought he didn't look that much older than eighteen. His blonde hair was cut short and he was clean-shaven. He was dressed in the cassock of the monks but his scapular did not have a hood.

"Father Abbot, your guest is waiting for you in your office," he said.

"Thank you, Dominic. Please show my guest to visitation room three. I'm having lunch sent there."

"Yes, Father," Dominic answered and hurried off to the Abbey.

"Well, son." Abbot Ambrose turned to Charlie. "There's someone I would like you to see. Come."

Charlie stood up and followed him back to the Abbey. He tried to think of who the Abbot's guest might be and why he would want him to see him.

They entered the main doors of the Abbey and then the student wing. The doors locked behind them. Abbot Ambrose led Charlie down the hall toward the visitation room. Suddenly Charlie remembered what had happened to Franklyn, how he was adopted out right away to a farmer and his wife. Panic swept over him and he froze. Abbot Ambrose turned to speak to him and noticed that Charlie was not by his side. He looked back and saw Charlie.

"What is it?" he asked. "Come here, son."

Charlie crept slowly closer to the Abbot. His eyes were wide with fear.

"What is it, Charlie?" he asked. "Why are you acting so strangely?"

"I'm sorry, Abbot Ambrose," he blurted. "I really am."

"Sorry? About what?" Abbot Ambrose was confused as he looked at Charlie.

"Please don't send me away." Charlie burst into tears. "I'm not an orphan. My parents will be looking for me. I don't want to leave. Please don't send me away."

Abbot Ambrose took Charlie by his shoulders and held him firmly.

"That's enough," he said. "Stop it, right now."

Charlie trembled as he tried to compose himself. He wiped the tears from his cheeks and took a shaky but deep breath.

"Charlie, no one is sending you away," he assured him. "You have a visitor. She is waiting for you. You will have lunch with her and she may be able to answer some of your questions."

Charlie was now more confused than ever. Who would be coming to see him? Could it be his mother? His fears were replaced by extreme nervousness. What would he say? How would he react to seeing her?

Abbot Ambrose opened the door to visitation room three and stepped inside. Charlie followed. The room was like all the others, warm, cozy and bright. The sunlight poured in through the tall window and reflected off the large mirror that hung above a brick fireplace. In front of the fireplace were two wingback chairs and a mahogany coffee table sat in front of them. A sofa faced the fireplace with its back toward them as they entered along the east wall.

A woman sat on the sofa, her back to them. The clean scent of Ivory soap and rose petals touched Charlie's nose and his heart leapt.

"Grandma!" he shouted and ran around to her.

Ophelia stood up, took him into her arms, and hugged him. She looked at Abbot Ambrose and smiled.

"Thank you, Dietrich," she said.

Charlie pulled away and looked at his grandmother.

"Grandma, his name is Father Abbot Ambrose," he whispered loudly.

Abbot Ambrose smiled. "That's okay, Ophelia." He nodded.

Ophelia looked at her grandson. "Charlie, Father Abbot is my brother, your great uncle."

Charlie looked at her in shock. He then looked at Abbot Ambrose. His mind was reeling again.

"We thought it best that you not know at first. We didn't want the other boys to think you were getting special treatment because your uncle is the Abbot," she explained.

"As you know, son, the boys already think you are my pet." Abbot Ambrose smiled.

"You know?" Charlie could not believe his ears.

"You will find, son, there is not much that goes on here that I don't know about. And I know how boys are. They can be very cruel at times," he explained.

"Forgive me?" Ophelia looked at Charlie.

Charlie smiled at her. "Yes, grandma."

"But Charlie," Abbot Ambrose spoke up. "You must not tell any of the boys about this. This is just between you, me and your grandmother. It's very important the other boys do not know. Understood?"

"Yes, ah?" Charlie hesitated. For the first time he did not know how he should address the Abbot.

"Abbot Ambrose," Abbot Ambrose nodded and finished Charlie's sentence. "Now, if you will excuse me, I believe it's time for lunch. I'll have Dominic bring your meal in right away. Enjoy your visit." He walked over to Ophelia and gave her a hug. "Good to see you again, Ophelia."

"We will talk later," she said as he let her go.

"Good." He smiled and left the room.

Charlie sat down on the sofa and looked around the room blindly. "I don't believe this," he said. "So much has happened. My head is hurting."

"Oh, you poor dear," Ophelia said as she sat down beside him. "Dietrich, Abbot Ambrose," she corrected herself. "Told me all about what happened last night. Charlie, I'm so happy you're okay."

Charlie nodded his head. "Grandma, was he the man that came to see you that day with Uncle Chester? I mean, was he Mr. Duggan?"

Ophelia shook her head. "No. I don't think that was his name," she said as she thought. "No. It wasn't him." She said more confidently.

"Oh." Charlie sighed. "That means whoever it was is still out there."

"Charlie, don't worry yourself about it." Ophelia said. "It's too dangerous for you to get involved."

Charlie nodded and rubbed his head.

"Oh, honey, is something wrong?" Ophelia felt Charlie's forehead.

"No." He shook his head. "It's just finding out that my dad

was here. Then the Abbot is my uncle. Now this man coming to see you and you saying it's too dangerous, Grandma, what's going on? What's with the key and the medal?" he asked.

Ophelia looked at Charlie and frowned. Her eyes showed her concern. "Not yet. I'm sorry. It is too dangerous," she said.

"Dangerous? But grandma, I was nearly thrown out of the attic window," Charlie's voice strained as he spoke. "Dangerous for who?"

"For whom," she corrected him. "Charlie, dear, I can't talk about it now. Please, you will just have to trust me. I will tell you when it is safe. I promise."

Charlie sighed heavily. He could not hide his disappointment. "Grandma, what was my father like?" he asked.

Ophelia smiled and stoked Charlie's short auburn hair. She touched his cheek.

"He was a lot like you." She smiled fondly. "He was gentle, kind, loving and caring. I think that is what caused your mom to fall in love with him."

"How did they meet?" Charlie asked.

"It was on a Sunday afternoon," Ophelia began and looked at the fireplace as though she were there again. "I had come to visit Dietrich and I brought along your mother. Your father had just come in with a message for Dietrich while we were visiting. When he left the Abbey, he came to see us, well, actually your mother. He moved into an apartment in town and secured a job. They began dating and the rest is history."

"Grandma, why have you never talked about them before?" he asked.

"Some things are best left alone. I'm only telling you this now because of what you have been through Charlie. Please don't ask any more questions, it isn't safe for you to know too much." She began to fidget. "Your uncle doesn't know that

Dietrich sent for me. I really must get back to the home before he finds out."

"Everyone will be in lunch right now," Charlie said.

There was a knock at the door. Ophelia jumped. Charlie smiled and put his hand on hers.

"It's just Brother Dominic with lunch," he said then went to answer the door.

Lunch was quiet as the two of them ate. Charlie just sat and smiled at his grandmother. He couldn't believe she was actually there. It felt good seeing her again, like old times.

Ophelia ate sparingly. She mainly picked at her food and moved it from one side of her plate to the other. She was too nervous to eat. The thought of Chester discovering that she had come to see Charlie frightened her, but she dared not tell anyone why.

After the meal was over, Abbot Ambrose returned to the visiting room. He intended to visit more with Ophelia and Charlie, but Ophelia said she had to get back right away. Abbot Ambrose nodded and summoned the car.

Charlie bid his grandmother goodbye, and promised to write her and let her know how his test turned out. Abbot Ambrose was a bit confused by Charlie's comment but let it pass. She agreed to keep writing but would be careful until she heard that everything was okay.

Charlie watched as the black Lincoln drove off and disappeared from view. Slowly he walked up the stairs to his dorm. He kept thinking about everything he had learned. His father, his mother, the Abbot, it was all too confusing. What was so dangerous in knowing about the key and medal?

Howard watched as Charlie walked over to his bed and sat down. He put his comic book down and sat up.

"I've read this one, five times," he said to make

conversation. "So, what's wrong?"

Charlie looked at Howard. Howard's dark brown hair looked a bit more messed up than usual. His cassock and surplice were laid across the footboard of his bed. His tee shirt was worn and grayed with age. He wore his favorite pair of faded jeans. Everything thing about him hadn't changed. He was the same as he was yesterday, but Charlie didn't feel the same.

"Everything is wrong," Charlie answered.

"Charlie, what happened upstairs?" Howard asked just as Gus stepped around the corner of the partition.

Charlie looked at Gus and smiled. "Come on in and sit down," he invited.

Gus sat down on Howard's bed. Howard didn't make his usual fuss since he was anxious to hear the news. Both boys looked at Charlie and waited.

Charlie looked around the dorm and then finally looked at his friends. "Last night I went to the attic to stake it out. Just as I told you, the noises were not a ghost. It turned out that it wasn't even Jeffrey. It was Dougary's father, Franklyn Duggan."

"What?" Howard gasped.

"I don't believe it!" Gus over-talked Howard.

"Yes, but there's more," Charlie said as he noticed Brother Simon just entering the dorm. "I found out that my father used to go here and that he and Franklyn were friends."

"You're kidding!" Gus said in disbelief.

"I wish I were. You see, my dad was one of the boys who locked Jeffrey in the attic," Charlie added.

"Are you sure?" Howard asked.

"I'm afraid so," Brother Simon said and looked at Charlie. "Only Patrick MacCready did the right thing. When he was asked about what had happened, he told the truth. Something

Franklyn did not do. Ever since then, it seems that Franklyn has had it in for Patrick and decided to take it out on young Charlie."

"He tried to throw me out of the window, but Brother Simon convinced him not to," Charlie added.

"Were you scared?" Gus asked.

"Yes." Charlie nodded.

"But what about Jeffrey?" Howard asked. "Did you see him up there?"

Brother Simon looked at Charlie and waited for Charlie to answer.

"The only one up there was Franklyn, until Brother Simon arrived and saved me," Charlie answered.

Howard slumped as he sat on his bed. "I guess we still have a mystery to solve, then."

Charlie shook his head. "The whole idea was to find out who was making the noises in the attic. We found out. It was Mr. Duggan. You know how Brother Tobias reacted when we asked him about Kenny. He just wants to put it behind him. Maybe Jeffrey feels the same? Maybe we should leave him alone. I know if it were me, I'd just want to forget it if I could."

Howard thought for a moment. He started to shake his head in disagreement but then he nodded. "I suppose you're right. I wouldn't want to be reminded of it either."

Brother Simon gave Charlie a slight smile and walked away.

THANK YOU

Abbot Ambrose clapped the block of wood against the head table signaling all to be silent. Slowly, he rose to his feet, and looked out at all of the boys in the refectory. He looked at the monks beside him, and then took a deep breath.

"As you all are quite well aware," his deep but gentle voice resounded. "Graduation is this coming weekend. As is our custom here at Saint Michael's, we will have the diploma ceremony after Mass on Saturday. Afterward, there will be a reception here in the refectory. There will be several visitors here during that time, and I hope that all of you will do your best to help tidy up the Abbey in preparation."

"Oh great," Howard sighed and whispered. "Not only do we have finals this week, but we will have extra work to do too."

"Well, if you had been studying all year instead of horsing around playing detective with Charlie—" Rick whispered harshly at him.

"Never mind." Howard rolled his eyes and brushed him off. Charlie smiled at them both. Things were back to normal.

"The lists of duties will be posted on the bulletin board in the common area after lunch. Please check to see where you are assigned to help out and please be prompt. The more hands helping out, the quicker the work will be done," Abbot Ambrose concluded.

After the prayer, Charlie, Howard, Rick and Gus met at the stairs. They waited until everyone had cleared out before they started up the stairs.

"Still no word from your grandmother?" Gus asked Charlie.

"No," he answered. "I'm not sure if she isn't writing or if the person is still stealing my mail."

"I can't believe after all of our hard work that your trap failed." Howard shook his head.

"I knew from the start it wasn't going to work," Rick chimed in and received glares from the other three.

"Then why didn't you tell us before we wasted our time?" Howard snapped.

"He didn't know anything of a sort." Charlie shook his head. "Never mind about the mail."

As the three headed down the hall toward their dorm, Charlie began to lag behind. He couldn't stop thinking about what Rick said. His trap couldn't have failed. It was carefully thought out and put together. Something else must have happened.

"Pssst, Charlie," a voice whispered to him as they passed the shower room.

Charlie looked when he heard his name called and saw Austin peeking out from behind the shower room door. He motioned for Charlie to come. Charlie hesitated, remembering Dougary's threats and what had happened the last time he had the unfortunate timing of being trapped by them.

"It's okay, I promise," Austin pleaded quietly.

Charlie looked back at his three friends who had continued on their way back to their dorm. He glanced around the hall to see if he could spot any sign of Dougary and his other goons lurking about. Then slowly he walked over to Austin.

"Come in here, I want to talk to you," Austin whispered.

Cautiously Charlie entered the shower room. Austin closed the door behind them. Charlie quickly looked up the long hall of shower stalls, checking for any signs of a trap.

Austin turned to Charlie. The look on his face was not his usual menacing expression. Charlie began to relax just a bit.

"I just wanted to apologize for what happened earlier in the year," Austin said sheepishly. "It wasn't nice of us and I am sorry." He looked at his hands and rubbed them nervously.

"Why are we whispering?" Charlie asked.

Austin looked over his shoulder at the door behind him. "I don't want Dougary to hear. You know how they are."

"Yeah." Charlie nodded.

"Anyway, I just wanted to tell you I'm glad you're okay and I'm sorry for Dougary's threats and all. I do like you and would like to be your friend but—" Again he looked over his shoulder. "You understand."

"I guess so." Charlie shrugged and glanced at Austin's hands. "What happened to your hands?" he asked curiously.

Austin quickly looked at his hands. They were red from his rubbing them and smeared with blue ink. "You mean the ink?" he asked.

"Yes." Charlie nodded. "How did you get ink all over yourself?"

"I spilled my ink bottle in Brother Vincent's class," he answered with a slight bit of hesitation.

"Oh," Charlie said. "Well, I guess I'll be going." He started for the door but Austin stepped in front of him.

"I really did spill my ink bottle," he said earnestly.

Charlie gave him a confused smile. "It's okay. It'll wear off."

"Yeah, I suppose you're right," Austin agreed. "Hey, I'll let you know if Dougary is planning anything."

"Okay." Charlie smiled. "For what it's worth, Austin, I've always thought you didn't belong with them."

"Thanks." he smiled.

Charlie threw open the shower rooms door and headed back to his dorm. He paused for a moment by the bulletin board in the common area. He wanted to see what Austin was up to so he pretended to read the postings.

Austin waited for a moment and then cautiously slipped out of the shower room. As he reached the water fountain Dougary and the other two walked around the corner. He quickly turned and took a drink of water as they approached.

"There you are," Dougary said in an irritated voice. "We've been looking all over for you."

"You have?" Austin said as he wiped his mouth on the back of his sweatshirt sleeve.

"Yah," Travis jumped in and glanced down the hall at Charlie. "Where've you been?"

"Nowhere special," Austin answered nervously. "Why? What's going on?"

"Dougary just found out that his father is going to be locked up in the nut house for a long time, thanks to Charlie," Larry spoke up. "He's going to be spending the summer here."

"So, we were thinking maybe we all should spend the summer here." Dougary smiled with a fiendish glint in his eyes. "We could spend all summer making life hell for the Abbot's little pet."

Austin thought for a moment. He really wanted to go home

for the summer, especially since he wasn't able to go last summer due to a court order. He shook his head.

"I really can't stay," he said. "My father is expecting me to be home to help him out with my new baby brother."

"Oh, isn't that special," Dougary snapped. "You ditch us for some smelly, diaper wetting, little baby? He's not even a full brother. He's your half-brother."

Austin's temper began to rise at the sound of those words. He clenched his teeth angrily and glared at Dougary.

"He's still my brother," he said. "And you had better watch how you talk about my family."

Dougary looked at Austin's clenched fists and took a step back. He held up his hands in a mock surrender. "Okay, okay, I'm sorry," he apologized. "Go home if you want to. There'll be plenty of fun to be had when you get back."

Travis and Larry both let out a sigh of relief as Austin and Dougary calmed down. They even chuckled lightly to relieve the tension in the air.

"Come on, we'll tell you what we have in mind," Larry said and put his arm around Austin's neck and led him off back to their dorm.

Moments later, Charlie sat down on his bed and stared at his hands in his lap. Howard sat up and looked that him.

"Uh oh," he breathed and shook his head. "I don't like that look."

"What look?" Charlie asked and turned his attention to Howard.

"The look that says something's up. What's wrong?"

"Nothing really," Charlie answered. "I just ran into Austin is all. He said he was glad I'm okay and he'd like to be my friend."

"I smell a trap," Howard said. "Don't trust him," he

warned.

"Oh, I know." Charlie nodded. "There was something else. He had ink all over his fingers."

Howard's eyebrows raised behind his glasses. "Oh? And did you ask him about it?"

"Yes." Charlie nodded. "He said he spilled his ink bottle in class the other day."

"Interesting." Howard nodded.

"You don't think he could be the one stealing my mail, do you?" Charlie asked and looked at Howard.

Howard thought for a moment. "He is part of their gang. Maybe Dougary has someone else open the letters for him, seeing how his father is a nut case and all. On the other hand, he could be telling the truth."

"Yeah." Charlie nodded. "That's what I was afraid of."

"So, did you see where we are assigned to help out cleaning this Friday, after our last exam?" Howard changed the subject.

"No, did you?"

"Yes. We are supposed to help Brother Owen clean the classrooms." Howard answered. "And you will never guess who else is on that list."

"Dougary?" Charlie guessed.

"No, but it's just as bad, Larry and Austin," Howard answered. "Dougary gets to help outside cleaning up the pathways."

"Great." Charlie nodded to himself. "At least we won't have to deal with him."

The week of exams was a lot harder than Charlie thought it would be. As usual Brother Simon's World Cultures exam was the last test and by far the hardest. It wouldn't have been so bad if he would've been able to keep up with all the reading. But no one was able to and Brother Simon knew it. It was as though he took great pleasure in making his class harder. At least that's what Charlie thought.

Brother Simon looked at the clock on the wall as he paced the floor. Howard shook his head as he read over the test questions.

"Sheesh!" he sighed.

Brother Simon stopped and turned around to face Howard.

"Is there a problem, Master Miller?" he asked coldly.

Howard looked up. "No, sir," he answered. "Everything's just fine."

"Then quiet down!" Brother Simon snapped back at him and then resumed his pacing.

Charlie looked at Howard. He appeared to be having just as hard a time with the test as he was. He glanced at Gus. His face showed it all. The tiny beads of sweat on his forehead, the tears in his eyes, his pink cheeks, even the teeth marks in his pencil showed how stressed he was. Charlie felt sorry for him but there was nothing he could do to help him. He looked at Rick who also appeared to be struggling. That gave Charlie a better feeling about himself and the test. He turned back to his paper.

The clock on the wall ticked away the seconds slowly. Ten, nine, eight, Brother Simon smiled to himself. Five, four, three, Brother Simon turned around and faced the class.

"Times up. Pencils down," he said firmly.

Charlie quickly did as instructed.

"That goes for you too, Master Walters." Brother Simon snapped.

The bell rang in the hall and signaled the end of the school year, but no one moved.

"Pick up your papers and bring them up here on your way out of the class." Brother Simon instructed.

Slowly the boys picked up their things and filed out of the class. First Gus handed his in. Then Rick, Howard and finally Charlie handed their papers over to Brother Simon.

"Well, looks like we'll be taking this class over next year," Gus sighed.

"Who cares, its summer vacation!" Howard shouted.

"So, what're you going to do this summer?" Charlie turned to Rick.

"I'm going home this year," he answered. "My parents have planned a trip to Disney World."

"You'll have to tell us all about it when you come back," Howard jumped in. "As I'm sure you will."

"Be nice, Howard," Charlie said as the boys headed off to their cleaning assignments.

They didn't have to go far. Brother Owen was waiting for them in their homeroom. He was dressed in jeans, an old sweatshirt and tennis shoes. He looked more like one of the students than he did a monk. Beside the desk sat buckets, mops, brooms and dust rags. Charlie sat down at his regular desk. Howard sat on top of his.

Austin walked into the room just a few minutes later. He looked at Charlie and then turned away as he took his seat. Once the rest of the crew arrived, Brother Owen gave them all instructions and sent them on their way.

Two hours later, Charlie wheeled his mop bucket into the last classroom. He had been following Howard and the other boys as they swept and dusted but now that they were finished, they had all gone upstairs to their dorm. As he began, he silently wished Howard had waited around for him.

Just then there was the sound of someone behind him. Charlie spun around, his heart pounding. He relaxed when he it was only Austin with his mop and bucket.

"I'm sorry," Austin apologized, seeing that he had startled Charlie.

"It's okay," Charlie gave a sigh. "Guess I'm still a bit edgy after that incident with Mr. Duggan."

"Yeah, I can imagine," Austin agreed. "I was wondering if you could use a hand in here. I mean since everyone else has left."

"Sure." Charlie nodded. "That would be great."

Austin set his mob bucket down and then began in the back corner, opposite Charlie. They worked together, moving toward the door. Charlie was glad for the help. It was going faster but he was not too sure about whether or not he should trust Austin. After all, he was still Dougary's friend.

"Hey, Charlie," Austin spoke in a near whisper. "The other day after our little talk, after you left, Dougary made some comments about getting revenge. He's really mad at you about his father being committed in the loony bin."

Charlie shrugged. "So, what else is new? Dougary has been out to get me ever since I arrived and his father told him who I was. He doesn't scare me."

"Good." Austin nodded. "Hey, I'm not going to be around this summer. I'm going home. It's been a long time since I've been able to spend the entire summer with my family. I'm really looking forward to it."

"So, when do you leave?" Charlie asked to be polite.

"After the graduation Mass tomorrow," Austin answered.

Charlie could tell that something was on Austin's mind by the way he kept looking around the room nervously, but he was not about to ask Austin what it was. He figured if Austin wanted him to know something, he would tell him in his time.

"Charlie," Austin spoke up in a whisper. "You be careful around Dougary and the others this summer."

"Sure." Charlie nodded.

"No." Austin stopped mopping and took Charlie's arm to get his full attention. "I mean it seriously. They are planning something very serious. I don't know what it is because they won't tell me, but I know it's not good."

Charlie looked at Austin, at his eyes. He was really concerned about Charlie.

"Okay." Charlie nodded. "I'll be careful."

They finished the rest of the mopping in silence. Charlie kept thinking about what Austin said. He had an uneasy feeling about Austin. He couldn't shake the feeling that he was being set up. He returned to his dorm and hoped Howard would be there. They needed to talk.

When he arrived, the dorm was filled with excited talking. Charlie looked around confused. He spotted Howard and headed straight for him.

"What's going on?" he asked.

"We're having our goodbye party for Roger, Tony and Clark. They graduate tomorrow, remember?" Howard answered and sipped his red punch. "Oh, and Brother Simon just came in to tell us that we all had passed his class."

"He did?" Charlie looked confused. "But—"

"Hey, don't question it, Charlie. I know it doesn't make sense, but I'm not going to look a gift horse in the mouth." Howard looked across the room at the gathering of boys. "Come on, get yourself a cup of this punch. It's really good."

Charlie shrugged off any misgivings he had about passing a test he was sure he failed and joined the party. As for Austin, there would be plenty of time to talk to Howard later.

Saturday morning came all too quickly for Charlie. He was in the middle of a dream about his parents, about them taking him and Howard on a grand picnic in the mountains far away, when the morning bell rang out. He opened his eyes to the reality that it was only a dream.

After breakfast, it was time to prepare for the Graduation Mass. Rick, Howard and Charlie met in the sacristy with the other Altar Boys members. It seemed strange that Steve and Randy weren't there. As seniors, they wouldn't be participating in the ceremony. Instead Robert, a junior, a member of Saint Thomas dorm, and the newly appointed sacristan, explained the ceremony. He was a lot different than Steve and Randy. His red hair was cut in a military style and his impatience seemed to have been as well. He constantly tightened his already thin lips in an angry glare at Howard and Charlie for one thing or another.

"I can't wait until this is over," Rick whispered to Charlie. "I'm leaving right after the Mass."

"But what about the party?" Charlie asked back in a whisper.

"I don't care about that," Rick answered. "I'm going to Disney World."

"Oh." Charlie nodded. He knew that Rick was excited about his trip but it came across as gloating. Now he couldn't wait for the Mass to be over. He wouldn't have to listen to Rick anymore for three months.

Charlie and Howard were assigned as candle bearers to walk on either side of Robert, who would be carrying the processional cross. Rick was assigned to carry the thurible and incense boat, despite his protests that he carried it the last time.

"Have you heard the news about this summer's games?" Howard asked Charlie as they readied their candles.

"Heard what?" Charlie answered distractedly. He was struggling with his candlestick that wouldn't stand straight in its holder.

"The summer softball games are canceled." Howard

replied. "There's going to be a big announcement this evening."

"No, I haven't heard." Charlie admitted and frowned at his candle. "This stupid candle," Charlie sighed and took it out of the holder. He took out a knife from the closet and carefully cleaned out the melted wax that had built up in the bottom of the holder.

"Come on, Charlie, we're ready to begin." Robert said as he entered the Altar Boys' room off the sacristy.

"I'm coming." Charlie said and stuck the candle back into the holder. To his surprise, it fit snuggly but still was not standing straight. He lit his candle and hurriedly took his place in the procession.

The Mass ran a little too long for Charlie. His arms began to tire as he held his candle during the final procession out of the Abbey Church. He was glad when they finally returned to the Altar Boys room and it was over. Rick was too. He hurriedly snuffed out the burning embers in the thurible and put it safely away. Then without a word he disappeared. After Charlie and Howard put away their candles, they met up with Gus outside the refectory.

"Hi guys," Gus greeted them. "You just missed Rick. I've never seen him move so quickly. He was out of here in record time."

"It's his trip to Disney World." Howard shook his head. "I hate that mouse."

"So, are we going inside?" Charlie asked.

"Sure." They nodded in agreement.

The refectory was unusually crowded. The tables had been removed and chairs lined the walls. The head table was draped in a golden yellow tablecloth. Two unlit candles sat at either end. In the center sat a large bouquet of colorful flowers. On the main floor in front of the head table was another long table draped in a navy-blue tablecloth. Large bowls of punch sat at either end and in the center, the remains of two sheet cakes.

"Guess we're a little late," Howard said. "Would've liked a piece of cake before they demolished them."

"Oh, there's still some," Gus said, his eyes taking quick inventory of the table. "I'm going to get some; you want me to bring you back a piece?"

"Sure." Howard nodded but Gus was gone before he could hear the answer.

"So, what do you think this big announcement's going to be?" Charlie asked.

"I don't know, but it has to be pretty big for Abbot Ambrose to cancel the baseball games. He loves the games."

"I guess we'll hear tonight," Charlie said.

"So, how was it working with Austin this afternoon?" Howard changed the subject.

"Oh, I'm glad you said that. I almost forgot," Charlie whispered. "Something is up with him and I don't know how to take it."

"What?" Howard cocked his head curiously.

"The other day he stopped me and said he was glad I was okay and that he wished he could be my friend. Then today he told me, actually he warned me that Dougary is out for revenge and is planning on doing something to me."

"Oh, I don't know. It still sounds like a trap." Howard shook his head wearily.

"That's what I thought," Charlie said as Gus walked up. He was trying to balance three plates of cake crumbs on top of three plastic cups of punch. From the look of his surplice, he wasn't very successful.

"Oh, don't worry, it'll wash out," he assured them as he handed them their cake and punch.

"You didn't have to get me anything," Charlie smiled. "But thanks."

"So, what're you guys talking about?" Gus asked.

"Austin," Howard replied with a mouthful of cake.

"What about him?" Gus looked at Charlie.

"How well did you get to know him when you lived in Saint Peter dorm?" Charlie asked.

"Well enough to wonder how he ever ended up with Dougary, Travis and Larry for friends," Gus replied as he ate his cake crumbs greedily.

"What do you mean?" Charlie continued to question.

"Just that he's a nice guy. He actually protected me many times from Travis' tormenting. Why?" Gus asked again.

"Oh, I was just wondering is all." Charlie shrugged and gave Howard the look that said, keep this between us.

"Yeah, I actually like Austin." Gus nodded. "He's okay."

Charlie sighed even more confused than before. He sipped his punch and handed Gus his cake. He didn't feel too much like eating. Summer was certainly going to be interesting, to say the least, he thought to himself.

After the party, Charlie, Howard and Gus returned to their dorm. They were tired from the morning's Mass and party. The dorm was quiet when they entered. It seemed they weren't the only ones tired.

"Just a quick nap before dinner," Charlie said as he and Howard returned to their cubicle.

As Charlie neared his bed, he noticed a flat package wrapped in brown paper and tied with a piece of twine. Tucked under the twine was a small envelope. Charlie looked around the dorm, confused about who would have left it for him.

Howard noticed the package too. He sat down on his bed and eagerly waited to see what it was.

Charlie sat down and picked it up.

"Oh, I bet it's a book." Howard guessed out loud.

"A book?" Charlie gave him a funny look. He opened the envelope and withdrew a flat card. Now he was more confused. He looked up at Howard. "Thank you."

"For what?" Howard looked at him confused.

"No," Charlie sighed. "The card just says, 'Thank you.'" He handed the typewritten card to Howard.

Slowly he untied the twine and laid it beside him on his bed. He glanced at Howard and then carefully unwrapped the package.

"Oh," Howard shook his head. "It's just the picture Prior Anselm gave you. I thought it was going to be something neat." He tossed the card back onto Charlie's bed and then lay back on his bed.

Charlie stared at the picture. It was not the same photograph that Prior Anselm had given him. It was black and white like the other one but the people were different. He looked at the faces and then noticed the grease pencil circle around one of them. He stared at the boy's face, and a tear came to his eyes. Suddenly his questions about who had given him the package were answered, and he knew who the boy was.

Howard sat back up when he noticed Charlie's reaction to the photograph. He became very concerned as he saw a tear fall from Charlie's eyes.

"What is it?" he asked and leaned forward, resting his elbows on his knees.

Charlie looked up and smiled through his tears. "It's my dad."

ABOUT THE AUTHOR

James M. McCracken spent much of his teenage years away from his family in a seminary boarding school. It was there that his love of writing began. It is his experiences while at the boarding school that serve as the inspiration for the Charlie MacCready series.

James M. McCracken currently resides in Central Oregon. He is a longtime member of the writing group Becoming Fiction and the Northwest Independent Writers Association.

www.ingramcontent.com/pod-product-compliance
Lightning Source LLC
LaVergne TN
LVHW022002060526
838200LV00003B/59